The Guest List

A Novel

Lucy Foley

HARPER LARGE PRINT
An Imprint of HarperCollins*Publishers*

Published in 2020 by HarperFiction, an imprint of HarperCollins UK.

FIRST HARPER LARGE PRINT EDITION

ISBN: 978-0-06-297873-8

Library of Congress Cataloging-in-Publication Data is available upon request.

20 21 22 23 24 LSC 10 9 8 7 6 5 4 3 2 1

For Kate and Robbie, the most supportive siblings a girl could hope for . . . Luckily nothing like the ones in this book!

NOW

THE WEDDING NIGHT

The lights go out.

In an instant, everything is in darkness. The band stop their playing. Inside the tent the wedding guests squeal and clutch at one another. The light from the candles on the tables only adds to the confusion, sends shadows racing up the canvas walls. It's impossible to see where anyone is or hear what anyone is saying: above the guests' voices the wind rises in a frenzy.

Outside a storm is raging. It shrieks around them, it batters the tent. At each assault the whole structure seems to flex and shudder with a loud groaning of metal; the guests cower in alarm. The doors have come free from their ties and flap at the entrance. The flames of the paraffin torches that illuminate the doorway snicker.

It feels personal, this storm. It feels as though it has saved all its fury for them.

This isn't the first time the electric has shorted. But last time the lights snapped back on again within minutes. The guests returned to their dancing, their drinking, their pill-popping, their screwing, their eating, their laughing . . . and forgot it ever happened.

How long has it been now? In the dark it's difficult to tell. A few minutes? Fifteen? Twenty?

They're beginning to feel afraid. This darkness feels somehow ominous, intent. As though anything could be happening beneath its cover.

Finally, the bulbs flicker back on. Whoops and cheers from the guests. They're embarrassed now about how the lights find them: crouched as though ready to fend off an attack. They laugh it off. They almost manage to convince themselves that they weren't frightened.

The scene illuminated in the three adjoining tents should be one of celebration, but it looks more like one of devastation. In the main dining section, clots of wine spatter the laminate floor, a crimson stain spreads across white linen. Bottles of champagne cluster on every surface; testament to an evening of toasts and celebrations. A forlorn pair of silver sandals peeks from beneath a tablecloth.

The Irish band begins to play again in the dance tent—a rousing ditty to restore the spirit of celebration. Many of the guests hurry in that direction, eager for some light relief. If you were to look closely at where they step you might see the marks where one barefoot guest has trodden in broken glass and left bloody footprints across the laminate, drying to a rusty stain. No one notices.

Other guests drift and gather in the corners of the main tent, nebulous as leftover cigarette smoke. Loath to stay, but also loath to step outside its sanctuary while the storm still rages. And no one can leave the island. Not yet. The boats can't come until the wind dies down.

In the center of everything stands the huge cake. It has appeared whole and perfect before them for most of the day, its train of sugar foliage glittering beneath the lights. But only minutes before the lights went out the guests gathered around to watch its ceremonial disemboweling. Now the deep red sponge gapes from within.

Then from outside comes a new sound. You might almost mistake it for the wind. But it rises in pitch and volume until it is unmistakable.

The guests freeze. They stare at one another. They are suddenly afraid again. More so than they were when the lights went out. They all know what they are hearing. It is a scream of terror.

THE DAY BEFORE

AOIFE

The Wedding Planner

Nearly all of the wedding party are here now. Things are about to crank into another gear: there's the rehearsal dinner this evening, with the chosen guests, so the wedding really begins tonight.

I've put the champagne on ice ready for the predinner drinks. It's vintage Bollinger: eight bottles of it, plus the wine for dinner and a couple of crates of Guinness—all as per the bride's instructions. It is not for me to comment, but it seems rather a lot. They're all adults, though. I'm sure they know how to restrain themselves. Or maybe not. That best man seems a bit of a liability—all of the ushers do, to be honest. And the bridesmaid—the bride's half sister—I've seen her on her solitary wanderings of the island, hunched over and walking fast like she's trying to outpace something.

You learn all the insider secrets, doing this sort of work. You see the things no one else is privileged to see. All the gossip that the guests would kill to have. As a wedding planner you can't *afford* to miss anything. You have to be alert to every detail, all the smaller eddies beneath the surface. If I didn't pay attention, one of those currents could grow into a huge riptide, destroying all my careful planning. And here's another thing I've learned—sometimes the smallest currents are the strongest.

I move through the Folly's downstairs rooms, lighting the blocks of turf in the grates, so they can get a good smolder on for this evening. Freddy and I have started cutting and drying our own turf from the bog, as has been done for centuries past. The smoky, earthy smell of the turf fires will add to the sense of local atmosphere. The guests should like that. It may be midsummer but it gets cool at night on the island. The Folly's old stone walls keep the warmth out and aren't so good at holding it in.

Today has been surprisingly warm, at least by the standards of these parts, but the same's not looking likely for tomorrow. The end of the weather forecast I caught on the radio mentioned wind. We get the brunt of all the weather here; often the storms are much worse than they end up being on the mainland, as if they've exhausted themselves on us. It's still sunny out but this afternoon the needle on the old barometer in the hallway swung from FAIR to CHANGEABLE. I've taken it down. I don't want the bride to see it. Though I'm not sure that she is the sort to panic. More the sort to get angry and look for someone to blame. And I know just who would be in the firing line.

"Freddy," I call into the kitchen, "will you be starting on the dinner soon?"

"Yeah," he calls back, "got it all under control."

Tonight they'll eat a fish stew based on a traditional Connemara fisherman's chowder: smoked fish, lots of cream. I ate it the first time I ever visited this place, when there were still people here. This evening's will be a more refined take on the usual recipe, as this is a refined group we have staying. Or at least I suppose they like to *think* of themselves as such. We'll see what happens when the drink hits them.

"Then we'll be needing to start prepping the canapés for tomorrow," I call, running through the list in my head.

"I'm on it."

"And the cake: we'll be wanting to assemble that in good time."

The cake is quite something to behold. It should be. I know how much it cost. The bride didn't bat an eyelid at the expense. I believe she's used to having the best of everything. Four tiers of deep red velvet sponge, encased in immaculate white icing and strewn with sugar greenery, to match the foliage in the chapel and the marquee's tents. Extremely fragile and made according to the bride's exact specifications, it traveled all the way here from a very exclusive cake-maker's in Dublin: it was no small effort getting it across the water in one piece. Tomorrow, of course, it will be destroyed. But it's all about the moment, a wedding. All about the day. It's not really about the marriage at all, in spite of what everyone says.

See, mine is a profession in which you orchestrate happiness. It is why I became a wedding planner. Life is messy. We all know this. Terrible things happen, I learned that while I was still a child. But no matter what happens, life is only a series of days. You can't control more than a single day. But you can control *one* of them. Twenty-four hours can be curated. A wedding day is a neat little parcel of time in which I can create something whole and perfect to be cherished for a lifetime, a pearl from a broken necklace.

Freddy emerges from the kitchen in his stained butcher's apron. "How are you feeling?"

I shrug. "A little nervous, to be honest."

"You've got this, love. Think how many times you've done this."

"But this is different. Because of who it is—" It was a real coup, getting Will Slater and Julia Keegan to hold their wedding here. I worked as an event planner in Dublin, before. Setting up here was all my idea, restoring the island's crumbling, half-ruined folly into an elegant ten-bedroom property with a dining room, drawing room and kitchen. Freddy and I live here permanently but use only a tiny fraction of the space when it's just the two of us.

"Shush." Freddy steps forward and enfolds me in a hug. I feel myself stiffening at first. I'm so focused on my to-do list that it feels like a diversion we don't have time for. Then I allow myself to relax into the embrace, to appreciate his comforting, familiar warmth. Freddy is a good hugger. He's what you might call "cuddly." He likes his food—it's his job. He ran a restaurant in Dublin before we moved here.

"It's all going to work out fine," he says. "I promise. It will all be perfect." He kisses the top of my head. I've had a great deal of experience in this business. But then I've never worked on an event I've been so invested in. And the bride is very particular—which, to be fair to her, probably goes with the territory of what she does, running her own magazine. Someone else might have been run a little ragged by her requests. But I've enjoyed it. I like a challenge.

Anyway. That's enough about me. This weekend is about the happy couple, after all. The bride and groom haven't been together for very long, by all accounts. Seeing as our bedroom is in the Folly too, with all the others, we could hear them last night. "Jesus," Freddy said as we lay in bed. "I can't listen to this." I knew what he meant. Strange how when someone is in the throes of pleasure it can sound like pain. They seem very much in love, but a cynic might say that's *why* they can't seem to keep their hands off each other. Very much in lust might be a more accurate description.

Freddy and I have been together for the best part of two decades and even now there are things I keep from him and, I'm sure, vice versa. Makes you wonder how much they know about each other, those two.

Whether they really know all of each other's dark secrets.

HANNAH

The Plus-One

The waves rise in front of us, whitecapped. On land it's a beautiful summer's day, but it's pretty rough out here. A few minutes ago we left the safety of the mainland harbor and as we did the water seemed to darken in color and the waves grew by several feet.

It's the evening before the wedding and we're on our way to the island. As "special guests," we're staying there tonight. I'm looking forward to it. At least—I *think* I am. I need a bit of a distraction at the moment, anyway.

"Hold on!" A shout from the captain's cabin, behind us. Mattie, the man's called. Before we have time to think the little boat launches off one wave and straight into the crest of another. Water sprays up over us in a huge arc.

"Christ!" Charlie shouts and I see that he's got soaked on one side. Miraculously I'm only a little damp.

"Would you be a bit wet up there?" Mattie calls.

I'm laughing but I'm having to force it a bit because it was pretty frightening. The boat's motion, somehow back and forth and side to side all at once, has my stomach turning somersaults.

"Oof," I say, feeling the nausea sinking through me. The thought of the cream tea we ate before we got on the boat suddenly makes me want to hurl.

Charlie looks at me, puts a hand on my knee and gives a squeeze. "Oh, God. It's started already?" I always get terrible motion sickness. Anything sickness really; when I was pregnant it was the worst.

"Mm-hmm. I've taken a couple of pills, but they've hardly taken the edge off."

"Look," Charlie says quickly, "I'll read about the place, take your mind off it." He scrolls through his phone. He's got a guidebook downloaded; ever the teacher, my husband. The boat lurches again and the iPhone nearly jumps out of his grasp. He swears, grips it with both hands; we can't afford to replace it.

"There's not that much here," he says, a bit apologetically, once he's managed to load the page. "Loads on Connemara, yeah, but on the island itself—I suppose it's so small . . ." He stares at the screen as though willing it to deliver. "Oh, here, I've found a bit." He clears his throat, then starts to read in what I think is probably the voice he uses in his lessons. "Inis an Amplóra, or Cormorant Island, in the English translation, is two miles from one end to the other, longer than it is wide. The island is formed of a lump of granite emerging *majestically* from the Atlantic, several miles off the Connemara coastline. A large bog comprised of peat, or 'turf' as it is called locally, covers much of its surface. The best, indeed the only, way to see the island is from a private boat. The channel between the mainland and the island can get particularly choppy—"

"They're right about that," I mutter, clutching the side as we seesaw over another wave and slam down again. My stomach turns over again.

"I can tell you more than all that," Mattie calls from his cabin. I hadn't realized he could overhear us from there. "You won't be getting much about Inis an Amplóra from a guidebook."

Charlie and I shuffle nearer to the cabin so we can hear. He's got a lovely rich accent, does Mattie. "First people that settled the place," he tells us, "far as it's known, were a religious sect, persecuted by some on the mainland."

"Oh, yes," Charlie says, looking at his guide. "I think I saw a bit about that—"

"You can't get everything from that thing," Mattie says, frowning and clearly unimpressed by the interruption. "I've lived here all my life, see—and my people have been here for centuries. I can tell you more than your man on the internet."

"Sorry," Charlie says, flushing.

"Anyway," Mattie says. "Twenty years or so ago the archeologists found them. All together in the turf bog they were, side by side, packed in tight." Something tells me that he is enjoying himself. "Perfectly preserved, it's said, because there's no air down in there. It was a massacre. They'd all been hacked to death."

"Oh," Charlie says, with a glance at me, "I'm not sure—"

It's too late, the idea is in my head now: long-buried corpses emerging from black earth. I try not to think about it but the image keeps reasserting itself like a glitch in a video. The swoop of nausea that comes as we ride over the next wave is almost a relief, requiring all my focus.

"And there's no one living there now?" Charlie asks brightly, trying for a change of conversation. "Other than the new owners?"

"No," Mattie says. "Nothing but ghosts."

Charlie taps his screen. "It says here the island was inhabited until the nineties, when the last few people decided to return to the mainland in favor of running water, electricity and modern life."

"Oh, that's what it says there, is it?" Mattie sounds amused.

"Why?" I ask, managing to find my voice. "Was there some other reason they left?"

Mattie seems to be about to speak. Then his face changes. "Look out for yourselves!" he roars. Charlie and I manage to grab the rail seconds before the bottom seems to drop out of everything and we are sent plunging down the side of one wave, then smashed into the side of another. Jesus.

You're meant to find a fixed point with motion sickness. I train my gaze on the island. It has been in view the whole way from the mainland, a bluish smudge on the horizon, shaped like a flattened anvil. Jules wouldn't pick anywhere less than stunning, but I can't help feeling that the dark shape of it seems to hunch and glower, in contrast to the bright day.

"Pretty stunning, isn't it?" Charlie says.

"Mm," I say noncommittally. "Well, let's hope there's running water and electricity there these days. I'm going to need a nice bath after this."

Charlie grins. "Knowing Jules, if they hadn't plumbed and wired the place before, they'll have done so by now. You know what she's like. She's so efficient."

I'm sure Charlie didn't mean it, but it feels like a comparison. I'm *not* the world's most efficient. I can't seem to enter a room without making a mess and since we've had the kids our house is a permanent dump. When we—rarely—have people round I end up throwing stuff in cupboards and cramming them closed, so that it feels like the whole place is holding its breath, trying not to explode. When we first went round for dinner at Jules's elegant Victorian house in Islington it was like something out of a magazine; like something out of *her* magazine—an online one called *The Download*. I kept thinking she might try and tidy me away somewhere, aware of how I stuck out like a sore thumb with my inch of dark roots and off-the-rack clothes. I found myself trying to smooth out my accent, even, soften my Mancunian vowels.

We couldn't be more different, Jules and I. The two most important women in my husband's life. I lean over the rail, taking deep breaths of the sea air.

"I read a good bit in that article," Charlie says, "about the island. Apparently it's got white sand beaches, which are famous in this part of Ireland. And the color of the sand means the water in the coves turns a beautiful turquoise color."

"Oh," I say. "Well, that sounds better than a peat bog."

"Yep," Charlie says. "Maybe we'll have a chance to go swimming." He smiles at me.

I look at the water, which is more of a chilly slate green than turquoise, and shiver. But I swim off the beach in Brighton, and that's the English Channel, isn't it? Still. There it feels so much tamer than this wild, brutal sea.

"This weekend will be a good distraction, won't it?" Charlie says.

"Yeah," I say. "I hope so." This will be the closest we'll have had to a holiday for a long time. And I really need one right now. "I can't work out why Jules would choose a random island off the coast of Ireland," I add. It seems particularly *her* to choose somewhere so exclusive that her guests might actually drown trying to get there. "It's not like she couldn't have afforded to hold it anywhere she wanted."

Charlie frowns. He doesn't like to talk about money, it embarrasses him. It's one of the reasons I love him. Except sometimes, just sometimes, I can't help wondering what it would be like to have a tiny bit more. We agonized over the gift registry and had a bit of an argument about it. Our max is normally fifty quid, but Charlie insisted that we had to do more, because he and Jules go back so far. As everything listed was from Liberty's, the £150 we finally agreed to only bought us a rather ordinary-looking ceramic bowl. There was a scented candle on there for £200.

"You know Jules," Charlie says now, as the boat makes another swoop downward before hitting something that feels much harder than mere water, bouncing up again with a few sideways spasms for good measure. "She likes to do things differently. And it could be to do with her dad being Irish."

"But I thought she doesn't get on with her dad?"

"It's more complicated than that. He was never really around and he's a bit of a dick, but I think she's always kind of idolized him. That's why she wanted me to give her sailing lessons all those years ago. He had this yacht, and she wanted him to be proud of her."

It's difficult to imagine Jules in the inferior position of wanting to make someone proud. I know her dad's a big-deal property developer, a self-made man. As the daughter of a train driver and a nurse who grew up constantly strapped for cash, I'm fascinated by—and a little bit suspicious of—people who have made loads of money. To me they're like another species altogether, a breed of sleek and dangerous big cats.

"Or maybe Will chose it," I say. "It seems very him, very Outward Bound." I feel a little leap of excitement in my stomach at the thought of meeting someone so famous. It's hard to think of Jules's fiancé as a completely real person.

I've been catching up on the show in secret. It's pretty good, though it's hard to be objective. I've been fascinated by the idea of Jules being with this man . . . touching him, kissing him, sleeping with him. About to get *married* to him.

The basic premise of the show, *Survive the Night*, is that Will gets left somewhere, tied up and blindfolded, in the middle of the night. A forest, say, or the middle of an Arctic tundra, with nothing but the clothes he's wearing and maybe a knife in his belt. He then has to free himself and make his way to a rendezvous point using his wits and navigational skills alone. There's lots of high drama: in one episode he has to cross a waterfall in the dark; in another he's stalked by wolves. At times you'll suddenly remember that the camera crew is there watching him, filming him. If it were really all that bad, surely they'd step in to help? But they certainly do a good job of making you feel the danger.

At my mention of Will, Charlie's face has darkened. "I still don't get why she's marrying him after such a short time," he says. "I suppose that's what Jules is like. When she's made up her mind, she acts quickly. But you mark my words, Han: he's hiding something. I don't think he's everything he pretends to be."

This is why I've been so secretive about watching the show. I know Charlie wouldn't like it. At times I can't help feeling that his dislike of Will seems a little like jealousy. I really hope it's *not* jealousy. Because what would that mean?

It could also be to do with Will's stag party. Charlie went, which seemed all wrong, as he's Jules's friend. He came home from the weekend in Sweden a bit out of sorts. Every time I even alluded to it he'd go all weird and stiff. So I shrugged it off. He came back in one piece, didn't he?

The sea seems to have got even rougher. The old fishing boat is pitching and rolling now in all directions at once, like one of those rodeo-bull machines, like it's trying to throw us overboard. "Is it really safe to keep going?" I call to Mattie.

"Yep!" he calls back, over the crash of the spray, the shriek of the wind. "This is a good day, as they go. Not far to Inis an Amplóra now."

I can feel wet hanks of hair stuck to my forehead, while the rest of it seems to have lifted into a huge tangled cloud around my head. I can only imagine how I'll look to Jules and Will and the rest of them, when we finally arrive.

"Cormorant!" Charlie shouts, pointing. He's trying to distract me from my nausea, I know. I feel like one of the children being taken to the doctor's for an injection. But I follow his finger to a sleek dark head, emerging from the waves like the periscope of a miniature submarine. Then it swoops down beneath the surface, a swift black streak. Imagine feeling so at home in such hostile conditions.

"I saw something in the article specifically about cormorants," Charlie says. He picks up his phone again. "Ah, here. They're particularly common along this stretch of coast, apparently." He puts on his schoolteacher voice: " 'The cormorant is a bird much maligned in local folklore.' Oh, dear. 'Historically, the bird has been represented as a symbol of greed, bad luck and evil.' " We both watch as the cormorant emerges from the water again. There's a tiny fish in its sharp beak, a brief flash of silver, before the bird opens its gullet and swallows the thing whole.

My stomach flips. I feel as though it's me that has swallowed the fish, quick and slippery, swimming about in my belly. And as the boat begins to list in the other direction, I lurch to the side and throw up my cream tea.

JULES

The Bride

I'm standing in front of the mirror in our room, the biggest and most elegant of the Folly's ten bedrooms, naturally. From here I only need to turn my head a fraction to look out through the windows toward the sea. The weather today is perfect, the sun shimmering off the waves so brightly you can hardly look at it. It bloody well better stay like this for tomorrow.

Our room is on the western side of the building and this is the westernmost island off this part of the coast, so there is nothing, and no one, for thousands of miles between me and the Americas. I like the drama of that. The Folly itself is a beautifully restored fifteenth-century building, treading the line between luxury and timelessness, grandeur and comfort: antique rugs on the flagstone floors, claw-footed baths, fireplaces lit with smoldering peat. It's large enough to fit all our guests, yet small enough to feel intimate. It's perfect. Everything is going to be perfect.

Don't think about the note, Jules.

I will *not* think about the note.

Fuck. *Fuck.* I don't know why it's got to me so much. I have never been a worrier, the sort of person who wakes up at three in the morning, fretting. Not until recently anyway.

The note was delivered through our letter box three weeks ago. It told me not to marry Will. To call it off.

Somehow the idea of it has gained this dark power over me. Whenever I think about it, it gives me a sour feeling in the pit of my stomach. A feeling like dread.

Which is ridiculous. I wouldn't normally give a second thought to this sort of thing.

I look back at the mirror. I'm currently wearing the dress. *The* dress. I thought it important to try it on one last time, the eve of my wedding, to double-check. I had a fitting last week but I never leave anything to chance. As expected, it's perfect. Heavy cream silk that looks as though it has been poured over me, the corsetry within creating the quintessential hourglass. No lace or other fripperies, that's not me. The nap of the silk is so fine it can only be handled with special white gloves which, obviously, I'm wearing now. It cost an absolute bomb. It was worth it. I'm not interested in fashion for its own sake, but I respect the power of clothes, in creating the right optics. I knew immediately that this dress was a queenmaker.

By the end of the evening the dress will probably be filthy, even I can't mitigate that. But I will have it shortened to just below the knee and dyed a darker color. I am nothing if not practical. I have always, *always* got a plan; have done ever since I was little.

I move over to where I have the table plan pinned to the wall. Will says I'm like a general hanging his campaign maps. But it is important, isn't it? The seating can pretty much make or break the guests' enjoyment of a wedding. I know I'll have it perfect by this evening. It's all in the planning: that's how I took *The Download* from a blog to a fully fledged online magazine with a staff of thirty in a couple of years.

Most of the guests will come over tomorrow for the wedding, then return to their hotels on the mainland—I enjoyed putting "boats at midnight" on the invites in place of the usual "carriages." But our most important invitees will stay on the island tonight and tomorrow, in the Folly with us. It's a rather exclusive guest list. Will had to choose the favorites among his ushers, as he has so many. Not so difficult for me as I've only got one bridesmaid—my half sister, Olivia. I don't have many female friends. I don't have time for gossip. And groups of women together remind me too much of the bitchy clique of girls at my school who never accepted me as their own. It was a surprise to see so many women at the bachelorette party—but then they were largely my employees from *The Download*—who organized it as a not entirely welcome surprise—or the partners of Will's mates. My closest friend is male: Charlie. In effect, this weekend, he'll be *my* best man.

Charlie and Hannah are on their way over now, the last of tonight's guests to arrive. It will be so good to see Charlie. It feels like a long time since we hung out as adults, without his kids there. Back in the day we used to see each other all the time—even after he'd got together with Hannah. He always made time for me. But when he had kids it felt like he moved into that other realm: one in which a late night means 11 P.M., and every outing without kids has to be carefully orchestrated. It was only then that I started to miss having him to myself.

"You look stunning."

"Oh!" I jump, then spot him in the mirror: Will. He's leaning in the doorway, watching me. "Will!" I hiss. "I'm in my dress! Get out! You're not supposed to see—"

He doesn't move. "Aren't I allowed to have a preview? And I've seen it, now." He begins to walk toward me. "No point crying over spilled silk. You look—*Jesus*—I can't wait to see you coming up the aisle in that." He moves to stand behind me, taking ahold of my bare shoulders.

I should be livid. I *am*. Yet I can feel my outrage sputtering. Because his hands are on me now, moving from my shoulders down my arms, and I feel that first shiver of longing. I remind myself, too, that I'm far from superstitious about the groom seeing the wedding dress beforehand—I've never believed in that sort of thing.

"You shouldn't *be* here," I say, crossly. But already it sounds a little halfhearted.

"Look at us," he says as our eyes meet in the mirror, as he traces a finger down the side of my cheek. "Don't we look good together?"

And he's right, we do. Me so dark-haired and pale, him so fair and tanned. We make the most attractive couple in any room. I'm not going to pretend it's not part of the thrill, imagining how we might appear to the outside world—and to our guests tomorrow. I think of the girls at school who once teased me for being a chubby nerd (I was a late bloomer) and think: *Look who's having the last laugh.*

He bites into the exposed skin of my shoulder. A pluck of lust low in my belly, a snapped elastic band. With it goes the last of my resistance.

"You nearly done with that?" He's looking over my shoulder at the table plan.

"I haven't quite worked out where I'm putting everyone," I say.

There's a silence as he inspects it, his breath warm on the side of my neck, curling along my collarbone. I can smell the aftershave he's wearing: cedar and moss. "Did we invite Piers?" he asks mildly. "I don't remember him being on the list."

I somehow manage not to roll my eyes. *I* did all of the invitations. *I* refined the list, chose the stationer's, collated all the addresses, bought the stamps, mailed every last one. Will was away a lot, shooting the new series. Every so often, he'd throw out a name, someone he'd forgotten to mention. I suppose he did check through the list at the end pretty carefully, saying he wanted to make sure we hadn't missed anyone. Piers was a later addition.

"He wasn't on the list," I admit. "But I saw his wife at those drinks at the Groucho. She asked about the wedding and it seemed total madness not to invite them. I mean, why wouldn't we?" Piers is the producer of Will's show. He's a nice guy and he and Will have always seemed to get along well. I didn't have to think twice about extending the invitation.

"Fine," Will says. "Yes, of course that makes sense." But there's an edge to his voice. For some reason it has bothered him.

"Look, darling," I say, curling one arm around his neck. "I thought you'd be delighted to have them here. They certainly seemed pleased to be asked."

"I don't mind," he says, carefully. "It was a surprise, that's all." He moves his hands to my waist. "I don't mind in the least. In fact, it's a *good* surprise. It will be nice to have them."

"OK. Right, so I'm going to put husbands and wives next to each other. Does that work?"

"The eternal dilemma," he says, mock-profoundly.

"God, I know . . . but people do really care about that sort of thing."

"Well," he says, "if you and I were guests I know where I'd want to be sitting."

"Oh, yes?"

"Right opposite you, so I could do this." His hand reaches down and rucks up the fabric of the silk skirt, climbing beneath.

"Will," I say, "the silk—"

His fingers have found the lace edge of my underwear.

•

"Will!" I say, half-annoyed, "what on earth are you—" Then his fingers have slipped inside my knickers and have begun to move against me and I don't particularly care about the silk anymore. My head falls against his chest.

This is not like me at all. I am not the sort of person who gets engaged only a few months into knowing someone . . . or married only a few months after that. But I would argue that it isn't rash, or impulsive, as I think some suspect. If anything, it's the opposite. It's knowing your own mind, knowing what you want and acting upon it.

"We could do it right now," Will says, his voice a warm murmur against my neck. "We've got time, haven't we?" I try to answer—*no*—but as his fingers continue their work it turns into a long, drawn-out groan.

With every other partner I've got bored in a matter of weeks, the sex has rather too quickly become pedestrian, a chore. With Will I feel like I am never quite sated—even when, in the baser sense, I am more sated than I have been with any other lover. It isn't just about him being so beautiful—which he is, of course, objectively so. This insatiability is far deeper than that. I'm aware of a feeling of wanting to possess him. Of each sexual act being an attempt at a possession that is never quite achieved, some essential part of him always evading my reach, slipping beneath the surface.

Is it to do with his fame? The fact that once you attain celebrity you become, in a sense, publicly owned? Or is it something else, something fundamental about him? Secret and unknowable, hidden from view?

This thought, inevitably, has me thinking about the note. *I will not think about the note.*

Will's fingers continue their work. "Will," I say, halfheartedly, "anyone might come in."

"Isn't that the thrill of it?" he whispers. Yes, yes, I suppose it is. Will has definitely broadened my sexual horizons. He's introduced me to sex in public places. We've done it in a nighttime park, in the back row of a near-empty cinema. When I remember this I am amazed at myself: I cannot believe that it was me who did these things. Julia Keegan does not break the law.

He's also the only man I have ever allowed to film me in the nude—once, even during sex itself. I only agreed to this once we were engaged, naturally. I'm not a fucking idiot. But it's Will's thing and, since we've started doing it, though I don't exactly *like* it—it represents a loss of control, and in every other relationship I have been the one in control—at the same time it is somehow intoxicating, this loss. I hear him unbuckle his belt and just the sound of it sends a charge through me. He pushes me forward, toward the dressing table—a little roughly. I grip the table. I feel the tip of him poised there, about to enter me.

"Hello-hello? Anybody in there?" The door creaks open.

Shit.

Will pulls away from me, I hear him scrabbling with his jeans, his belt. I feel my skirt fall. I almost can't bear to turn.

He stands there, lounging in the doorway: Johnno, Will's best man. How much did he see? *Everything.* I feel the heat rising into my cheeks and I'm furious with myself. I'm furious with him. I *never* blush.

"Sorry, chaps," Johnno says. "Was I interrupting?" Is that a smirk? "Oh—" He catches sight of what I'm wearing. "Is that . . . ? Isn't that meant to be bad luck?"

I'd like to pick up a heavy object and hurl it at him, scream at him to get out. But I am on best behavior. "Oh, for God's sake!" I say instead, and I hope my tone asks: *Do I look like the sort of cretin who would believe something like that?* I raise my eyebrow at him, cross my arms. I am past master at the raised eyebrow game—I use it at work to fantastic effect. I *dare* him to say another word. For all Johnno's bravado, I think he's a little scared of me. People are, generally, scared of me.

"We were going through the table plan," I tell him. "So you interrupted that."

"Well," he says. "I've been such a bellend . . ." I can see that he's a little cowed. Good. "I've just realized I've forgotten something pretty important."

I feel my heart begin to beat faster. Not the rings. I told Will not to trust him with the rings until the last minute. If he's forgotten the rings I cannot be held responsible for my actions.

"It's my suit," Johnno says. "I had it all ready to go, in the liner . . . and then, at the last minute . . . well, I dunno what happened. All I can say is, it must be hanging on my door in Blighty."

I look away from them both as they leave the room. Concentrate hard on not saying anything I'll regret. I have to keep a handle on my temper this weekend. Mine has been known to get the better of me. I'm not proud of the fact, but I have never found myself able to completely control it, though I'm getting better. Rage is not a good look on a bride.

I don't get why Will is friends with Johnno, why he hasn't cut him out of his life by now. It's definitely not the witty conversation that keeps him hanging in there. The guy's harmless, I suppose . . . at least, I assume he's harmless. But they're so different. Will is so driven, so successful, so smart in the way he presents himself.

Johnno is a slob. One of life's dropouts. When we collected him from the local train station on the mainland he stank of weed and looked like he'd been sleeping rough. I expected him to at least get a shave and a haircut before he came out here. It's not too much to ask that your groomsman doesn't look like a caveman, is it? Later I'll send Will over to his room with a razor.

Will's too good to him. He even, apparently, got Johnno a screen test for *Survive the Night* which, of course, didn't come to anything. When I asked Will why he sticks with Johnno, he put it down to simple "history." "We don't have much in common, these days," he said. "But we go back a long way."

But Will can be fairly ruthless. To be honest, that was probably one of the things that attracted me to him when we first met, one of the things I immediately recognized we had in common. As much as his golden looks, his winning smile, the thing that drew me was the ambition I could smell coming off him, beneath his charm.

So this is what worries me. Why would Will keep a friend like Johnno around simply because of a shared past? Unless that past has some sort of hold over him.

JOHNNO

The Best Man

Will climbs out of the trapdoor carrying a pack of Guinness. We're up on the Folly's battlements, looking through the gaps in the stonework. The ground's a long way down and some of the stones up here are pretty loose. If you didn't have a good head for heights it would do a number on you. From here you can see all the way to the mainland. I feel like a king up here, with the sun on my face.

Will breaks a can out of the case. "Here you go."

"Ah, the good stuff. Thanks, mate. And sorry I walked in on you back there." I give him a wink. "Thought you were meant to save it for after marriage, though?"

Will raises his eyebrows, all innocence. "I don't

know what you're talking about. Jules and I were going through the table plan."

"Oh, yeah? That's what they call it now? Honest, though," I say, "I'm sorry about the suit, mate. I feel like such a tool for forgetting." I want him to know I feel bad—that I'm serious about being a good best man to him. I really am, I want to do him proud.

"Not an issue," Will says. "Not sure my spare's going to fit, but you're welcome to it."

"You're sure Jules is going to be all right about it? She didn't look all that happy."

"Yeah." Will waves a hand. "She'll be fine." Which I guess means she probably isn't fine, but he'll work on it.

"OK. Thanks, mate."

He takes a swig of his Guinness, leans against the stone wall behind us. Then he seems to remember something. "Oh. By the way, you haven't seen Olivia, have you? Jules's half sister? She keeps disappearing. She's a little—" He makes a gesture: *cuckoo,* that's what it means, but "fragile" is what he says.

I met Olivia earlier. She's tall and dark-haired, with a big, sulky mouth and legs that go up to her armpits. "Shame," I say. "'Cause . . . well, don't tell me you haven't noticed?"

"Johnno, she's nineteen, for Christ's sake," Will

says. "Don't be disgusting. Besides, she also happens to be my fiancée's sister."

"Nineteen; so she's legal, then," I say, looking to wind him up. "It's tradition, isn't it? The best man has the pick of the bridesmaids. And there's only one, so it's not like I have all that much choice . . ."

Will twists his mouth like he's tasted something disgusting. "I don't think that rule applies when they're fifteen years younger than you, you idiot," he says. He's acting all prim now, but he's always had an eye for the ladies. They've always had an eye for him in return, lucky bastard. "She's off-limits, all right? Get that through your thick skull." He knocks my head with his knuckles.

I don't like the "thick skull" bit. I'm not necessarily the brightest penny in the till. But I don't like being treated like a moron, either. Will knows that. It was one of the things that always got my back up at school. I laugh it off, though. I know he didn't mean it.

"Look," he says. "I can't have you blundering around making passes at my teenage sister-in-law. Jules would *kill* me. She'd kill you, too."

"All right, all right," I say.

"Besides," he says, lowering his voice, "there's also the fact that she's, you know . . ." He makes that *cuckoo* gesture again. "She must get it from Jules's mum. Thank God Jules missed out on any of those genes. Anyway, hands off, all right?"

"Fine, fine . . ." I take a swig of my Guinness and do a big belch.

"You had a chance to do much climbing lately?" Will asks me, obviously trying to change the subject.

"Nah," I say. "Not really. That's why I've got this." I pat my gut. "Hard to find time when you're not being paid for it, like you are."

The funny thing is, it was always me who was more into that stuff. All the Outward-Bound stuff. Until recently, it's what I did for a living too, working at an adventure center in the Lake District.

"Yeah. I guess so," Will says. "It's funny—it's not quite as much fun as it looks, really."

"I doubt that, mate," I say. "You get to do the best thing on earth for a living."

"Well—you know . . . but it's not that authentic; a lot of smoke and mirrors . . ."

I'd bet anything he uses a stuntman to do the harder stuff. Will has never liked getting his hands that dirty. He claims he did a lot of training for the show, but still.

"Then there's all the hair and makeup," he says, "which seems ridiculous when you're shooting a program about survival."

"Bet you love all that," I say with a wink. "Can't fool me."

He's always been a bit vain. I say it with affection, obviously, but I enjoy getting him riled. He's a good-looking bloke and he knows it. You can tell all the clothes he's wearing today, even the jeans, are good stuff, expensive. Maybe it's Jules's influence: she's a stylish lady herself and you can imagine her marching him into a shop. But you can't imagine him minding much either.

"So," I say, clapping him on the shoulder. "You ready to be a married man?"

He grins, nods. "I am. What can I say? I'm head over heels."

I was surprised when Will told me he was getting married, I'm not going to lie. I've always thought of him as a lad about town. No woman can resist that golden boy charm. On the stag, he told me about some of the dates he went on, before Jules. "I mean, in a way it was crazy good. I've never had so much action with so many different women as when I joined those apps, not even at uni. I had to get myself tested every couple of *weeks*. But there were some crazy ones out there, some clingy ones, you know? I don't have time for all that anymore. And then Jules came along. And she was . . . perfect. She's so sure of herself, of what she wants from life. We're the same."

I bet the house in Islington didn't hurt either, I didn't say. *The loaded dad.* I don't dare rib him about it—people get weird talking about money. But if there's one thing Will has always liked, maybe even more than the ladies, it's money. Maybe it's a thing from childhood, never having quite as much as anyone else at our school. I get that. He was there because his dad was headmaster, while I got in on a sports scholarship. My family aren't posh at all. I was spotted playing rugby at a school tournament in Croydon when I was eleven and they approached my dad. That sort of thing actually happened at Trevs: it was that important to them to field a good team.

A voice comes from down below us. "Hey hey hey! What's going on up there?"

"Boys!" Will says. "Come up and join us! More the merrier!"

Bollocks. I was quite enjoying it being just Will and me.

They're climbing up out of the trapdoor—the four ushers. I shift over to make room, giving each a nod as they appear: Femi, then Angus, Duncan, Peter.

"Fuck me, it's high up here," Femi says, peering over the edge.

Duncan grabs hold of Angus's shoulders and pretends to give him a shove. "Whoa, saved you!"

Angus lets out a high-pitched squeal and we all laugh. "Don't!" he says angrily, recovering himself. "Jesus—that's *fucking* dangerous." He's clinging on to the stone as though for dear life, inching his way along to sit down next to us. Angus was always a bit wet for our group, but got social credit for arriving in his dad's chopper at the start of term.

Will hands out the cans of Guinness I'd been eyeing up for seconds.

"Thanks, mate," Femi says. He looks at the can. "When in Rome, hey?"

Pete nods to the drop beneath us. "Think you might have to have a few of these to forget about that, Angus, mate."

"Yeah but you don't want to drink *too* many," Duncan says. "Or you won't care enough about it."

"Oh shut it," Angus says crossly, coloring. But he's still pretty pale and I get the impression he's doing everything he can not to look over the edge.

"I've got gear with me this weekend," Pete says in an undertone, "that would make you think you could jump off and fucking fly."

"Leopards don't change their spots, eh, Pete?" Femi says. "Raiding your mum's pill cabinet—I remember that kit bag of yours rattling when you came back after exeat."

"Yeah," Angus says. "We all owe her a thank-you."

"*I'd* thank her," Duncan says. "Always remember your mum being a bit of a MILF, Pete."

"You better share the love tomorrow, mate," Femi says.

Pete winks at him. "You know me. Always do well by my boys."

"How about now?" I ask. I suddenly feel I need a hit to blur the edges and the weed I smoked earlier has worn off.

"I like your attitude, J-dog," Pete says. "But you gotta pace yourself."

"You better behave yourselves tomorrow," Will says, mock-sternly. "I don't want my groomsmen showing me up."

"We'll behave, mate," Pete says, throwing an arm around his shoulder. "Just want to make sure our boy's wedding is an occasion to remember."

Will's always been the center of everything, the anchor of the group, all of us revolving round him. Good at sport, good enough grades—with a bit of extra help here and there. Everyone liked him. And I guess it seemed effortless, as though he didn't work for anything. If you didn't know him like I did, that is.

We all sit and drink in silence for a few moments in the sun.

"This is like being back at Trevs," Angus says, ever the historian. "Remember how we used to smuggle beers into the school? Climb up onto the roof of the sports hall to drink them?"

"Yeah," Duncan says. "Seem to remember you shitting yourself then, too."

Angus scowls. "*Fuck* off."

"Johnno smuggled them in really," Femi says, "from that shop in the village."

"Yeah," Duncan says, "because he was a tall, ugly, hairy bastard, even at fifteen, weren't you, mate?" He leans over, punches me on the shoulder.

"And we drank them warm from the can," Angus says, " 'cause we didn't have any way to cool them down. Best thing I've ever drunk in my life, probably—even now, when we could all drink, you know, chilled fucking Dom every day of the week if we wanted to."

"You mean like we did a few months ago," Duncan says. "At the RAC."

"When was this?" I ask.

"Ah," Will says. "Sorry, Johnno. I knew it would be too far for you to come, you being in Cumbria and everything."

"Oh," I say. "Yeah, that makes sense." I think of them having a nice old champagne lunch together at the Royal Automobile Club, one of those posh members-only places. Right. I take a big long swig of my Guinness. I could really do with some more weed.

"It was the kick of it," Femi says, "back at school, at Trevs. That's what it was. Knowing we could get caught."

"Jesus," Will says. "Do we really have to talk about Trevs? It's bad enough that I have to hear my dad talking about the place." He says it with a grin, but I can see he's got this slightly pinched look, as if his Guinness has gone down the wrong way. I always felt sorry for Will having a dad like his. No wonder he felt he had to prove himself. I know he'd prefer to forget his whole time at that place. I would too.

"Those years at school seemed so grim at the time," Angus says, "but now, looking back—and Christ knows what this says about me—I think in some ways they feel like the most important of my life. I mean, I definitely wouldn't send my own kids there—no offense to your dad, Will—but it wasn't all bad. Was it?"

"I dunno," Femi says doubtfully. "I got singled out a lot by the teachers. Fucking racists." He says it in an offhand way but I know it wasn't always easy for him, being one of the only black kids there.

"I loved it," Duncan says, and when the rest of us look at him, he adds: "Honest! Now I look back on it

I realize how important it was, you know? Wouldn't have had it any other way. It bonded us."

"Anyway," says Will, "back to the present. I'd say things are pretty good now for all of us, wouldn't you?"

They're definitely good for him. The other blokes have done all right for themselves too. Femi's a surgeon, Angus works for his dad's development firm, Duncan's a venture capitalist—whatever that means—and Pete's in advertising, which probably doesn't help his coke habit.

"So what are you up to these days, Johnno?" Pete asks, turning to me. "You were doing that climbing instructor stuff, right?"

I nod. "The adventure center," I say. "Not just climbing. Bushcraft, building camps—"

"Yeah," Duncan says, cutting me off, "you know, I was thinking of a team-bonding day—was going to talk to you about it. Cut me some mates' rates?"

"I'd love to," I say, thinking someone as minted as Duncan doesn't need to ask for mates' rates. "But I'm not doing it anymore."

"Oh?"

"Nah. I've set up a whiskey business. It'll be coming out pretty soon. Maybe in the next six months or so."

"And you've got outlets?" Angus asks. He sounds

rather put out. I suppose it doesn't fit with his image of big, stupid Johnno. I've somehow managed to avoid the boring office job and come out on top.

"I have," I say, nodding. "I have."

"Waitrose?" Duncan asks. "Sainsbury's?"

"And the rest."

"There's a lot of competition out there," Angus says.

"Yeah," I say. "Lots of big old names, celebrity brands—even that UFC fighter, Connor MacGregor. But we wanted to go for a more, I dunno, artisanal feel. Like those new gins."

"We're lucky enough to be serving it tomorrow," Will says. "Johnno brought a case with him. We'll have to give it a try this evening, too. What's the name again? I know it's a good one."

"Hellraiser," I say. I'm quite proud of the name, actually. Different from those fusty old brands. And a little annoyed Will's forgotten—it's only on the labels of the bottles I gave him yesterday. But the bloke's getting married tomorrow. He's got other stuff on his mind.

"Who'd have thought it?" Femi says. "All of us, respectable adults. And having come out of that place? Again, no offense to your dad, Will. But it was like somewhere from another century. We're lucky we got out alive—four boys left every term, as I recall."

I couldn't ever have left. My folks were so excited when I got the rugby scholarship, that I got to go to a posh school—a *boarding* school. All the opportunities it would give me, or so they thought.

"Yeah," Pete says. "Remember, there was that boy who drank ethanol from the science department because he was dared to—they had to rush him to hospital? Then there were always the kids who had nervous breakdowns—"

"Oh, shit," Duncan says, excitedly, "and there was that little weedy kid, the one who died. Only the strong survived!" He grins round at us all. "The ones who raised hell, am I right, boys? All back together this weekend!"

"Yeah," Femi says. "But look at this." He leans over and points to the patch where he's going a bit thin on top. "We're getting old and boring now, aren't we?"

"Speak for yourself, mate!" Duncan says. "I reckon we could still fire things up if the occasion demanded it."

"Not at my wedding you won't," Will says, but he's smiling.

"*Especially* at your wedding we will," Duncan says.

"Thought you'd be the first to get married, mate," Femi says to Will. "Being such a hit with the ladies."

"And I thought you never would," Angus says, sucking up like always, "too *much* of a hit with them. Why settle?"

"Do you remember that girl you shagged?" Pete asks. "From the local comp? That topless Polaroid you had of her? Jesus."

"One for the wank bank," Angus says. "Still think about that photo sometimes."

"Yeah, because you never get any action yourself," Duncan says.

Will winks. "Anyway. Seeing as we're all together again—even if we're old and boring, as you so charmingly put it, Femi—I think that deserves a toast."

"I'll drink to that," Duncan says, raising his can.

"Me too," says Pete.

"To the survivors," Will says.

"The survivors!" We echo him. And just for a moment, when I look at the others, they look different, younger. It's like the sun has gilded them. You can't see Femi's bald spot from this angle, or Angus's paunch, and Pete looks less like he only goes out at night. And, if possible, even Will looks better, brighter. I have this sudden sense that we're back there, sitting on that sports hall roof and nothing bad has happened yet. I'd give a fair amount to return to that time.

"Right," Will says, draining the dregs of his Guinness. "I better get downstairs. Charlie and Hannah will be arriving soon. Jules wants a welcoming party on the jetty."

I suppose once everyone's here the weekend will kick off in earnest. I wish for a moment we could go back to just Will and me, shooting the breeze, like we were before the others arrived. I haven't seen all that much of Will recently. Yet he's the person who knows more about me than anyone in the world, really. And I know the most about him.

OLIVIA

The Bridesmaid

My room used to be a maid's quarters, apparently. I worked out pretty quickly that I'm directly below Jules and Will's room. Last night I could hear *everything*. I did try not to, obviously. But it was like the harder I tried, the more I heard every tiny sound, every groan and gasp. Almost as if they *wanted* to be heard.

They did it this morning too, but at least then I could get out, escape the Folly. We're all under instructions not to go walking around the island after dark. But if it happens again this evening there's no way I'm going to stay here. I'd prefer to take my chances with the peat bog and the cliffs.

I toggle my phone on to Airplane mode and off again, to see if anything happens to the little NO SIGNAL message, but it does fuck all. I doubt I have any new messages. I've sort of lost contact with all my mates. It's not like we've fallen out. It's more that I've left their world since I dropped out of uni. They sent me messages at first:

Hope you're OK babes

Call if you need to chat Livs

See you soon, yeah?

We miss you! 💔

What happened????

Suddenly I feel like I can't breathe. I reach for the bedside table. The razor blade is there: so small, but so sharp. I pull down my jeans and press the razor's edge to my inner thigh, up near my knickers, drag it into my flesh until the blood wells. The color's such a dark red against the blue-white skin there. It's not a very big cut; I've made bigger. But the sting of it focuses everything to a point, to the metal entering my flesh, so that for a moment nothing else exists.

I breathe a little easier. Maybe I'll do one more—

There's a knock on my door. I drop the blade, fumbling to get my jeans closed. "Who is it?" I call.

"Me," Jules says, pushing the door open before I tell her she can come in, which is so Jules. Thank God I reacted quickly. "I need to see you in your bridesmaid dress," she says. "We've got a bit of time before Hannah and Charlie arrive. Johnno's forgotten his *bloody* suit so I want to make sure that at least one member of the wedding party looks good."

"I've already tried it on," I say. "It definitely fits." *Lie.* I have no idea whether it fits or not. I was meant to come to the shop to try it on. But I found an excuse every time Jules tried to get me there: eventually she gave up and bought it, on condition I tried it on and told her it fitted straightaway. I told her it did but I couldn't make myself put it on. It's been in its big stiff cardboard box since Jules had it delivered.

"*You* may have tried it on," Jules says, "but *I* want to see it." She smiles at me, suddenly, like she's just remembered to do so. "You can do it in our bedroom, if you like." She says it as if she's offering some amazing privilege.

"No thanks," I say. "I'd prefer to stay here—"

"Come on," she says. "We've got a nice big mirror." I realize it isn't optional. I go to the wardrobe and lift out the big duck-egg-blue box. Jules's mouth tightens. I know she's pissed off I haven't hung it up yet.

Growing up with Jules sometimes felt like having a second mother, or one who was like other mums—bossy, strict, all that stuff. Mum was never really like that, but Jules was.

I follow her up to their bedroom. Even though Jules is *super* tidy and even though there's a window open to let the fresh air in, it smells of bodies in here, and men's aftershave and, I think (*I don't want to think*), of sex. It feels wrong being in here, in their private space.

Jules closes the door and turns to me with her arms folded. "Go on, then," she says.

I don't feel like I have much choice. Jules is good at making you feel that. I strip down to my underwear, keeping my legs pressed together in case my thigh's still bleeding. If Jules sees I'll have to tell her I've got my period. My skin prickles into goose bumps in the slight breeze coming through the window. I can feel her watching me; I wish she'd give me a bit of privacy. "You've lost weight," she says critically. Her tone is caring, but it doesn't quite ring true. I know she's probably jealous. Once, when she got drunk, she went on about how kids had got at her at school for being "chubby." She's always making comments about my weight, like she doesn't know I've always been skinny, ever since I was a little girl. But it's possible to hate your body when you're thin, too. To feel like it's kept secrets from you. To feel like it's let you down.

Jules is right, though. I have lost weight. I can only wear my smallest jeans at the moment, and even they slip down off my hips. I haven't been trying to lose weight or anything. But that feeling of emptiness I get when I don't eat as much . . . it matches how I feel. It seems right.

Jules is taking the dress out of the box. "Olivia!" she says crossly. "Has this been in here the whole time? Look at these creases! This silk's so delicate . . . I thought you'd look after it a bit better." She sounds as though she's talking to a child. I guess she thinks she is. But I'm not a child anymore.

"Sorry," I say. "I forgot." *Lie.*

"Well. Thank *goodness* I've brought a steamer. It'll take ages to get all of these out, though. You'll have to do that later. But for now just try it on."

She has me put out my arms, like a child, while she shrugs the dress down over my head. As she does I spot an inch-long, bright pink mark on the inside of her wrist. It's a burn, I think. It looks sore and I wonder how she did it: Jules is so careful, she's never normally clumsy enough to burn herself. But before I can get a better look she has taken hold of my upper arms and is steering me toward the mirror so both of us can look at me in the dress. It's a blush pink color, which I would never wear, because it makes me look even paler. The same color, almost, as the swanky manicure Jules made me get in London last week. Jules wasn't happy with the state of my nails: she told the manicurist to "do the best you can with them." When I look at my hands now it makes me want to laugh: the prissy princess-pink shimmer of the polish next to my bitten down, bleeding cuticles.

Jules steps back, her arms folded and eyes narrowed. "It's quite loose. God, I'm sure this was the smallest size they had. For *Christ's sake,* Olivia. I wish you'd told me it didn't fit properly—I would have had it taken in. But . . ." She frowns, moving around me in a slow circle. I feel that breeze through the window again, and shiver. "I don't know, maybe it works a little loose. I suppose it's a *look,* of sorts."

I study myself in the mirror. The shape of the dress itself isn't too offensive: a slip, bias cut, quite nineties. Something I might even have worn if it was another color. Jules isn't wrong; it doesn't look terrible. But you can see my black pants and my nipples through the fabric.

"Don't worry," Jules says, as though she's read my

mind. "I've got a stick-on bra for you. And I've bought you a nude thong—I knew you wouldn't have one yourself."

Great. That will make me feel a lot less fucking naked.

It's weird, standing together in front of the mirror, Jules behind me, both of us looking at my reflection. There are obvious differences between us. We're totally different shapes, for one, and I have a slimmer nose—Mum's nose—while Jules has better hair, thick and shiny. But when we're together like this I can see that we're more similar than people might think. The shape of our faces is the same, like Mum's. You can see we're sisters, or nearly.

I wonder if Jules is seeing it too: the similarity between us. Her expression is all odd and pinched-looking.

"Oh, Olivia," she says. And then—I see it happen, in the mirror in front of us, before I actually feel it—she reaches out and takes my hand in hers. I freeze. It's so unlike Jules: she is not big on physical contact, or affection. "Look," she says, "I know we haven't always got along. But I *am* proud to have you as my bridesmaid. You do know that—don't you?"

"Yes," I say. It comes out as a bit of a croak.

Jules gives my hand a squeeze, which for her is like

a full-blown hug. "Mum says you broke up with that guy? You know, Olivia, at your age it can feel like the end of the world. But then later you meet someone who you *really* click with and you understand the difference. It's like Will and me—"

"I'm fine," I say. "It's fine." *Lie.* I do *not* want to talk about any of this with anyone. Jules least of all. She's the last person who would understand if I told her I can't remember why I ever bothered to put makeup on, or nice underwear, or buy new clothes, or go and get my hair cut. It seems like someone else did all those things.

Suddenly I feel really weird. Sort of faint and sick. I sway a bit, and Jules catches me, her hands gripping my upper arms hard.

"I'm fine," I say, before she can even ask what's wrong. I bend down and unfasten the over-fancy gray silk shoes Jules has chosen for me, with their jeweled buckles, which takes ages because my hands have become all clumsy and stupid. Then I reach up and drag the dress over my head, so hard that Jules gives a little gasp, like she thinks it might tear. I didn't use her pillow.

"Olivia!" she says. "What on *earth* has gotten into you?"

"Sorry," I say. But I only mouth the word, no actual sound comes out.

"Look," she says. "Just for these few days I'd like you to try and make a bit of an effort. *OK?* This is my wedding, Livvy. I've tried so hard to make it perfect. I bought this dress for you—I'd like you to wear it because I want you there, as my bridesmaid. That *means* something to me. It should mean something to you, too. Doesn't it?"

I nod. "Yeah. Yeah, it does." And then, because she seems to be waiting for me to go on, I add, "I'm OK. I don't know what . . . what that was before. I'm fine now."

Lie.

JULES

The Bride

I push open the door to my mother's room into a cloud of Shalimar perfume and, possibly, cigarette smoke. She better not have been smoking in here. Mum is sitting at the mirror in her silk kimono, busy outlining her lips in her signature carmine. "Goodness, that's a murderous expression. What do you want, darling?"

Darling.

The strange cruelty of that word.

I keep my tone calm, reasonable. I am being my best self, today. "Olivia is going to behave herself tomorrow, isn't she?"

My mother gives a weary sigh. Takes a sip of the drink she's got next to her. It looks suspiciously like a martini. Great, so she's already on the strong stuff.

"I made her my bridesmaid," I say. "I could have

picked from twenty other people." Not quite true. "But she's acting as though it's this big drag. I've hardly asked her to do anything. She didn't come to the hen do even though there was a room free in the villa for her. It did look odd—"

"I could have come instead, darling."

I stare at her. It would never have occurred to me that she might have wanted to come. Besides, no bloody *way* was I ever going to invite my mother to the hen do. It would, inevitably, have morphed into the Araminta Jones show.

"Look," I say. "None of that really matters. It's in the past now, I suppose. But is she at least going to try and *look* happy for me?"

"She's had a difficult time," Mum says.

"You mean because her boyfriend broke up with her or whatever it was? They were only going out for a few months according to what I've seen on Instagram. Clearly a romance of epic proportions!" A note of petulance has crept in, despite my best intentions.

My mother is now concentrating on the more precise work of outlining her Cupid's bow. "But, darling," she says, once she has finished, "when you think about it, you and the gorgeous Will haven't been together all *that* long, have you?"

"That's rather different," I say, nettled. "Olivia's

nineteen. She's still a teenager. Love is what teenagers *think* has happened when actually they're just stuffed full of hormones. *I* thought I was in love when I was about her age."

I think of Charlie at eighteen: the deep biscuit tan, the white line sometimes visible beneath his board shorts. It occurs to me that my mother never knew—or cared to know—about my adolescent affairs of the heart. She was too busy with her own love life. Thank God; I'm not sure any teenager wants that kind of scrutiny. And yet I can't help but feel that this all proves she and Olivia are much closer than we ever were.

"When your father left me," Mum says, "you have to remember that I was about the same age. I had a newborn baby—"

"I know, Mum," I say, as patiently as I can. I've heard more times than I ever needed to about how my birth ended what definitely, probably, *maybe,* would have been a highly successful career for my mother.

"Do you know what it was like for me?" she asks. Ah, here it comes: the same old script. "Trying to have a career and a tiny baby? Trying to make a living, to make something of myself? Just so I could put food on the table?"

You didn't have to continue trying to get acting jobs, I think. *If you'd really wanted to put food on the table that probably wasn't the most sensible way to do it. We didn't have to spend your tiny income on an apartment off Shaftesbury Avenue in Zone One and not be able to afford to eat as a result. It's not my fault you made some bad decisions when you were a teenager and got yourself knocked up.*

As usual, I don't say any of this. "We were talking about Olivia," I say, instead.

"Well," Mum says, "let's just say that there was a little more to Olivia's experience than a bad breakup." She examines the glossy finish of her nails—carmine, too, as though her fingers have been dipped in blood.

Of course, I think. This is Olivia, so it had to be special and different in some way. *Careful, Jules. Don't be bitter. Best behavior.* "What, then?" I ask. "What else was there?"

"It's not my place to say." This is surprisingly discreet, coming from my mother. "And besides," she says, "Olivia's like me in that—an empath. We can't simply . . . smother our feelings and put a brave face on it like some people can."

I know that in a sense this is true. I know that Olivia *does* feel things deeply, too deeply, that she does take them to heart. She's a dreamer. She was always coming home from school with playground scrapes, and bruises from bumping into things. She's a nail-biter, a hairsplitter, an overthinker. She's "fragile." But she's also spoiled.

And I can't help sensing implied criticism in Mum's reference to "some people." Just because the rest of us don't wear our hearts on our sleeves, just because we have found a way of *managing* our feelings—it doesn't mean they're not there.

Breathe, Jules.

I think of how Olivia looked so oddly at me when I told her I was happy to have her as my bridesmaid. I couldn't help feeling a small pang as, trying on the dress, she slipped out of her clothes and revealed her slender, stretch mark–free body. I know she felt me staring. She is definitely too thin and too pale. And yet she looked undeniably gorgeous. Like one of those nineties heroin-chic models: Kate Moss lounging in a bedsit with a string of fairy lights behind her. Looking at her, I was caught between those two emotions I always seem to feel when it comes to Olivia: a deep, almost painful tenderness, and a shameful, secret envy.

I suppose I haven't always been as warm toward her as I might. Now she's older, she's wised up a little—and of late, since the engagement party especially, she has been noticeably cool. But when Olivia was younger she used to trail around after me like an adoring puppy.

I got quite used to her displays of unrequited affection. Even as I envied her.

Mum turns around on her chair now. Her face is suddenly very somber, uncharacteristically so. "Look. She's had a difficult time, Jules. You can't possibly begin to know the half of it. That poor kid has been through a lot."

That poor kid. I feel it, at that. I thought I'd be immune to it by now. I'm ashamed to find that I am not: the little dart of envy, under my ribs.

I take a deep breath. Remind myself that here I am, getting married. If Will and I have kids their childhood will be nothing like mine was—Mum with her string of boyfriends, all actors, always "on the verge of a big break." Someone finding me a place to sleep on the coats at all the inevitable Soho afterparties, because I was six years old and all my classmates would have been tucked up hours before.

Mum turns back to the mirror. She squints at herself, pushes her hair one way, then the other, twists it up behind her head. "Got to look good for the new arrivals," she says. "Aren't they *handsome,* all of Will's friends?"

Oh, *Christ.*

Olivia doesn't know how good she had it, how lucky she was. To her it was all normal. When her dad, Rob, was around, Mum became this proper mother figure: cooked meals, insisted on bed by eight, there was a playroom full of toys. Mum eventually got bored of playing happy family. But not before Olivia had had a whole, contented childhood. Not before I had begun half *hating* that little girl for everything she didn't even know she had.

I'm itching with the need to break something. I pick up the Cire Trudon candle on the dressing table, heft it in my hand, imagine how it would feel to watch it splinter to smithereens. I don't do this anymore—I've got it under control. I definitely wouldn't want Will to see this side of me. But around my family I find myself regressing, letting all the old pettiness and envy and hurt come rushing back until I am teenage Jules, plotting to get away. I must be bigger than this. I have forged my own path. I have built it all on my own, something stable and powerful. And this weekend is a statement of that. My victory march.

Through the window I hear the sound of a boat's engine guttering. It must be Charlie arriving. Charlie will make me feel better.

I put the candle back down.

HANNAH

The Plus-One

By the time we finally reach the stiller waters of the island's inlet I've been sick three times and I'm soaked and cold to the bone, feeling as wrung out as an old dish cloth and clinging to Charlie like he's a human life raft. I'm not sure how I'm going to walk off the boat, as my legs feel like they've got no bones left. I wonder if Charlie's embarrassed to be turning up with me in the state I'm in. He always gets a bit funny around Jules. My mum would call it "putting on airs."

"Oh, look," Charlie says, "see those beaches over there? The sand really is white." I can see the way the sea turns an astonishing aquamarine color in the shallows, the light bouncing off the waves. At one end the land shears away in dramatic cliffs and giant stacks that have become separated from the rest. At the other end is an improbably small castle, right out on a promontory, perched over a few shelves of rocks and the crashing sea below.

"Look at that castle," I say.

"I think that's the Folly," Charlie says. "That's what Jules called it, anyway."

"Trust posh people to have a special name for it."

Charlie ignores me. "We'll be staying in there. It should be fun. And it'll be a nice distraction, won't it? I know this month's always tough."

"Yeah," I nod.

Charlie squeezes my hand. We both fall silent for a moment.

"And, you know," he says, suddenly, "being without the kids for a change. Being adults again."

I shoot him a look. Is there a touch of wistfulness in his tone? It's true that we haven't done very much recently other than keep two small people alive. I even feel, sometimes, that Charlie's a bit jealous of how much love and attention I lavish on the kids.

"Remember those days in the beginning," Charlie said an hour ago, as we drove through the beautiful countryside of Connemara, admiring the red heather and the dark peaks, "when we'd get on a train with a tent and go camping somewhere wild for the weekend? God, that seems a long time ago."

We'd spend whole weekends having sex back then, surfacing only to eat or go for walks. We always seemed to have some spare cash. Yeah, our lives are rich now in another way, but I know what Charlie's getting at. We were the first in our group of friends to have kids—I got pregnant with Ben before we got married. Even though I wouldn't change any of it, I've wondered whether we missed out on a couple more years of carefree fun. There's another self that I sometimes feel I lost along the way. The girl who always stayed for one more drink, who loved a dance. I miss her, sometimes.

Charlie's right. We've needed a weekend away, the two of us. I only wish that our first proper escape in ages didn't have to be at the glamorous wedding of Charlie's slightly terrifying friend.

I don't want to think too hard about when the last time we had sex was, because I know the answer will be too depressing. A while, anyway. In honor of this weekend I've had my first bikini wax in . . . Jesus, quite a long time, anyway, if you don't count those little boxes of DIY strips mainly left unused in the bathroom cupboard. Sometimes, since the kids, it's as though we're more like colleagues, or partners in a small, somewhat shaky start-up that we have to devote all our attention to, rather than lovers. *Lovers.* When was the last time we thought of ourselves as that?

"Crap," I say, to distract myself from this line of thought, "look at that marquee! It's enormous." It's so big it looks like a tented city rather than a single structure. If anyone were going to have a *really* fancy marquee, it would be Jules.

The rest of the island looks, if possible, even more hostile than it did from far away. It seems incredible that this forbidding place is going to accommodate us for the next few days. As we get closer I can see a cluster of small, dark dwellings behind the Folly. And on the crest of a hill rising up beyond the marquee is a bristle of dark shapes. At first I think they're people; an army of figures awaiting our arrival. Only they seem oddly, impossibly still. As we draw closer I realize that the strange, upright forms seem to be grave markers. And what looked like large bulbous heads are crosses, Celtic ones, the round circle enclosing the even-sided cross.

"There they are!" Charlie says. He gives a wave.

I see the cluster of figures on the jetty now, waving. I comb my fingers through my hair, although I know from long experience that I'm probably making it more wild. I wish I had a bottle of water to swig from to help the sour taste in my mouth.

As we draw closer, I can make them all out a little better. I see Jules, and even from this distance, I can see that she looks immaculate: the only person who could wear all white in a place like this and not immediately stain her clothes. Near Jules and Will stand two women who I can only assume must be Jules's family—the glossy dark hair gives them away.

"There's Jules's mum," Charlie says, pointing to the elder woman.

"Wow," I say. She's not what I expected at all. She wears black skinny jeans and little cat's-eye black glasses pushed back onto a glossy dark bob. She doesn't look old enough to have a thirty-something daughter.

"Yeah, she had Jules pretty young," Charlie says, as if reading my mind. "And that must be—Jesus Christ! I suppose that must be Olivia. Jules's little half sister."

"She doesn't look so little now," I say. She's taller than both Jules and her mum; a totally different shape to Jules, who's all curves. She's very striking-looking, beautiful, even, and her skin is pale pale pale in the way that only really looks good with black hair, like hers. Her legs in her jeans look as though they've been drawn with two long thin lines of charcoal. God, I'd kill for legs like that.

"I can't believe how much older she is," Charlie says. He's half whispering now, we're close enough that they might hear us. He sounds a bit freaked out.

"Is she the one who used to have a crush on you?" I

ask, dredging this fact up from some half-remembered conversation with Jules.

"Yes," he says, with a rueful grin. "God, Jules used to tease me about it. It was pretty embarrassing. Funny, but embarrassing, too. She used to find excuses to come and talk to me and lounge around in that disturbingly provocative way thirteen-year-olds can."

I look at the gorgeous creature on the jetty and think—*I bet he wouldn't be so embarrassed now.*

Mattie is suddenly busying himself around us, putting out fenders on one side, readying a rope.

Charlie steps forward: "Let me help—"

Mattie waves him away, which I suspect Charlie's a little offended by.

"Chuck it here!" Will strides up the jetty toward us. On TV, he's good-looking. In the flesh, he's . . . well, he's pretty breathtaking. "Let me help you!" he calls to Mattie.

Mattie throws him a rope and Will catches it expertly in midair, revealing a slice of muscular stomach beneath his Aran knit sweater. I wonder if I'm imagining Charlie bristling next to me. Boats are his thing: he was a sailing instructor in his youth. But *everything* outdoorsy, it seems, is Will's thing.

"Welcome, you two!" He grins and reaches out a hand to me. "Need a lift?" I don't really, but I take it anyway. He grabs me under my armpit and lifts me over the side of the boat as though I'm as light as a child. I catch a gust of some subtle, masculine scent—moss and pine—and realize with dismay how I must smell in return, like vomit and seaweed.

He has it in real life, I can tell already, that charm, that magnetism. In one of the articles I read about him, while watching the show—because obviously I had to start googling everything I could find about him—the journalist joked that she basically just watched it because she couldn't tear her eyes away from Will. Lots of people became outraged, claimed it was objectification, that if the same piece had been written by a man the journalist would have been roasted alive. But I bet the show's PR team opened the champagne.

If I'm honest, I can see what she meant. There are lots of shots of Will stripped to the waist, or grunting his way up a rock face, always looking incredibly attractive. But it's more than that. He has a particular way of talking to the camera, an intimacy, so that you feel you might be lying next to him in the temporary shelter he's built out of branches and tree bark, blinking in the light of his headlamp. It's the feeling of a companionable solitude, that it's just you and him in the wilderness. It's a seduction.

Charlie reaches out a hand to Will. "Oh, what the

hell?" Will says, ignoring it to envelop Charlie in a big hug. I can see the tension in Charlie's back from here.

"Will," Charlie says, with a curt nod, stepping away immediately. It's borderline rude when Will's being so welcoming.

"Charlie!" Jules is coming forward now, reaching out her arms. "It's been so long. God, I've missed you."

Jules, the other woman in Charlie's life. The most significant woman in his life—until I came along. They hug for a long time.

At last we follow Jules and Will up toward the Folly. Will tells us it was originally built as a coastal defense, then converted by some wealthy Irishman into a holiday home a century ago: a place to retreat to for a few days, entertain friends. But if you didn't know you could almost believe it was medieval. There's a small turret and in among the bigger windows are tiny ones: "false arrow slits," Charlie says—he's quite into castles.

As we make our way there we see a chapel, or what remains of a chapel, hidden behind the Folly. The roof seems to be completely gone, leaving only the walls and five tall pillars—what might once have been the spires—reaching for sky. The windows are gaping empty holes in the stone and the whole front of it must have fallen away. "That's where the ceremony will take place tomorrow," Jules says.

"It's beautiful," I say. "So romantic." All the right things. And I suppose it is beautiful, in a stark way. Charlie and I got married in the local registry office. Definitely not beautiful: a poky municipal room, a bit scuffed and cramped. Jules was there, too, of course, looking rather out of place in her designer outfit. The whole thing was over in what felt like twenty minutes, we met the next couple coming in on our way out.

But I wouldn't have wanted to get married in a place like the chapel. It is beautiful, yes, but there's definitely something tragic about its beauty, even slightly macabre. It stands out against the sky like a twisted, long-fingered hand, reaching up from the ground. There's a haunted look about it.

I watch Will and Jules as we follow them. I would never have had Jules down as a very tactile person but her hands are all over him, it's as if she can't not touch him. You can tell they are having sex. A lot of it. It's hard to watch as her hand slides into the back pocket of his jeans, or up beneath the fabric of his T-shirt. I bet Charlie's noticed, too. I won't mention it, though. That would only draw attention to the lack of sex we're having. We used to have really good, adventurous sex. But these days we're so knackered all the time. And I find myself wondering whether, since kids, I feel different to Charlie, or whether he fancies me as much now my boobs are not the same boobs they were before breastfeeding, now I have all this strange slack skin on my belly. I know I *shouldn't* ask, because my body has performed a miracle; two, in fact. And yet it is important for a couple to still desire each other, isn't it?

Jules has never really had a lasting relationship in all the time Charlie and I have been together. I always sensed she didn't have time for anything serious, so focused was she on *The Download.* Charlie liked predicting how long they would last: "Three months, tops." Or, "This one's already past its expiry date, if you ask me." And he was always the one she called when she did break up with them. Part of me wonders how he feels now, seeing her settled at last. I'd guess not entirely happy. My suspicions about the two of them threaten to surface. I push them back down.

As we near the building a big cackle of laughter erupts from somewhere above. I glance up and see a group of men on top of the Folly's battlements, looking down at us. There's a mocking note to the laughter and I'm suddenly very aware of the state of my clothes and hair. I'm convinced that we're the butt of their joke.

OLIVIA

The Bridesmaid

Seeing Charlie again reminds me of how I used to moon about after him. It was only a few years ago, really, but I was a kid then. It's embarrassing, thinking of the girl I used to be. But it also makes me kind of sad.

I'm looking for somewhere to hide from them all. I take the track past the ruined houses, left over from when people used to live on this island. Jules told me that the islanders abandoned their homes because they found it easier to live on the mainland, that they wanted electricity and stuff. I get that. Just the fact of being stuck here would drive you mental. Even if you managed to get a boat to the mainland you'd still be a million miles away from anywhere. Your nearest, I don't know, H&M, say, would be hundreds of miles away. I've always felt like Mum and I lived out in the sticks, but now I'm just grateful that we don't live on an island in the middle of the Atlantic. So, yeah, I can see why you'd want to leave. But looking at these deserted houses with their empty windows and tumbledown appearance, it's hard not to feel like bad things happened here.

Yesterday, I saw something on one of the beaches; it was bigger than the rest of the rocks, gray but smoother, softer-looking somehow. I went to get a closer look. It was a dead seal. A baby, I think, because it was so small. I crept a bit closer and then I got a shock. On the other side, which had been hidden from me before, the seal's body was all open, dark red, spilling out. I can't get the image of it out of my head. Since then this place has made me think of death.

It only takes me a few minutes to get down to the cave, which is marked on a map of the island in the Folly. The Whispering Cave, it's called. It's like a long wound in the ground—open at both ends. You could fall into it without realizing it was there because the opening is hidden by all this long grass. When I came across it yesterday I nearly did fall in. I would have broken my neck. That would ruin Jules's perfect wedding, wouldn't it? The thought almost makes me smile.

I climb down into the cave, down the rocks at the

side that resemble a flight of steps. All the noise in my head dials down a notch and I start to breathe easier, even if there is a weird smell in this place—like sulfur, and maybe also of things rotting. It could be coming from the seaweed, lying all around in here in big dark ropes. Or maybe the stink's coming from the walls, which are spotted with yellow lichen.

In front of me is a tiny shingled beach, and the sea beyond. I sit down on a rock. It's damp, but then this whole place is damp. I could feel it on my clothes when I dressed this morning, like they'd been washed and hadn't quite dried. If I lick my lips I can taste salt on my skin.

I think about staying here for a long time, even overnight. I could hide here until after the ceremony is over, until it's all done and dusted. Jules would be livid, of course. Although . . . maybe she'd *pretend* to be angry, but actually she'd be secretly relieved. I don't think she really wants me at her wedding at all. I think she resents me because Mum gets on better with me and because I have a dad who wants to see me at least occasionally. I know I'm being a bitch. Jules does do nice stuff for me, sometimes, like when she let me stay in her flat in London last summer. And when I remember that, I feel bad, like there's a nasty taste in my mouth.

I take out my phone. Because of the rubbish signal here my Instagram is stuck with one photo at the top.

Of course it would be Ellie's latest post. It's like they're mocking me. The comments underneath:

You GUYS! ❤ ❤ ❤

OMG sooooo cute. 😍

mum + dad

#mood ❤

so can we assume its official now, yeh? *winks*

It hurts, still. A pain at the center of my chest. I look at their smug, smiling faces, and part of me wants to lob my phone as hard as I can at the wall of the cave. But that wouldn't sort my problems out. They're all right here with me.

I hear a noise in the cave—footsteps—and almost drop my phone in shock. "Who's there?" I say. My voice sounds small and scared. I really hope it's not the best man, Johnno. I caught him looking at me earlier.

I stand up and start to clamber out of the cave, keeping close to the wall, which is covered with thousands of tiny rough barnacles that graze my fingertips. Finally I put my head around the wall of rock.

"Oh Jesus!" The figure stumbles backward and puts a hand to her chest. It's Charlie's wife. "*Christ!* You gave me a right shock. I didn't think anyone was down here." She's got a nice accent, Northern. "You're Olivia, aren't you? I'm Hannah, I'm married to Charlie."

"Yeah," I say. "I got that. Hi."

"What are you doing down here?" She does a quick glance over her shoulder, like she's checking there's no one listening. "Looking for a place to hide? Me too."

I decide I like her a little bit for that.

"Oh," she says, "that probably sounded bad, didn't it? I just—I guess Charlie and Jules will catch up better if I'm not around. You know, they have all this history and it doesn't include me."

She sounds a bit fed up. History. I'm like 90 percent sure Charlie and Jules have screwed at some point in the past. I wonder if Hannah's ever thought about that.

Hannah sits down on a shelf of rock. I sit, too, because I was here first. I really wish she'd take the hint and leave me alone. I take my pack of cigarettes out of my pocket and tip one out. I wait to see if Hannah's going to say anything. She doesn't. So I go one step further, to test her, I suppose, and offer her one, along with my lighter.

She screws up her face. "I shouldn't," she says. Then she sighs. "But why not? We had such a mental crossing over here—I've got the shakes now." She holds up a hand to show me.

She lights up, takes a deep drag and gives another

big sigh. I can see she's gone a bit dizzy. "Wow. That's gone straight to my head. Haven't had one for so long. Gave up when I got pregnant. But I smoked a lot in my clubbing days." She gives me a look. "Yeah, I know—you're thinking that must have been a million years ago. Certainly feels like it."

I feel a bit guilty, because I had thought it. But looking at her more closely I can see that she has four piercings in one ear and there's a tattoo on the inside of her wrist, half-hidden by her sleeve. Maybe there's another side to her.

She takes another big drag. "God, that's good. I thought when I gave them up that I'd eventually go off the taste, or wouldn't miss them anymore." She gives a big, deep laugh. "Yeah. Didn't happen." She blows out four perfect rings of smoke.

I'm kind of impressed, despite myself. Callum used to try that but he never got the hang of it.

"So you're at uni, right?" she asks.

"Yeah," I say.

"Whereabouts?"

"Exeter."

"That's a good one, isn't it?"

"Yeah," I say. "I suppose so."

"I didn't go," Hannah says. "No one in my family went to uni," she coughs, "except for my sister, Alice."

I don't know what to say to that. I don't really know anyone who didn't go to uni. Even Mum went to acting school.

"Alice was always the clever one," Hannah goes on. "I used to be the wild one, if you can believe it. We both went to this crummy school but Alice came out of there with amazing grades." She taps ash from her cigarette. "Sorry, I know I'm banging on. She's on my mind a lot at the moment."

Her face has changed, I notice. But I don't feel like I can ask her about it, seeing as we're total strangers.

"Anyway," Hannah says. "You like Exeter?"

"I'm not there anymore," I say. "I dropped out." I don't know what made me say it. It would have been so much easier to play along, pretend I was still there. But I suddenly felt like I didn't want to lie to her.

Hannah frowns. "Oh, yeah? You weren't enjoying it, then?"

"No," I say. "I guess . . . I had this boyfriend. And he broke up with me." Wow, that sounds pathetic.

"He must have been a real shit," Hannah says, "if you left uni because of him."

When I think about everything that happened in the last year my mind goes hot, and blank, and I can't think about it properly or sort it all out in my head. None of it makes sense, especially now, trying to piece it all together. I can't explain it, I think, without telling her everything. So I shrug and say, "Well, I guess he was my first proper boyfriend."

Proper as in more than someone to hook up with at house parties. But I don't say this to Hannah.

"And you loved him," she says.

She doesn't say it like a question, so I don't feel I have to answer. All the same, I nod my head. "Yeah," I say. My voice comes out very small and cracked. I didn't believe in love at first sight until I saw Callum, across the bar at Fresher's Week, this boy with black curls and beautiful blue eyes. He gave me a sort of slow smile and it was like I knew him. Like we had always meant to come together, to find each other.

Callum said he loved me first. I was too scared of making an arse of myself. But eventually I felt like I *had* to say it too, like it was bursting out of me. When he broke up with me, he told me that he would love me forever. But that's total crap. If you love someone, really, you don't do *anything* to hurt them.

"I didn't leave just because he broke up with me," I say, quickly. "It was . . ." I take a big drag on my cigarette. My hand's trembling. "I guess if Callum hadn't broken up with me, none of the rest would have happened."

"None of the rest?" Hannah asks. She's sitting forward, interested.

I don't answer. I'm trying to think of a way to go on, but I can't find the right words. She doesn't push me. So there's a long silence, both of us sitting there and smoking.

Then: "Shit!" Hannah says. "Is it me or has it got quite a lot darker while we've been sitting here?"

"I think the sun's started to set," I say. We can't see it from here as we're not facing in the right direction, but you can make out the pink glow in the sky.

"Oh dear," Hannah says. "We should probably make our way back to the Folly. Charlie hates being late for anything. He's such a teacher. I reckon I can hide for another ten minutes but—" She's stubbing out her cigarette now.

"You go," I say. "It's fine. It's not important."

She squints at me. "It kind of sounded like it was."

"No," I say. "Honestly."

I can't believe how close I came to telling her about it all. I haven't told anyone the other stuff. Not even any of my mates. It's a relief, really. If I'd told her, there'd be no taking it back. It would be out there in the world: what I've done.

AOIFE

The Wedding Planner

Seven o'clock. The table is laid for dinner in the dining room. Freddy's got supper covered, which means it's a free half hour, which means I decide to pay a visit to the graveyard. The flowers need refreshing and tomorrow we'll be run off our feet.

When I step outside the sun is just beginning to go down, spilling fire upon the water. It tinges pink the mist that has begun to gather over the bog, that shields its secrets. This is my favorite hour.

The ushers are sitting up on the battlements: I hear their voices floating down as I leave the Folly—louder and slightly more slurred than earlier, the work of the Guinness, I'll bet.

"Got to send them off with a bang."

"Yeah, we should do *something.* Would only be traditional . . ."

I'm half-tempted to stay and listen, to check they aren't plotting mayhem on my watch. But it sounds harmless. And I've only got this brief window of time to myself.

The island looks at its most starkly beautiful this evening, lit up by the glow of the dying sun. But perhaps it will never seem quite so beautiful to me as I remember from those trips we took here when I was a child. The four of us, my family, here to stay for the summer holidays. Nowhere on earth could possibly live up to those halcyon days. But that's nostalgia for you, the tyranny of those memories of childhood that feel so golden, so perfect.

There is a whispering in the graveyard when I get there, the beginnings of a breeze stirring between the stones. A harbinger of tomorrow's weather, maybe. Sometimes, when the wind is really up, it seems to carry from here the echoes of women from centuries past performing the *caoineadh,* their keening for the dead.

The graves here are unusually close together, because true dry land is in short supply on the island. Even then, at the outer edges the bog has begun to nibble away at it, swallowing several of the graves until only the top few inches remain. Some of the stones have moved closer still, leaning in toward one another as though sharing a secret. The names, the ones that remain visible, are common to Connemara: Joyce, Foley, Kelly, Conneely.

It's a strange thing when you consider that the dead on this island far outnumber the living, even now that some of the guests have arrived. Tomorrow will redress the balance.

There is a great deal of local superstition about the island. When Freddy and I bought the Folly a year or so ago, there was no other bidder. The islanders were always mistrusted, seen as a species apart.

I know the mainlanders view Freddy and me as outsiders. Me the townie "Jackeen" from Dublin and Freddy the Englishman, a couple who don't know better, who have probably bitten off more than we can chew. Who don't know about Inis an Amplóra's dark history, its ghosts. Actually, I know this place better than they think. It is more familiar to me in some ways than any other place I have known in my life. And I'm not worried about it being haunted. I have my own ghosts. I carry them with me wherever I go.

"I miss you," I say, as I crouch down. The stone stares back at me, blank and mute. I touch it with my fingertips. It is rough, cold, unyielding—so far from the warmth of a cheek, or the soft, springy hair that I recall so vividly. "But I hope you'd be proud of me." I feel it as I do every time I crouch here: the familiar, impotent anger, rising up in me to leave its bitter taste in my mouth.

And then I hear a cackling, from somewhere above me, as though in mockery of my words. No matter how many times I hear it, that sound will never cease to make my blood run cold. I look up and see it there: a big cormorant perched on the highest part of the ruined chapel, its crooked black wings hung open to dry like a broken umbrella. A cormorant on a steeple: that's an ill omen. The devil's bird, they call it in these parts. The *cailleach dhubh*, the black hag, the bringer of death. Here's hoping that the bride and groom don't know this . . . or that they aren't the superstitious sort.

I clap my hands, but the creature doesn't budge. Instead it rotates its head slowly so I can see its stark profile, the cruel shape of its beak. And I realize that it is watching me, sidewise, out of its beady gleaming eye, as though it knows something I do not.

Back at the Folly, I carry a tray of champagne flutes through to the dining room, ready for this evening's drinks. As I open the door I see a couple sitting there on the sofa. It takes me a moment to realize that it's the bride and another man: one of the couple that Mattie brought across on the boat. The two of them are sitting very close together, their heads touching, talking in low voices. They don't exactly spring apart on noticing my entrance, but they do move a few inches away from one another. And she takes her hand off his knee.

"Aoife," the bride calls out. "This is Charlie."

I remember his name from the list. "Our MC for tomorrow, I believe?" I say.

He coughs. "Yes, that's me."

"Sure, and your wife's Hannah, isn't she?"

"Yes," he says. "Good memory!"

"We were going through Charlie's duties for tomorrow," the bride tells me.

"Of course," I say. "Good." I wonder why she felt the need to explain anything to me. They looked rather cozy together on the sofa but I'm not here to cast any moral judgment upon my clients, or even to have likes and dislikes, to have opinions on things. That isn't how this sort of thing works. Freddy and I, if everything goes well, should simply fade into the background. We will only stand out if things go wrong, and I shall take care to ensure they will not. The bride and groom and their nearest and dearest should feel that this place is theirs, really, that they are the hosts. We are merely here to facilitate everything, to ensure that the whole weekend runs smoothly. But to do that I can't be completely passive. It is the strange tension of my role. I'll have to keep an eye on all of them, watch for any threatening developments. I will have to try and stay one step ahead.

NOW

THE WEDDING NIGHT

The sound of the scream rings in the air after it has finished, like a struck glass. The guests are frozen in its wake. They are looking, all of them, out of the marquee and into the roaring darkness from where it came. The lights flicker, threatening another blackout.

Then a girl stumbles into the marquee. Her white shirt marks her out as a waitress. But her face is a wild animal's, her eyes huge and dark, her hair tangled. She stands there in front of them, staring. She does not appear to blink.

Finally a woman approaches her, not one of the guests. It is the wedding planner. "What is it?" she asks gently. "What's happened?"

The girl doesn't answer. It seems to the guests that

all they can hear is her breathing. There is something animal about that too: rough and hoarse.

The wedding planner steps toward her, places a tentative hand on her shoulder. The girl doesn't react. The guests are transfixed, rooted to the spot. Some of them vaguely remember this girl from earlier. She was one of many who smilingly handed them their starters and main courses and desserts. She cleared their plates and refreshed their wineglasses, pouring expertly, her red ponytail bobbing smartly with every step, her shirt white and clean and crisp. Some of them recall her gentle singsong accent: Could she top them up, could she get them anything more? Otherwise she was, for want of a better expression, part of the furniture. Part of the well-oiled machinery of the day. Less worthy of proper notice, really, than the chic arrangements of greenery, the wavering flames atop the silver candlesticks.

"What happened?" the wedding planner asks again. Her tone is still compassionate, but this time there's more firmness in it, a note of authority. The waitress has begun to tremble, so much so that she looks as though she might be having some sort of fit. The wedding planner puts a hand on her shoulder again, as though to quiet her. The girl holds a hand over her mouth, and it seems for a moment that she might vomit. Then, finally, she speaks.

"Outside." It is a rasp of sound, hardly human.

The guests crane in to listen.

She lets out a low moan.

"Come on," the wedding planner says, calmly, quietly. She gives the girl a gentle shake, this time. "Come on. I'm here, I want to help—we all do. And it's OK, you're safe in here. Tell me what has happened."

Finally, in that terrible rasping voice, the girl speaks again. "Outside. *So much blood.*" And then, right before she collapses: "A body."

THE DAY BEFORE

HANNAH

The Plus-One

I bite down on a tissue to blot my lipstick. This place seems worthy of lipstick. Our room here is huge, twice the size of our bedroom back home. Not a single detail has been forgotten: the ice bucket with a bottle of expensive white wine in it, two glasses; the antique chandelier in the high ceiling; the big window looking out to sea. I can't go too close to the window or I'll get vertigo, because if you look straight down you can see the waves smashing on the rocks below and a tiny wet sliver of beach.

This evening the dying glow of the sunset lights the whole room rose gold. I've had a big glass of the wine, which is delicious, while getting ready. On an empty stomach and after the cigarettes I smoked with Olivia I already feel a bit light-headed.

It was fun smoking in the cave—it felt like a blast from the past. It's inspired me to go for it this weekend. I've felt jittery and sad all month: now here's a chance to cut loose a bit. So I've squeezed myself into a pre-kids black silky dress from & Other Stories; I've always felt good in it. I've blow-dried my hair smooth. It's worth the effort, even if it comes into contact with the moist air from outside and turns into a massive ball of frizz again, like a hairdo version of Cinderella's pumpkin. I thought Charlie would be waiting for me, crossly, but he only returned to the room a couple of minutes ago himself, so I've had time to brush my teeth and remove any scent of cigarettes, feeling like a naughty teenager. I'd half-hoped he would be here, though. We could have had a bath together in the claw-footed tub.

I've barely seen Charlie since we got off the boat, in fact: he and Jules spent the early evening cozied up together, going through his duties as MC. "Sorry, Han," he said, when he got back. "Jules wanted to go through all this stuff for tomorrow. Hope you didn't feel abandoned?"

Now he does an appreciative once-over as I emerge from the bathroom. "You look," he raises his eyebrows, "*hot.*"

"Thank you," I say, doing a little shimmy. I *feel* hot; I suppose it's been a while since I've gone all out. And

I know I shouldn't mind that I can't remember the last time he said that.

We join the others in the drawing room, where we're having drinks. It's as well put together as our room: an ancient brick floor, a candelabra bristling with candles, glass boxes on the walls holding vast glistening fish, which I think may be real. How on earth do you taxidermy a fish, I wonder. Small windows show rectangles of blue twilight and everything outside now has a misty, slightly otherworldly quality.

Standing surrounded by a cluster of guests, Jules and Will are lit by candlelight. Will seems to be telling some anecdote: the others all listening to whatever he's saying, hanging off his every word. I notice that he and Jules are holding hands, as though they can't bear not to be touching. They look so good together, impossibly tall and elegant, she in a tailored cream jumpsuit and he in dark trousers and a white shirt that makes his tan appear several shades darker. I'd been feeling good about myself but now my own outfit feels inadequate by comparison: while for me, & Other Stories is a wild extravagance, I'm sure Jules hardly ventures into high-street chains.

I end up standing quite near to Will, which isn't a total accident—I seem to be drawn to him. It's a heady experience, being so close to someone you've seen on your TV screen. This feeling of familiarity and strangeness at the same time. I can feel my skin tingling, being in such close proximity. I was aware when I walked over of his gaze raking my face, quickly up and down my person, before he went back to finishing his anecdote. So I *am* looking good. A guilty thrill goes through me. In the years since I've had kids—probably because I'm always *with* the kids—I've apparently become invisible to men. It only dawned on me, when I stopped feeling them on me, that I had taken men's glances for granted. That I enjoyed them.

"Hannah," Will says, turning to me with that famous, generous smile of his. "You look stunning."

"Thanks." I take a big gulp of my champagne, feeling sexy, a little bit reckless.

"I meant to ask, on the jetty—did we meet at the engagement drinks?"

"No," I say, apologetically. "We couldn't make it up from Brighton, sadly."

"Maybe I've seen you in one of Jules's photos, then. You seem familiar."

"Maybe," I say. I don't think so. I can't imagine Jules displaying a photo that includes me; she's got plenty of just her and Charlie. But I know what Will's doing: helping me feel welcome, one of the gang. I appreciate the kindness. "You know," I say, "I think I'm getting the same feeling about you. Might I have seen *you* somewhere before? You know . . . like on my TV set?"

It was corny but Will laughs anyway, a rich, low sound, and I feel as though I've just won something. "Guilty!" he says, raising his hands. As he does I get a gust of that cologne again: moss and pine, a forest floor via an expensive department store perfume hall. He asks me about the kids, about Brighton. He seems fascinated by what I'm saying. He's one of those people who makes you feel wittier and more attractive than normal. I realize I'm enjoying myself, enjoying the delicious glass of chilled champagne.

"Now," Will says, palm on my back as a gentle steer, warm through my dress, "let me introduce you to some people. This is Georgina."

Georgina, thin and chic in a column of fuchsia silk, gives me a wintry smile. She can't move her face much and I try hard not to stare—I'm not sure I've ever seen Botox in real life. "Were you on the hen do?" she asks. "I can't remember."

"I had to give it a miss," I say. "The kids . . ." Partly true. But there's also the fact that it was at a yoga retreat in Ibiza and I could never in a million years have afforded it.

"You didn't miss much." A man—slender, dark-red hair—swoops into the conversation. "Just a load of bitches burning their tits off and gossiping over bottles of Whispering Angel. Goodness," he says, giving me a once-over before bending in to kiss my cheek. "Don't *you* scrub up well?"

"Er—thanks." His smile suggests it was meant kindly, but I'm not totally sure it was a compliment.

This man is Duncan, apparently, and he's married to Georgina. He's also one of the ushers, along with the other three guys. Peter—hair slicked back, a party-boy look. Oluwafemi, or Femi—tall, black, seriously handsome. Angus—Boris Johnson blond and similarly pot-bellied.

But in a funny way they all look quite similar. They're all wearing the same striped tie plus crisp white shirts, polished brogues and tailored jackets that definitely don't come from Next, like Charlie's. Charlie bought his especially for this weekend and I hope he's not feeling too put out by the comparison. But at least he looks fairly dapper next to the best man, Johnno, who despite his size somehow reminds me of a kid wearing clothes from the school lost property cupboard.

On the face of it they're so charming, these men. But I remember the laughter from the tower as we walked up to the Folly. And even now there's definitely an undercurrent beneath the charm. Smirks, raised eyebrows, as though they're having a secret joke at someone's expense—possibly mine.

I move over to chat to Olivia, who looks ethereal in a gray dress. It felt like we bonded a bit earlier in the cave but now she answers me in monosyllables, darting her eyes away.

A couple of times my gaze snags with Will's over her shoulder. I don't think it's my fault: sometimes I'll have the impression that his eyes have been on me for a while. It shouldn't be, but it's exciting. It reminds me—I know it's totally inappropriate to say this—but it reminds me most of that feeling you get when you start to suspect that someone you're attracted to fancies you back.

I catch myself in the thought. Reality check, Hannah. You're a married mother of two and your husband is right there and you're talking to a man who is about to get married to your husband's best friend, who is standing looking like Monica Bellucci, only better dressed. *Probably* ease off the champagne a little. I've been knocking it back. It's partly nerves, surrounded by this lot. But it's also the sense of freedom. No babysitter to embarrass ourselves in front of later, no small people to have to wake up for in the morning. There's something exotic about being all dressed up with only other adults for company, a plentiful supply of booze, no responsibility.

"The food smells incredible," I say. "Who's cooking?"

"Aoife and Freddy," Jules says. "They own the Folly. Aoife's our wedding planner, too. I'll introduce you all at dinner. And Freddy is doing the catering for us tomorrow."

"I can tell it's going to be delicious," I say. "God, I'm hungry."

"Well, your stomach's completely empty," Charlie says. "Got rid of it all on the boat, didn't you?"

"Had a vom?" Duncan asks, delighted. "Fed the fish?"

I shoot Charlie an icy look. I feel like he's just undone some of the effort I made this evening. I feel like he's playing for laughs, trying to get in on the joke at my expense. I swear he's put on a different voice—posher—but I know if I called him out on it he'd pretend he hadn't a clue what I was talking about.

"*Anyway,*" I say, "it'll make a nice change from chicken nuggets, which I seem to end up eating every other night with the kids."

"Do you have any good restaurants in Brighton, these days?" Jules asks. Jules always acts like Brighton is the sticks.

"Yes," I say, "there are—"

"Except we never go to them," Charlie says.

"That's not true," I say. "We went to that new Italian place . . ."

"It's not new now," Charlie counters. "That was about a year ago."

He's right. I can't think of the last time we ate out, other than that. Money has been a bit tight and you have to add the cost of a babysitter on top of the meal. But I wish he hadn't said it.

Johnno tries to top up Charlie's champagne and Charlie quickly puts his hand over his glass. "No thanks."

"Oh come on, mate," Johnno says. "Night before the wedding. Got to get a little loose."

"Come on!" Duncan chides. "It's only bubbly, not crack. Or are you going to tell us you're pregnant?"

The other ushers snicker.

"No," Charlie says again, tightly. "I'm taking it easy tonight." I can tell he's embarrassed saying it. But I'm glad he hasn't forgotten himself on this front.

"So Charlie boy," Johnno says, "tell us. How did you two first meet?"

I think at first he means Charlie and I. Then I realize he's looking between Charlie and Jules. Right.

"A million years ago . . ." Jules says. She and Charlie raise their eyebrows at each other in perfect unison.

"I taught her to sail," Charlie says. "I lived in Cornwall. It was my summer job."

"And my dad has a house there," Jules says. "I hoped if I learned he might take me out on his boat with him. But it turns out taking your sixteen-year-old daughter for a sail along the south coast wasn't quite the same as having your latest girlfriend sunbathe on the prow in St. Tropez." It comes out more bitterly than I think she might have intended. "Anyway," she says. "Charlie was my instructor." She looks at him. "I had a *big* crush on him."

Charlie smiles back at her. I laugh along with the others but I'm not really feeling it. It's hardly the first time I've heard this story. It's like a double act they do together. The local boy and the posh girl. Still, my stomach twists as Jules continues.

"*You* were mainly concerned with trying to sleep with as many girls of your own age as possible before you went to uni," Jules says to Charlie. It's suddenly like she's speaking only to him. "It seemed to work for you, though. That permanent tan and the body you had back then probably helped—"

"Yes," Charlie says. "Best body of my life. It was like having a gym membership with the job, working out on the water every day. Sadly you don't get quite as ripped teaching geography to fifteen-year-olds."

"Let's have a look at those abs now," Duncan says, leaning forward and grabbing the bottom of Charlie's shirt. He lifts the hem to show a few inches of pale, soft stomach. Charlie steps back, reddening, tucks himself in.

"And he seemed so grown-up," Jules says, heedless of the interruption. She touches Charlie's arm, proprietary. "When you're sixteen, eighteen seems so much older. I was shy."

"That's hard to believe," Johnno mumbles.

Jules ignores him. "But I know at first you thought I was this stuck-up princess."

"Which was probably true," Charlie says, raising an eyebrow, getting back into his stride.

Jules flicks him with champagne from her glass. "Oi!"

They're *flirting.* There's no other word for it.

"But no, I realized you were actually quite cool in the end," he says. "Discovered that wicked sense of humor."

"And then I suppose we just stayed in touch," Jules says.

"Mobiles had started to become a thing," Charlie says.

"*You* were the shy one the next year," Jules said. "I'd finally got some boobs. I remember seeing you do a double take when I walked down the jetty."

I take a big swig of my champagne. I remind myself that they were teenagers. That I am feeling envious of a seventeen-year-old who no longer exists.

"Yeah and you had that boyfriend and everything," Charlie says. "He wasn't my biggest fan."

"Yes," Jules says, with a secretive smile. "He didn't last very long. He was very jealous."

"So did you ever fuck?" Johnno asks. And just like that: it's the question I've never been able to ask outright.

The ushers are delighted. "He went there!" they cry. "Holy shit!" They crowd in, excited, gleeful, the circle growing tighter. Maybe that's why I'm suddenly finding it harder to breathe.

"Johnno!" Jules says. "Do you mind? This is my *wedding*!" But she hasn't said they didn't.

I can't look at Charlie. I don't want to know.

Then, thank God, there's an interruption: a big bang. Duncan has opened the bottle of champagne he's been holding.

"Christ, Duncan," Femi says. "You nearly took my eye out!"

"How do you guys all know each other?" I ask Johnno, keen to capitalize on the distraction.

"Ah," Johnno says, "we go back years." He puts a hand on Will's shoulder, and somehow this gesture sets him and Will apart from the others. Next to him Will looks even more handsome. They're like chalk and cheese. And there's something a bit weird about Johnno's eyes. I spend a while trying to work out exactly what's off about them. Are they too close together? Too small?

"Yup," Will says. "We were at school together." I'm surprised. The other men have that public schoolboy polish, while Johnno seems rougher—no cut-glass accent.

"Trevellyan's," Femi says. "It was like that book with all the boys on a desert island together, killing each other, oh Christ, what's it called—"

"*Lord of the Flies,*" Charlie says, the faintest trace of superiority in his tone. *I might have gone to state school,* it says, *but I'm better read than you.*

"It wasn't as bad as all that," Will says quickly. "It was more . . . boys running a bit wild."

"Boys will be boys!" Duncan chips in. "Am I right, Johnno?"

"Yeah. Boys will be boys," Johnno echoes.

"And we've been friends ever since," Will says. He slaps Johnno on the back. "Johnno here used to drive up in his ancient banger while I was at Edinburgh for uni, didn't you, Johnno?"

"Yeah," Johnno says. "I'd take him out into the

mountains for climbing and camping trips. Make sure he didn't get too soft. Or spend all his time shagging around." He pretends to look contrite. "Sorry, Jules."

Jules tosses her head.

"Who do we know who went to Edinburgh, Han?" Charlie says. I stiffen. How can he possibly have forgotten who it was? Then I see his expression change to one of horror as he realizes his mistake.

"You know someone?" Will says. "Who?"

"She wasn't there for very long," I say quickly. "You know, Will, I've been wondering. That bit in *Survive the Night*, in the Arctic tundra. How cold was it? Did you really nearly get frostbite?"

"Yep," says Will. "Lost all the feeling in the pads of these fingers." He holds up one hand toward me. "The fingerprints have gone from a couple of them." I squint. They don't actually look all that different to me. And yet I find myself saying, "Oh yes, I think I can see that. Wow." I sound like a fangirl.

Charlie turns to me. "I didn't realize you'd seen the show," he says. "When did you watch it? We've never watched it together." *Oops.* I think of those afternoons, setting the kids up with CBeebies, and watching Will's show on my iPad in the kitchen as I heated up their dinner. He looks to Will. "No offense, mate—I do keep meaning to catch it." This isn't true. You can tell from the way he says it that it isn't true. He hasn't made any attempt to sound genuine.

"No offense taken," Will says mildly.

"Oh," I say. "I've never watched the whole thing. I . . . caught the highlights, you know."

"Methinks the lady does protest too much," Peter says. He takes hold of Will's shoulder, grinning. "Will, you've got a fan!"

Will laughs it off. But I can feel the heat prickling up my neck into my cheeks. I'm hoping it's too dark in here for anyone to see that I'm blushing.

Fuck it. I need more champagne. I hold my glass out for a top-up.

"At least your wife knows how to party, mate," Duncan says to Charlie. Femi pours for me, filling the flute close to the top. "Whoa," I say, as it reaches the rim, "that's plenty."

Suddenly there's a loud *plink!* and a little splash up over my wrist. I look in surprise to see that something has been dropped into my drink.

"What was that?" I say, confused.

"Have a look," Duncan says, grinning. "Pennyed you. Have to drink it all now." I stare at him, then at my glass. Sure enough, at the bottom of my very full glass sits the little copper coin, the Queen's stern profile.

"Duncan!" Georgina says, giggling. "You're *too* awful!"

I don't think I've been pennyed since I was about eighteen. Suddenly everyone's looking at me. I look to Charlie, for agreement that I don't have to drink it. But his expression is oddly pleading. It's the sort of look Ben might give me: *Please don't embarrass me in front of my friends, Mum.*

This is crazy, I think. I don't have to drink it. I'm a thirty-four-year-old woman. I don't even know these people, they have no hold over me. I won't be made to do it—

"Down it . . ."

"Down it!"

God, they've started to chant.

"Save the Queen!"

"She's drowning!"

"*Down it down it down it.*"

I can feel my cheeks reddening. To get their eyes off me, to stop their chanting, I knock the glass back and gulp it all down. I'd thought the champagne was delicious before but it's awful like this, sour and sharp, stinging my throat as I cough mid-swallow, rushing up inside my nose. I feel some of it spill out over my bottom lip. I feel my eyes tear up. I'm humiliated. It's like everyone has understood the rules of whatever is happening. Everyone but me.

Afterward, they cheer. But I don't think they're cheering me. They're congratulating themselves. I feel like a child who's been surrounded by a ring of playground bullies. When I glance in Charlie's direction he gives me a kind of apologetic wince. I suddenly feel very alone. I turn away from the others to hide my face.

As I do I catch sight of something that makes my blood run cold.

There is someone at the window, looking in at us out of the blackness, observing silently. The face is pressed against the glass, its features distorted into a hideous gargoyle mask, its teeth bared in a horrible grin. As I continue to stare, unable to look away, it mouths a single word.

BOO.

I'm not even aware of the champagne glass leaving my hand until it explodes at my feet.

NOW
THE WEDDING NIGHT

It is a few moments before the waitress regains consciousness. She is, it appears, uninjured, but whatever she has seen out there has struck her nearly mute. The most they can get from her are low moans, wordless nonsense.

"I sent her over to the Folly for a couple more bottles of champagne," the head waitress—only twenty or so herself—says helplessly.

There is a palpable hush in the tent. The guests are looking among the throng of people for their loved ones, to check that they are safe and accounted for. But it is difficult to spot anyone among the seething crowd, all a little worse for wear after a day of carousing. It is difficult, too, because of the structure of this state-of-the-art venue: the dance floor in one tent, the bar in another, the main dining section in the largest.

"She could have had a scare," a man suggests. "She's a teenage girl. It's pitch-black out there and it's blowing a gale."

"But it sounds like someone needs help," another man says. "We should go and see—"

"We can't have everyone wandering all over the island." They listen to the wedding planner. She has an innate authority, though she looks as shocked as the rest of them, her face drawn and white. "It *is* blowing a gale," she says. "It's dark. And there's the bog, the cliffs. I don't want someone else to . . . to injure themselves, if that is what has happened."

"Must be shitting herself about her insurance," a man mutters.

"We should go and look," one of the ushers says. "Some of us blokes. Safety in numbers and all that."

THE DAY BEFORE

JULES

The Bride

"Dad!" I say. "You terrified poor Hannah!" I mean it was a *bit* of an overreaction from her, dropping her glass like that. Did she really have to make such a scene? I stifle my annoyance as Aoife begins sweeping up the shards, moving discreetly around us with a broom.

"Sorry." Dad grins at us all as he enters the room. "Thought I'd give ye all a little fright." His accent is more pronounced than usual, presumably as he's on home turf, or nearly. He grew up in the Gaeltacht, the Irish-speaking part of Galway, not far from here. Dad's not a big man but he manages to take up quite a bit of space and presents an imposing figure: the set of his shoulders, the broken nose. It's difficult for me to see him objectively, because of what he is to me. But I suppose an outsider might assume he was a boxer or something similarly pugilistic, rather than a very successful property developer.

Séverine, Dad's latest wife—French, not far off my age, one part décolletage and three parts liquid eyeliner—slinks in behind him, tossing her long mane of red hair.

"Well," I say to Dad, ignoring Séverine (I can't be bothered to spend much time on her until she passes the five-year mark, Dad's record to date). "You've made it . . . at last." I'd known they were scheduled to arrive about now—I had to ask Aoife to arrange the boat. But even then I'd wondered if there might be some excuse, some delay that meant they couldn't make tonight. It wouldn't be the first time.

I notice Will and Dad sizing each other up surreptitiously. In Dad's company, oddly, Will seems a little diminished, a little less himself. Looking at him, in his pressed shirt and trousers, I'm worried that to Dad he might seem privileged and glib, very much the ex-public schoolboy.

"I can't believe this is the first time you've met," I say. Not for want of bloody trying. Will and I flew to New York specially a few months ago. At the last minute, we learned, Dad had been called away on business in Europe. I imagined our planes crossing somewhere over the Atlantic. Dad is a Very Busy Man. Too busy, even, to meet his daughter's fiancé until the eve of her wedding. Story of my bloody life.

"It's a pleasure to meet you, Ronan," Will says, holding out a hand.

Dad ignores the gesture and cuffs him on the shoulder instead. "The famous Will," he says. "We meet at last."

"Not particularly famous yet," Will says, giving Dad a winning grin. I wince. It's a rare misstep. It sounded like a humblebrag and I'm fairly sure Dad didn't mean "famous" as a reference to the TV stuff. Dad's not a fan of celebrities, of anyone making their fortune by anything other than proper hard work. He's a proudly self-made man.

"And this must be Séverine," Will says, reaching across to give her a kiss on both cheeks. "Jules has told me so much about you—and about the twins."

No, I haven't. The twins, Dad's latest progeny, were not invited.

Séverine simpers, melting beneath Will's charm. This does not seem likely to endear Will further to Dad. I wish it didn't matter to me what my father thinks. And yet I stand, transfixed, watching as the two of them circle each other in the small space. It is excruciating. It's some relief when Aoife comes through and tells us that dinner is about to be served.

Aoife is a woman after my own heart: organized, capable, discreet. There's a coolness to her, a detachment, which I suppose some might not like. I prefer it. I don't want someone pretending to be my best friend when I'm paying her to do something. I liked Aoife the moment we first spoke on the phone and I'm half-tempted to ask if she'd consider leaving all of this and coming to work at *The Download.* She might look quite homely, but she has a steelier side.

We make our way through to the dining room. Mum and Dad, as planned, are seated either end of the table, as physically distant from one another as it is possible to get. I'm genuinely not sure if my parents have spoken more than a few words to one another since the nineties and it's probably better for the harmony of the weekend if that continues. Séverine, meanwhile, is sitting so close to Dad that she might as well be on his lap. Ugh: she may not be far off half his age but she's still a thirty-something, not a teenager.

Tonight, at least, everyone seems to be on pretty good behavior. I think the several bottles of 1999 Bollinger we've drunk are probably helping. Even Mum is being fairly gracious, acting the role of mother of the bride with aplomb. Her skills as an actress have always seemed to come to the fore in real life rather than on the stage.

Now Aoife and her husband come in bearing our starters: a creamy chowder flecked with parsley. "This is Aoife and Freddy," I tell the others. I don't say that they're our hosts because, really, I'm the host. I'm paying for that privilege. So I settle on: "The Folly belongs to them."

Aoife gives a neat little nod. "If you need anything, come to either of us," she says. "I hope you'll all enjoy your stay here. And the wedding tomorrow is our first on the island, so it will be particularly special."

"It's beautiful," Hannah says graciously. "And this looks delicious."

"Thank you," Freddy says, finding his voice. He's English, I realize—I'd assumed he was Irish like Aoife.

Aoife nods. "We picked the mussels ourselves this morning."

Once we're all served the conversation around the table resumes, with the exception of Olivia, who sits there mutely, staring at her plate.

"Such fond memories of Brighton," Mum is saying to Hannah. "You know, I performed down there a couple of times." Oh God. Not long before she starts telling everyone about that time she had penetrative sex on-screen for an art-house film (never got a release, probably now on PornHub).

"Oh," Hannah replies, "we feel a bit guilty about

not getting to the theater more often. Where did you perform? The Theatre Royal?"

"No," Mum says, with that slightly haughty tone that creeps into her voice when she's been shown up. "It's a little more boutique than that." A toss of her head. "It's called the Magic Lantern. In the Lanes. Do you know it?"

"Er—no," Hannah says. And then, quickly, "But as I say, we're so out of the loop we wouldn't know anywhere, even if it's the place to go."

She's kind, Hannah. That is one of the things I know about her. It sort of . . . spills out of her. I remember meeting Hannah for the first time and thinking: oh, that's who Charlie wants. Someone nice. Someone soft, and warm. I'm too much for him. I'm too angry, too driven. He would never have picked me.

I'm not envious of Hannah anymore, I remind myself. Charlie might once have been the sailing club hottie but he's softened now, a paunch where that flat brown stomach used to be. And he's settled in his career, too. If I had anything to do with it he'd be gunning for a deputy head position. There's nothing less sexy than a lack of ambition, is there?

I watch Charlie until his gaze snags on mine—I make sure I'm the first to glance away. And I wonder: *Is* he *now the jealous one?* I've seen the mistrustful way he acts around Will, as though he's trying to find the flaw. I caught him observing the two of us over drinks. And I felt it again, how good we look together, imagining it through his eyes.

"How *sweet*," Mum's saying to Hannah. "Five's a lovely age." She's certainly doing a very good job of acting interested. "And how are your two, Ronan?" she calls down the table. I wonder if it is an intentional slight, not to have included Séverine in her question. Actually—scrap that, I don't need to wonder. Despite the impression she works hard to convey of bohemian vagueness, very little my mother does is unintentional.

"They're good," he says. "Thank you, Araminta. They're starting at nursery soon, aren't they?" He turns to Séverine.

"*Oui*," she says. "We are looking for a French-speaking nursery for them. So important that they grow up—ah—bileengual, like me."

"Oh, you're bilingual?" I ask. I can't help the slight.

If Séverine notices, she doesn't react. "*Oui*," she says with a shrug. "I went to a girls' boarding school in the UK when I was leetle. And my brudders, they attended a school for boys there too."

"Goodness," Mum says, still speaking only to Dad. "It must all be so *exhausting* at your age, Ronan." Before he has a chance to reply she claps her hands.

"While we're between courses," she says, getting to her feet, "I'd like to say a little something."

"You don't have to, Mum," I call. Everyone laughs. But I'm not joking. Is she drunk? It's difficult to gauge, we've all had quite a bit. And I'm not sure it makes much of a difference with Mum anyway. She's never had any inhibitions to lose.

"To my Julia," she says, raising her glass. "Ever since you were a little girl you've known *exactly* what you wanted. And woe betide anyone who got in your way! I've never been like that—what I want always changes from week to week, which is probably why I've always been so bloody unhappy.

"Anyway: you've always known. And what you want, you go after." Oh, God. She's doing this because I've banned her from doing a speech at the wedding itself. I'm sure of it. "I knew it from the moment you told me about Will that he was what you wanted."

Not *quite* so clairvoyant as it sounds, seeing as I told her, in the same conversation, that we were already engaged. But Mum has never let inconvenient facts get in the way of a good story.

"Don't they *look* wonderful together?" she asks. Murmurs of assent from the others. I don't like the way the emphasis seemed to land on the "look."

"I knew Jules would need to find someone as driven

as her," Mum says. And was there an edge to the way she said "driven"? It's difficult to be sure. I catch Charlie's eye across the table—he knows of old what Mum is like. He winks at me and I feel a secret fizz of warmth deep in my belly. "And she has such style, my daughter. We all know that about her, don't we? Her magazine, her beautiful house in Islington, and now this stunning man here." She puts a red-nailed hand on Will's shoulder. "You've always had a good eye, Jules." Like I picked him out to go with a pair of shoes. Like I'm marrying him just because he fits perfectly into my life—

"And it might seem like madness to anyone else," Mum goes on. "To haul everyone out to this freezing godforsaken island in the middle of nowhere. But it is important to Jules, and that's what matters."

I don't like the sound of that, either. I'm laughing along with the others. But I'm secretly bracing myself. I want to stand up and say my own piece, as though she's the prosecuting barrister, and I'm the defense. That's not how you're meant to feel, listening to a speech from a loved one, is it?

Here's the truth my mother won't speak: if I hadn't known what I wanted, and worked out how to get it, I wouldn't have got anywhere. I had to learn how to get my way. Because my mother wasn't going to be any bloody help. I look at her, in her frothy black chiffon—like a negative of a wedding gown—and her glittering earrings, holding her sparkling glass of champagne, and I think: You don't get this. This isn't your moment. You didn't create it. I created it in *spite* of you.

I grip the edge of the table with one hand, hard, anchoring myself. With the other I pick up my glass of champagne and take a long swig. *Say you're proud of me*, I think. And it will just about make everything all right. *Say it, and I'll forgive you.*

"This might sound a little immodest," Mum says, touching her breastbone. "But I have to say that I'm proud of myself, for having brought up such a strong-willed, independent daughter."

And she does a little bow, as though to an adoring audience. Everyone claps dutifully as she sits down.

I'm trembling with anger. I look at the champagne flute in my hand. I imagine, for one delicious, delirious second, smashing it against the table, bringing everything to a halt. I take a deep breath. And instead I rise to make my own toast. I will be gracious, grateful, affectionate.

"Thank you so much for coming," I say. I strive to make my tone warm. I'm so used to giving talks to my employees that I have to work to keep the note of authority out of my voice. I know some women complain about not being able to get people to take them seriously. If anything, I have the opposite problem. At our Christmas party one of my employees, Eliza, got drunk and told me I have permanent resting bitch face. I let it go, because she was drunk and wouldn't remember saying it in the morning. But *I* certainly haven't forgotten it.

"We're so happy to have you all here," I say. I smile. My lipstick feels waxy and unyielding on my lips. "I know it was a long way to come . . . and difficult to get time away from everything. But from the moment this place came to my attention I knew it was perfect. For Will, so Outward Bound. And as a nod to my Irish roots." I look to Dad, who grins. "And to see you all gathered here—our nearest and dearest—it means so much to me. To both of us." I raise my glass to Will, and he raises his in return. He's so much better at this than I am. He exudes charm and warmth without even trying. I can get people to do what I want, sure. But I haven't always been able to get them to like me. Not in the way that my fiancé can. He gives me a grin, a wink, and I find myself imagining carrying on what we started earlier, in the bedroom—

"I didn't believe this day would ever come," I say, remembering myself. "I've been so busy with *The Download* over the last few years that I thought I'd never have the time to meet someone."

"Don't forget," Will calls. "I had to work pretty hard to persuade you to go on a date."

He's right. It seemed somehow too good to be true. He told me later that he'd recently got out of something toxic, that he wasn't looking for anything either. But we really hit it off at that party.

"I'm so glad you did." I smile down at him. It still feels like a kind of miracle, how quickly and easily it all happened. "If I believed in it," I say, "I might think we were brought together by Fate."

Will beams back at me. Our gazes lock, it's like there's no one else here. And then out of nowhere I think of that bloody note. And I feel the smile waver slightly on my lips.

JOHNNO

The Best Man

It's pitch-black outside now. The smoke from the fire fills the room, so that everyone looks different, hazy around the edges. Not quite themselves.

We're on to the next course, some fiddly dark chocolate tart. I try to cut into it and it goes shooting off my plate, crumbs of pastry exploding everywhere.

"Need someone to cut your food for you, big boy?" Duncan jeers, from the far end of the table. I hear the other blokes laugh. It's like nothing has changed. I ignore them.

Hannah turns to me. "So, Johnno," she says, "do you live in London too?" I like Hannah, I've decided. She seems kind. And I like her Northern accent and the studs in the top of her ear which make her look like a party girl, even though she's apparently a mum of two. I bet she can be pretty wild when she wants to be.

"Christ no," I tell her. "I hate the city. Give me the countryside any day. I need space to roam free."

"Are you pretty outdoorsy yourself?" Hannah asks.

"Yeah," I say. "I guess you could say that. I used to work at an adventure center in the Lake District. Teaching climbing, bushcraft, all that."

"Oh wow. I suppose that makes sense, because it was you who organized the stag, right?" She smiles at me. I wonder how much she knows about it.

"Yeah," I say, "I did."

"Charlie hasn't said much about any of it. But I heard there was going to be some kayaking and climbing and stuff."

Ah, so he didn't tell her anything about what went down. I'm not surprised. I probably wouldn't if I were him, come to think of it. The less said about all of that the better. Let's hope he's decided to let bygones be bygones on that front. Poor bloke. It wasn't my idea, all of that.

"Well, yeah," I continue. "I've always been into that sort of thing."

"Yes," Femi interjects. "It was Johnno who worked out how to scale the wall to get up on top of the sports hall. And you climbed that massive tree outside the dining hall, didn't you?"

"Oh God," Will says to Hannah. "Don't get this lot started on our school days. You'll never hear the end of it."

Hannah smiles at me. "It sounds like you could have your own TV series, Johnno."

"Well," I say. "Funny you should say that, but I did actually do a tryout for the show."

"You did?" Hannah asks. "For *Survive the Night*?"

"Yeah." Ah, Christ. Why did I say anything? *Stupid Johnno, always shooting my mouth off.* Jesus, it's humiliating. "Yeah, well, they did a screen test, with the two of us, and—"

"And Johnno decided he wasn't up for any of that crap, didn't you?" Will says. It's good of him to try to save my blushes. But there's no point in lying now, I might as well say it. "He's being a good mate," I say. "Truth is I was shit at it. They basically told me I didn't work on-screen. Not like our boy here—" I lean over and muss up Will's hair, and he ducks away, laughing. "I mean, he's right. It wasn't for me anyway. Couldn't stand any of that makeup they slap on you, the clothes they make you wear. Not that that's any shade on what you do, mate."

"No offense taken," Will says, putting up his hands.

He's a natural on-screen. He has this ability to be whoever people want him to be. When he's on the program I notice he drops his "h's," sounds a bit more like "one of the people." But when he's with posh, public school–educated blokes, blokes who came from the better versions of the sort of school we both went to, he's one of them—100 percent.

"Anyway," I say to Hannah. "It makes sense. Who'd ever want this ugly mug on TV, eh?" I pull a face. I see Jules glance away from me as though I've just exposed myself. Stuck-up cow.

"So where did the idea for the show come from, Will?" Hannah asks. I appreciate that she's trying to move the conversation on, spare me any more humiliation.

"Yeah," Femi says. "You know, I was wondering about that. Was it Survival?"

"Survival?" Hannah turns to him.

"This game we used to play at school," Femi explains.

Duncan's wife, Georgina, chips in: "Oh God. Duncan's told me stories about it. Really awful stuff. He told me about boys being taken out of their beds at night, left in the middle of nowhere—"

"Yeah, that's what happened," Femi says. "They'd kidnap a younger boy from his bed and take him as far as they could away from the school, deep into the grounds."

"And we're talking big grounds," Angus says. "And the middle of nowhere. Pitch-black. No light from anything."

"It sounds barbaric," Hannah says, her eyes wide.

"It was a big tradition," Duncan says. "They'd been doing it for hundreds of years, since the start of the school."

"Will never had to do it, did you, mate?" Femi turns to him.

Will holds up his hands. "No one ever came and got me."

"Yeah," Angus says, "because they were all shit-scared of your dad."

"The chap would have a blindfold on at the start," Angus says, turning to Hannah, "so he didn't know where he was. Sometimes he'd even be tied to a tree or a fence, and had to get free. I remember when I did mine—"

"You pissed yourself," Duncan finishes.

"No I didn't," Angus replies.

"Yeah you *did*," Duncan says. "Don't think we've forgotten that. Pisspants."

Angus takes a gulp of wine. "Fine, well, *loads* of people did. It was fucking terrifying."

I remember my Survival. Even though you knew it would happen at some point, nothing prepared you for when they actually came to get you.

"The *craziest* thing is," Georgina says, "Duncan doesn't seem to think it was a bad thing." She turns to him. "Do you, darling?"

"It was the making of me," Duncan says.

I look over at Duncan who's sitting there with his hands in his pockets and his chest thrown out, like he's king of all he surveys, like he owns this place. And I wonder what it made him into, exactly.

I wonder what it made me into.

"I suppose it was harmless," Georgina says, "it's not like anyone died, is it?" She gives a little laugh.

I remember waking up, hearing the whispers in the dark all around me. *Hold his legs . . . you go for the head.* Then how they laughed as they held me down and tied the blindfold round my eyes. Then voices. Whoops and cheers, maybe—but with the blindfold over my ears too they sounded like animals: howls and screeches. Out into the night air, freezing on my bare feet. Rattling fast over the uneven ground—a wheelbarrow I guess it was—for so long I thought we must have left the school grounds. Then they left me, in the woods. All alone. Nothing but the beat of my heart and the secret noises of the woods. Getting the blindfold off and finding it just as dark, no moon to see by. Tree branches scratching at my cheeks, trees so close it felt like there was no way between them, like they were pressing in on me. So cold, a metallic taste like blood at the back of my throat. Crackle of twigs beneath my bare feet. Walking for miles, in circles probably. The whole night, through the woods, until the dawn came.

When I got back to the school building, I felt like I'd been reborn. Fuck the teachers who told me I'd never amount to much. Like they'd ever survived a night like that. I felt like I was invincible. Like I could do anything.

"Johnno," Will says, "I was saying I reckon it's time to get your whiskey out. Give it a sample." He jumps up from the table, and goes and gets one of the bottles.

"Oh," Hannah says, "can I look?" She takes it from Will. "This is such a cool design, Johnno. Did you work with someone on it?"

"Yeah," I say. "I've got a mate in London who's a graphic designer. He's done a good job, hasn't he?"

"He really has," she says, nodding, tracing the type with her finger. "That's what I do," she says. "I'm an illustrator, by trade. But it feels like a million years ago now. I'm on permanent maternity leave."

"Can I have a look?" Charlie says. He takes it from her and reads the label, frowning. "You must have had to partner with a distillery? Because it says here it's been aged twelve years."

"Yeah," I say, feeling like I'm being interviewed, or doing a test. Like he's trying to catch me out. Maybe it's the whole schoolteacher thing. "I did."

"Well," says Will, opening the bottle with a flourish. "The acid test!" He calls into the kitchen, "Aoife . . . Freddy. Could we have some glasses for whiskey please?"

Aoife carries some in on a tray.

"Get one for yourself too," Will says, like he's lord of the manor, "and for Freddy. We'll all try it!" Then, as Aoife tries to shake her head: "I insist!"

Freddy shuffles in to stand next to his wife. He keeps his eyes down and fiddles with the cord of his apron as they both stand there awkwardly. *Fucking weirdo,* Duncan mouths at the rest of us. It's probably a good thing the bloke's looking at the floor.

I check Aoife out. She's not as old as I thought at first: maybe only forty or so. She just dresses older. She's good-looking, too—in a refined kind of way. I wonder what she's doing with such a wet blanket of a husband.

Will pours out the rest of the whiskey. Jules asks for a couple of drops: "I've never been much of a whiskey drinker, I'm afraid." She takes a sip and I see her wince, before she has time to cover it by putting her hand over her mouth. But the hand only draws attention to it. Which maybe, come to think of it, she meant it to do. It's pretty clear she's not my biggest fan.

"It's good, mate," Duncan says. "It *kind* of reminds me of a Laphroaig, you know?"

"Yeah," I say. "I guess so." Trust Duncan to know his whiskies.

Aoife and Freddy down theirs as quickly as possible and hightail it back to the kitchen. I get that. My mum used to work at the local country club—the sort of place Angus and Duncan's parents probably had memberships to. She said the golfers sometimes tried to buy her a drink, thinking they were being so generous, but it only made her feel awkward.

"I think it's dead tasty," Hannah says. "I'm surprised. I have to tell you, Johnno, I'm not normally a whiskey fan." She takes another sip.

"Well," Jules says. "Our guests are very lucky." She smiles at me. But you know that thing they say about someone's eyes not smiling? Hers aren't.

I grin at them all. But I'm feeling a bit out of sorts. I think it's all that talk about Survival. Hard to remind myself that to them—to pretty much all the other ex-Trevellyan boys—it's all just a game.

I look over at Will. He's got his hand on the back of

Jules's head and he's grinning round at everyone. He looks like a man who has everything in life. Which, I suppose, he does. And I think: Does it not affect him too, all the talk about the old days? Not even the tiniest bit?

I've got to shake off this weird mood. I lunge toward the middle of the table and pick up the bottle of whiskey. "I think it's time for a drinking game," I say.

"Ah—" says Jules, probably about to call it off, but she's drowned out by the howls of approval from the blokes.

"Yes!" Angus shouts. "Irish snap?"

"Yeah," Femi says. "Like we played at school! Remember doing shots of Listerine mouthwash? 'Cause we worked out it was fifty percent proof?"

"Or that vodka you smuggled in, Dunc," Angus says.

"Right," I say, jumping up from the table. "I'll go get us a deck." I'm already feeling better now I've got a purpose to distract myself with.

I go to the kitchen and find Aoife standing with her back to me, going through some sort of list on a clipboard. When I cough she gives a little jump.

"Aoife, love," I say, "you got a deck of cards?"

"Yes," she says, taking a step away from me, like

she's scared of me. "Of course. I think there's one in the drawing room." She's got a nice accent. I've always liked an Irish girl. "Tink" rather than "think"—that makes me smile.

Her husband's in there too, busying himself with the oven.

"You making stuff for tomorrow?" I ask him, while I wait for Aoife.

"Mm-hmm," he says, without making eye contact. I'm glad when Aoife returns after a minute or so with the cards.

Back at the table I deal the deck out to the others.

"I'm off to get my beauty sleep," Jules's mum says. "I've never been one for the hard stuff." *Not true,* I see Jules mouth. Jules's dad and the hot French step-mum excuse themselves too.

"Nor me," Hannah says. She looks over at Charlie. "We've had a long day, haven't we, love?"

"I don't know—" Charlie says.

"Come on, Charlie boy," I call to Charlie. "It'll be fun! Live a little!"

He doesn't look convinced.

Things got a bit loose on the stag. Charlie, poor bloke, didn't go to a school like ours, so he wasn't really prepared for it. He's just such a . . . geography teacher.

I felt like he went to a dark place that night. Anyone would have, I guess. He barely talked to any of us for the rest of the weekend.

It was being back together with that group of blokes again, I suppose. Most of them went to Trevellyan's. We were all bonded by that place. Not in the same way that Will and I are bonded—that's only the two of us. But we are tied by the other stuff. The rituals, the male bonding. When we get together there's this kind of pack mentality.

We get carried away.

HANNAH

The Plus-One

Since the pennying incident I've become very wary of the ushers. The more they drink the more it emerges: something dark and cruel hiding behind the public schoolboy manners. And I hate that right now my husband's behaving like a teenager who wants to be accepted into their gang.

"Right," Johnno says. "Everyone ready?" He looks around the table. I've worked out what's weird about his eyes. They're so dark you can't tell where the irises end and the pupils begin. It gives him a strange, blank look, so that even while he's laughing, it's like his eyes aren't quite playing along. And the rest of his face is a bit too expressive by comparison, changing every couple of seconds, his mouth very large and mobile. There's this kind of manic energy about him. I hope it's harmless. Like a dog that jumps up at you, big and scary, but all it really wants is to be thrown a ball—not to maul your face.

"Charlie," Johnno says. "You *are* joining us?"

"Charlie," I whisper, trying to catch my husband's eye. He's barely looked my way all evening, too wrapped up in Jules or trying to be one of the lads. But I want to get through to him.

Charlie's such a mild man: hardly ever raises his voice, hardly ever gets cross with the kids. If they get a telling off, it's normally from me. So it isn't like he becomes a more intense version of himself when he drinks, or that alcohol amplifies his bad qualities. In ordinary life he doesn't really have many bad qualities. Yeah, maybe all that anger is there, hidden, somewhere beneath the surface. But I could swear, on the couple of times I have seen him drunk, that it is like my husband has been taken over by someone else. That's what makes it all the more frightening. Over the years I've learned to spot the smallest signs. The slight slackening of his mouth, the drooping of his eyelids. I've had to learn because I know that the next stage isn't pretty. It's like a small firework has suddenly detonated in his brain.

Finally Charlie glances in my direction. I shake my head, slowly, deliberately, so he can make no mistake of my meaning. *Don't do it.*

"What the fuck's going on here?" Duncan crows. Oh God, he's caught me doing it. He swivels to Charlie. "She keep you on a leash, Charlie boy?"

Charlie's ears have gone bright red. "No," he says. "Obviously not. Yeah, fine. I'm in."

Shit. I'm torn between wanting to stay so I can try to stop him doing anything stupid and thinking I should leave him to it and let him take himself out, no matter the consequences. Especially after all that unsubtle flirting with Jules.

"I'm going to deal," Johnno says.

"Wait," Duncan says, getting to his feet, clapping his hands. "We should do the school motto first."

"Yeah," Femi agrees, joining him. Angus stands too. "Come on, Will, Johnno. Old times' sake and all that."

Johnno and Will rise.

I look at them—all, except Johnno, so elegantly dressed in their white shirts and dark trousers, expensive watches at their wrists. I wonder why on earth these men, who have apparently done so well for themselves since, are still obsessing about their school days. I can't imagine banging on about crappy old Dunraven High. I never had any resentment toward it but it's also not somewhere I think about all that much. Like everyone else, I left in a scribbled-on leaver's shirt and never really looked back. No leaving school at 3:30 P.M. and heading home to watch *Hollyoaks* for these guys—they must have spent a chunk of their childhoods locked in that place.

Duncan begins to drum slowly with a fist on the table. He looks around, encouraging the others to join him. They do. Gradually it gets louder and louder, the drumming faster, more frenzied.

"*Fac fortia et patere*," Duncan chants, in what I guess must be Latin.

"*Fac fortia et patere*," the others follow.

And then, in a kind of low, intent murmur:

Flectere si nequeo superos,
Acheronta movebo.
Flectere si nequeo superos,
Acheronta movebo!

I watch the men, how their eyes seem to gleam in the flickering candlelight. Their faces are flushed—they're excited, drunk. There's a prickle up my spine. With the candles and the dark pressing in at the windows and the strange rhythm of the chanting, the drumming, I feel suddenly like I'm watching some satanic ritual being performed. There's a menacing element to it, tribal. I put a hand to my chest and I can feel my heart beating too fast, like a frightened animal's.

The drumming intensifies to a climax, until it's so frenzied that the crockery and cutlery are leaping about all over the place. A glass hops its way off the corner of the table and smashes on the floor. No one apart from me pays it any attention.

Fac fortia et patere!
Flectere si nequeo superos,
Acheronta movebo!

And then, finally, right when I feel I can't bear it any longer, they all give a roar and stop. They stare at each other. Their foreheads glisten with sweat. Their pupils seem bigger, like they've taken a hit of something. Big hyena laughs now, teeth bared, slapping each other on the back, punching each other hard enough to hurt. I notice Johnno's not laughing as hard as all the others. His grin doesn't convince, somehow.

"But what does it mean?" Georgina asks.

"Angus," Femi slurs, "you're the Latin geek."

"The first part," Angus says, "is: 'Do brave deeds and endure,' which was the school motto. The second part was added in by us boys: 'If I can't move heaven, then I shall raise hell.' It used to get chanted before rugby matches."

"And the rest," says Duncan, with a nasty smile.

"It's so menacing," Georgina says. But she's staring up at her red, sweaty, wild-eyed husband as though she's never found him so attractive.

"That was kind of the point."

"Right, *ladies*," Johnno shouts. "Time to stop fannying around and get some drinking done!"

Another roar of approval from the others. Femi and Duncan mix the whiskey with wine, with sauce left over from the meal, with salt and pepper, so it forms a disgusting brown soup. And then the game begins—all of them slamming down their hands on the table and yelling at the top of their voices.

Angus is the first to lose. As he drinks, the mixture slops onto the immaculate white of his shirt, staining it brown. The others jeer him.

"You idiot!" Duncan shouts. "Most of it's going down your neck."

Angus swallows the last gulp, gags. His eyes bulge.

Will's next. He puts it away expertly. I watch the muscles of his throat working. He turns the glass upside down above his head and grins.

Next to end up with all the cards is Charlie. He looks at his glass, takes a deep breath.

"Come on, you pussy!" Duncan shouts.

I can't watch this. I don't have to watch this. Sod Charlie, I think. This was meant to be our weekend away together. If he wants to take himself down it's his bloody lookout. I'm his wife, not his mother. I stand up.

"I'm going to bed," I say. "Night all."

But no one answers, or even glances in my direction.

I push into the drawing room next door and as I walk through I stop short in shock. A figure's sitting there on the sofa, in the gloom. After a moment I recognize it to be Olivia. "Oh, hey there," I say.

She looks up. Her long legs stick out in front of her, her feet bare. "Hey."

"Had enough in there?"

"Yeah."

"Me too," I say. "You staying up for a bit?"

She shrugs. "No point in going to bed. My room's right next to *that*."

As if on cue, from the dining room comes a burst of mocking laughter. Someone roars: "Drink it—drink it all down!"

And now a chant: *Down it, down it, down it*—switching suddenly into *raise hell, raise hell, RAISE HELL!* Sounds of the table being smashed with fists. Then of something else shattering—another glass? A slurred voice: "Johnno, you fucking idiot!"

Poor Olivia, unable to escape from all that. I hover in the doorway.

"It's fine," Olivia says. "I don't need anyone to keep me company."

But I feel I should stay. I feel bad for her. And actually, I realize I *want* to stay. I liked sitting with her in the cave earlier, smoking. There was something exciting about it, a strange thrill. Talking to her, with the taste of the tobacco on my tongue, I could almost imagine I was nineteen again, talking about the boys I'd slept with—not a mum of two and mortgaged up to the eyeballs. And there's also the fact that Olivia reminds me of someone. But I can't think who. It bothers me, like when you're trying to think of a word and you know it's there on the tip of your tongue, just out of reach.

"Actually," I say, "I'm not all that tired. And I don't have to get up early tomorrow morning to deal with two crazy kids. There's some wine in our room—I could go and grab it."

She gives a small smile at this, the first I've seen. And then she reaches behind the sofa cushion and pulls out an expensive-looking bottle of vodka. "I nicked it from the kitchen earlier," she says.

"Oh," I say. "Well, even better." This really *is* like being nineteen again.

She passes me the bottle. I unscrew the cap, take a

swig. It burns a freezing streak down my throat and I gasp. "Wow. Can't think of the last time I did that." I pass the bottle to her and wipe my mouth. "We got cut off, earlier, didn't we? You were telling me about that guy—Callum? The breakup."

Olivia shuts her eyes, takes a deep breath. "I guess the breakup was only the beginning," she says.

Another big roar of laughter from the next room. More hands thumping the table. More drunken male voices shouting over each other. A crash against the door, then Angus falls through it, trousers about his ankles, his dick flopping out obscenely.

"Sorry, ladies," he says, with a drunken leer. "Don't mind me."

"Oh for Christ's sake," I explode, "just . . . just fuck off and leave us alone!"

Olivia looks at me, impressed, like she didn't think I had it in me. I didn't, either. I'm not quite sure where it came from. Maybe it's the vodka.

"You know what?" I say. "This probably isn't the best place to chat, is it?"

She shakes her head. "We could go to the cave?"

"Er—" I hadn't planned on a nighttime foray about the island. And I'm sure it's dangerous to wander around at night, with the bog and things.

"Forget it," Olivia says, quickly. "I get it. I just—it's weird—I just felt it was easier talking in there."

And suddenly I have the same feeling I did earlier. An odd thrill, the feeling of breaking the rules. "No," I say. "Let's do it. And bring that bottle."

We sneak out of the Folly via the rear entrance. It's really creepy at night, this place. It's so quiet, apart from the sound of the waves on the rocks in the near distance. Occasionally there comes a strange, guttural cackling that raises all the hairs on my arms. I finally realize that the noise must be made by some sort of bird. A pretty big one from the sound of it.

As we continue, the ruined houses loom up next to us in the beam of my flashlight. The dark, gaping windows are like empty eye sockets and it feels unnervingly as though someone might be in there, looking out, watching us pass. I can hear noises coming from inside, too: rustles and creaks and scratchings. It's probably rats—but then, that's not a particularly reassuring thought either.

I'm aware of things moving around us as we walk—too fast to see properly, caught momentarily by the weak light of the moon. Something flies so near to my face that I feel it brush the sensitive skin of my cheek. I jump back, put a hand up to fend it off. A bat? It was definitely too big to be an insect.

As we climb down into the cave a dark figure appears on the rock wall in front of us, human shaped. I almost drop the bottle in shock until, after a beat, I realize it is my own shadow.

This place is enough to make you believe in ghosts.

NOW
THE WEDDING NIGHT

The four ushers have formed a search party. They take a first-aid kit. They take the big paraffin torches from the brackets at the entrance of the marquee for illumination.

"Right, boys," Femi says. "Everyone ready?"

There has been a strange, fervent energy about their preparations, bordering on an inappropriate excitement. They might be scouts preparing for a mission, the schoolboys they once were on some midnight dare.

The other guests gather around silently watching the preparations, relieved that the thing has been taken out of their hands, that they are permitted to stay here in the light and warmth.

To those inside the marquee who watch them go, they look like medieval villagers on a witch hunt: the lighted torches, the fervor. The wind and the blackout have added to the sense of the surreal. The macabre discovery that supposedly lies in wait out there has taken on a fantastical dimension: not quite real. Besides, it's difficult to know what to believe, whether they can really trust the word of a hysterical teenager. Some of them are still hoping that it has all just been a terrible misunderstanding.

They watch, silently, as the small group marches through the thrashing flaps of the marquee entrance. Out into the loud ragged night, into the storm, holding their torches aloft.

THE DAY BEFORE

OLIVIA

The Bridesmaid

In the cave the sea has come in, so it's practically lapping at our feet, the water black as ink. It makes the space feel smaller, more claustrophobic. Hannah and I have to sit nearer to each other than we did before, our knees touching, a candle we nicked from the drawing room perched on the rock in front of us in its glass lantern.

Now I understand why it's called the Whispering Cave. The high water has changed the acoustics in here so that this time everything we say is whispered back to us, as though someone's standing there in the shadows, repeating every word. It's hard to believe there isn't. I find myself turning to check, every so often, to make certain we're alone.

I can't make Hannah out all that well in the soft light

of the candle. But I can hear her breathing, smell her perfume.

We pass the bottle of vodka between us. I'm already a bit drunk, I think, from dinner. I couldn't eat much and the booze went straight to my head. But I need to be drunker to tell her, drunk enough that my brain can't stop the words. Which seems silly, as recently I have been needing to tell someone about it so badly that sometimes I feel like it's going to erupt out of me, without any warning. But now it has actually come down to it, I feel tongue-tied.

Hannah speaks first. "Olivia."

The cave replies in a whisper: *Olivia, Olivia, Olivia.*

"God," Hannah says, "that echo. Did your ex . . . did he do anything to you? Someone I know—" She stops, starts again: "My sister, Alice. She had this boyfriend when she was at university. And he reacted really badly to the breakup. I mean, really *really* badly—"

I wait for Hannah to say more, but she doesn't. Instead she takes the bottle from me and has a very long drink, about four shots' worth.

"No, it wasn't anything like that," I say. "Yeah, Callum was a bit of a shit. I mean, he wasn't very subtle about hooking up with Ellie straight after. But he was the one who broke it off, so it wasn't that." I grab the bottle from her, take a big gulp. I can taste her lipstick on the rim. "It was in the summer holidays after term had ended. I was staying at Jules's place in Islington, while she was away for work for a few days."

I speak into the darkness, the cave whispering my own words back to me. I find myself telling Hannah how lonely I felt. How I was in this great big city, which I've always found so exciting, but realized I had no one to share it with. How it was Friday night and I'd gone to the Sainsbury's down the road from Jules's flat and bought myself some crisps, milk and cereal for the morning, and how my walk home took me past all these people standing outside pubs, drinking, having a laugh in the sun. How I felt like such a fucking saddo, with my orange carrier bag and a night of Netflix to look forward to. How it was at times like that I always thought of Callum, and what we might be doing together, which made me feel even more alone.

I still can't quite believe I'm telling her all this, when I hardly know her. But maybe that's the point. Maybe, of all the people here, she's the one person I can tell, *because* she's basically a stranger. The vodka definitely helps, too, and the fact that it's so gloomy in here that I can hardly see her face. Even so, I don't think I can tell her all of it. The thought of doing that makes me feel panicky. But maybe I can start at the beginning and see if, once I've told her most of it, I'm brave enough to tell her the whole thing.

"I was on my phone," I say, "and I could see that Callum was with Ellie. She'd shared all these pics on Snapchat. There was one of her sitting on his lap. And then another one of her kissing him, while she held one middle finger up to the camera like she didn't want anyone to take the picture . . . except then she went and shared it for the whole world to see, for fuck's sake."

Hannah takes a drink from the bottle, breathes out. "That must have made you feel pretty awful," she says. "Seeing that. Jeez, social media has a lot to answer for."

"Yeah." I shrug. "It did make me feel a bit . . . shit." In case I sound like a total stalker I don't tell her how many times I looked at those photos, how I sat there clutching my Sainsbury's bag and crying while I did it. "My mates had been saying I should have some fun," I say. "You know, like show Callum what he was missing. They kept telling me to get myself on some dating apps, but I didn't want to do it at uni, where it was all so incestuous."

"What, apps like Tinder?"

I think she's trying to show she's down with the kids. "Yeah, but no one really uses Tinder anymore."

"Sorry," she says. "I'm ancient, remember. What do I know?" She says it a bit wistfully.

"You're not that old," I tell her.

"Well . . . thanks." Her knee bumps against mine.

I take another swig of vodka. And remember how that night in Jules's flat I drank some of her wine, which made me realize how all the stuff we drank at uni for £3 a glass in the local bars tasted like absolute piss. I remember how I felt quite sophisticated walking around in my pants and bra with one of her big glasses. I imagined it was my flat, that I was going to go out and find some man and bring him back here and screw him. And *that* would show Callum.

Obviously I didn't *actually* plan to do that. I'd only had sex with one person before, with Callum. And even that had been pretty tame.

"I set up a profile," I tell Hannah. "I decided in London it was different. In London I could go on a date and it wouldn't be all over the whole of campus the next morning."

"I'm kind of impressed," Hannah says. "I'd never have been brave enough to do something like that. But weren't you, you know . . . worried about safety?"

"No," I say. "I'm not an idiot. I didn't use my real name. Or my age."

"Ah," Hannah nods. "Right." I get the impression she's not convinced by that and is trying very hard not to say anything else.

I put my age as twenty-six, in fact. The profile photo I put up didn't even look like me. I ransacked Jules's closet, did my makeup perfectly. But it was kind of the *point* not to look like me.

"I called myself Bella," I say. "You know, as in Hadid?"

I tell Hannah how I sat there on the bed and scrolled through photos of all these guys until my eyes burned. "Most of them were rank," I say. "In the gym, like lifting up their shirts, or wearing sunglasses that they thought made them look cool." I almost gave up.

"But I did match with this one guy," I tell Hannah. "He caught my eye. He was . . . different."

I made the first move. So unlike me, but I was a bit pissed from Jules's wine.

Free to meet up? I wrote.

Yes, his reply came. I'd like that, Bella. When suits you?

How about this evening?

There was a long pause. Then: You don't hang about.

This is my only free evening for the next few weeks. I liked how that sounded. Like I had better places to be.

Fine, he messaged back. It's a date.

"What was he like?" Hannah asks, her chin in her hand. She seems fascinated, watching me closely.

"Hotter than his photo. And a bit older than me."

"How much older?"

"Um . . . maybe fifteen years?"

"OK." Is she trying not to sound shocked? "And what was he like? When you actually met up?"

I think back. It's hard for me to see him as he appeared at the beginning. "I guess I thought he was hot. And . . . he seemed like more of a man. He made Callum look like a boy in comparison." He had broad shoulders, like he worked out a lot, and a tan. In comparison Callum was a scrawny little pretty boy. Proper men were my new thing, I decided. "But," I shrug, even though she can't see me, "I don't know. I suppose however hot he was, at first, a part of me would have preferred him to be Callum."

Hannah nods. "Yeah," she says sympathetically. "I get that. When you've got your heart set on someone Brad Pitt could walk in and he wouldn't be enough—"

"Brad Pitt is really fucking *old,*" I say.

"Um—Harry Styles?"

That almost makes me smile. "Yeah. Maybe. Or Timothée Chalamet." I always thought Callum looked a bit like him. "But Callum probably hadn't thought about me for a moment, especially not while Ellie's stupid big tits were in his face." I told myself I had better stop fucking thinking about him.

"And did this guy . . . what was his name?"

"Steven."

"Did he say anything? When you met, about you being so much younger?"

I give her a look. That sounded a bit judge-y.

"Sorry," she says, with a laugh. "But, seriously, did he?"

"Yeah, he did. He asked me if I was really twenty-six. But he didn't say it in a suspicious way, more like it was, I dunno—a joke we were both in on. It didn't really seem to matter to him, not then. And he was nice," I say, though it's hard to remember that now. "I was having a good time. He laughed at all my jokes. He asked me *loads* of questions about myself."

I cast my mind back to that night. Being in that bar with the drinks going to my head—I was drinking Negronis because I thought that would make me seem older. "My original plan was to get a photo," I say, "post it to my Instagram." Let Callum see what he was missing.

"I'm guessing . . . ," Hannah looks at me, "a bit more than that happened?"

"Yeah." I take a gulp of vodka.

There was this moment, I remember, when I thought maybe he was going to say goodbye, but he opened the door of the cab and turned to me and said: "Well, are you getting in?" And in the taxi (not even an Uber, a proper black cab), how this little voice kept piping up: *What are you doing? You hardly know him!* But the drunk part of me, the part of me that was up for it, kept telling it to shut up.

We went back to Jules's place, because he'd just moved house and didn't have any proper furniture. I felt a bit bad about it, but I told myself I'd wash the sheets.

"Wow," he said. "*This* is impressive. And it all belongs to you?"

"Yeah," I said, feeling like I'd got a whole lot more sophisticated in his eyes.

"And then we had sex," I tell Hannah. "I guess I wanted to do it before the booze wore off."

"Was it good?" Hannah asks. She sounds excited. And then: "I haven't had sex for ages. Sorry. I know that's TMI."

I try not to think of her and Charlie having sex. "Yeah," I say. "It was a bit—y'know. A bit rough? He pushed me up against the wall, pushed my skirt up around my waist, pulled my knickers down. And he—Can I have a bit more of that?" Hannah passes me the bottle and I take a quick slug. "He went down on me, even though I hadn't had a shower. He said he preferred it like that."

"Right," Hannah says. "OK. Wow."

Callum and I had never done anything very adventurous. I guess the sex I had with Steven was better than anything I'd had with Callum, even if, after he'd made me come with his mouth that first time, I weirdly felt like crying for a moment.

"I saw him, like, quite a few times after that," I tell Hannah.

I feel rather than see Hannah nod, her head so close to mine that I sense the movement of the air. I find myself telling her how I liked seeing myself the way he seemed to: as someone sexy, someone adventurous. Even if sometimes I felt like I was out of my depth, not always totally comfortable with all the stuff he asked me to do in bed.

"I mean," I say, "it wasn't like it was with Callum, when it felt like we were . . ."

"Soul mates?" Hannah asks.

"Yeah," I say. It's a pretty cringe word, but it's also exactly right. "This was different, I guess. With Steven it was like he only showed me a tiny bit of himself, which—"

"Left you wanting to see more?"

"Yeah. I was sort of obsessed by him, I think. And he was so grown-up and so sophisticated, but he wanted *me*. And then—" I shrug. "I fucked up."

Hannah frowns. "What do you mean?"

"I dunno. I suppose I wanted to prove to him I was *mature*. And we never seemed to *do* anything together, other than meet up and, you know, have sex. I had this—this feeling that he might only be interested in me for that."

Hannah nods.

"But at the end of the summer Jules's magazine was throwing this party at the V&A, and I thought it would be a cool thing to bring him to. A proper date. Like, impress him a bit. Make him think I was grown-up and mature."

I tell Hannah about walking up those steps and seeing all these very grown-up, glamorous people milling around inside, all looking like film stars. And how the guy who checked our names looked over me like he didn't think I should be there, whereas Steven seemed to fit in so perfectly.

"I got a bit nervous," I say. "Especially of having to introduce him to Jules. And there were all these free drinks. I had way too many of them, to try and feel more confident. I made a total twat of myself. I had to go and be sick in the loos—I was a state. And then Steven put me in a cab back to Jules's, and I couldn't even ask him to come with me because she would be there later on. I remember him counting out the notes to the cabdriver. And then asking him to make sure I got home safe, like I was a child."

"He should have gone with you," Hannah says. "*He* should have made sure you were all right. Not left it to some taxi driver."

I shrug. "Maybe. But I was such a fucking embarrassment. I'm not surprised he wanted to be rid of me."

I remember watching him out of the window and thinking: *I've blown it.* And thinking, if I were him, maybe I'd just go back inside and hang out with people my own age who could hold their booze.

"After that he started ghosting me." In case she doesn't know what that means I say, "You know, like not replying? Even though I could see the two little blue ticks."

She nods.

"I went back to uni. One night I got a bit drunk and sad after a night out and I sent him *ten* messages. I tried to call him on the walk to Halls at two A.M. He didn't answer. Didn't reply to my texts. I knew I'd never see him again."

"Shit," Hannah says.

"Yeah."

"So was that it?" she asks, when I don't say any more. "*Did* you see him again?" And then, when I don't answer: "Olivia?"

But I can't speak. It's like I was under some sort of spell before, it was so easy to talk. Now it feels as though the words are stuck in my throat.

There's this image in my brain. Red on white. All the blood.

When we get back to the Folly, Hannah says she's knackered. "Straight to bed for me," she says. I get it. It was different in the cave. Sitting there in the dark with the vodka and the candlelight, it felt like we could say anything. Now it feels almost like we overshared. Like we crossed a line.

I know I won't be able to go to sleep, though, especially not while all the blokes are still playing their game outside my room. So I stand against the wall outside for a bit and try to slow down the thoughts racing round my head.

"Hello there."

I nearly jump out of my skin. "What the fuck—"

It's the best man, Johnno. I don't like him. I saw how he looked at me earlier. And he's drunk—I can tell that, and *I'm* pretty drunk. In the light spilling from the dining room I can see him give a big grin, more of a leer. "Fancy a puff?" He holds out a big joint, sickly smell of weed. I can see it's wet on the end where it's been in his mouth.

"No thanks," I say.

"Very well behaved."

I make to go inside, but as I reach for the door he catches my arm, his hand tight about it. "You know, we should have a dance tomorrow, you and I. Best man and the bridesmaid."

I shake my head.

He steps nearer, pulls me closer to him. He's so much bigger than me. But he wouldn't do anything right here, would he? Not with everyone upstairs?

"You should think about it," he says. "Might surprise you. An older man."

"Get the fuck off me," I hiss. I think of my razor blade, upstairs. I wish I had it with me, just so I knew it was there.

I yank my arm out of his grip as I fumble with the door, my fingers not working properly. I feel him watching me the whole time.

JOHNNO

The Best Man

I'm back up in my room, having finished my joint. I managed to pick up the grass in Dublin when I arrived, hanging around Temple Bar with all the tourists. Not sure it's as strong as the stuff I get from my usual guy but hopefully it will help me sleep. I need a bit of help tonight.

Here on the island it's like we're back there, at Trevellyan's. Maybe it's to do with the land. The cliffs, the sea. All I can hear is the sound of the waves outside the windows, slamming into the rocks below. I remember the dorm room: the rows of beds and the bars outside the windows. To keep us safe or to keep us in—maybe a bit of both. And the sound of the waves there, too, rushing up the beach. *Shush, shush, shush.* Reminding me to keep the secret.

I haven't thought about it, not properly, for years. I can't. Some things you've got to put behind you. But it's like being here is forcing me to look right at it. And when I do I can't fucking breathe properly.

I lie in bed. I've drunk enough to pass out, and then the weed on top. But I feel like something's crawling all over my skin, a million cockroaches in the bed with me. They're here to stop me getting any rest. I want to scratch at myself, tear into my skin if I have to, to make it stop. And I'm afraid that if I do sleep I'll have dreams like I did last night. I haven't had them for as long as I can remember . . . years and years. It's the company. It's this place.

It's so dark in here. It's too dark. I feel like it's pressing down on me. Like I'm drowning in it. I sit up in bed, remind myself that I'm fine. Nothing trying to suffocate me, no cockroaches. It could be the weed—different stuff, making me more paranoid. I'll go take a shower, that's what I'll do. Get the water nice and hot, have a good scrub.

Then I think I see this thing, in the corner of the room. Growing, gathering itself together, out of the darkness.

Nah. I'm imagining it. Must be. Don't believe in ghosts.

It's got to be the weed, the whiskey. My brain playing tricks on me. Fuck, but I'm sure there's something there. I can see it out of the corner of my eye, but when I look directly at it, it seems to disappear. I shut my eyes like a little kid scared of monsters under the bed, press my eyelids with my fingers until I see silver spots. It's no good. I can see it even with my eyes closed. It had a face. And it's not an it, it's a someone. I know who it is.

"Get the fuck away from me," I whisper. Then I try a different way: "I'm sorry. It wasn't my fault. I didn't think—"

My stomach gives a heave. I just make it to the bathroom in time before I'm spewing over the bowl of the toilet, my whole body shaking with fear.

JULES

The Bride

Charlie and I are up on the battlements, looking out at the glitter of lights along the mainland. We left the others to their disgusting game. There's something illicit about it, just the two of us up here. Something reckless. Perhaps it's being on top of the world with the steep drop beneath us—invisible but very much there—adding a frisson of excitement, making everything feel slightly freighted with danger. Or that we're cloaked by darkness. That anything could happen up here and no one would know.

"It's so good to have you here," I tell him. "You know you're *my* best man, really?"

"Thanks," he says. "It's good to be here. Why did you choose this place?"

"Oh, you know. My Irish roots. And it's so exclusive, I like the idea of being first. There's the remoteness, too: good for deterring any paps."

"They'd really try and get photos of his wedding?" He sounds incredulous, like he doesn't believe Will's celebrity justifies it.

"They might. And it's so on-brand for Will, having his wedding in such a wild place."

All of what I've told him is true, in a way. But not the whole truth.

I rest my head against his shoulder. I think I feel him go still. Perhaps it doesn't feel quite so natural as it once did, being physically close like this. Come to think of it, did it ever?

Charlie clears his throat. "Can I ask you a question?"

He sounds serious. I sense a touch of wariness. "Go ahead."

"He does makes you happy, doesn't he?"

I lift my head a fraction off his shoulder. "What do you mean?"

I feel him shrug. "Just that. You know how much I care about you, Jules."

"Yes," I say. "He does. And I could ask you the same about Hannah."

"That's *very* different—"

"Really? How so?" I don't want to hear his reply; I don't need yet another person telling me that it has all been so quick, between Will and me. And then, because I've drunk more than I meant to this evening—and because when else am I going to be able to?—I say it: "Are you saying that *you* would have made me happier?"

"Jules—" He says it as a kind of groan. "Don't do that."

"Do what?" I ask innocently.

"We wouldn't have worked. We're friends, good friends. You know that." At that I feel him pulling away from me, retreating from the cliff edge.

Do I, though? And is he *really* so convinced of that? I know he wanted me once. I still think about that night. The memory I have returned to so many times . . . when I have needed some inspiration in the bath, for example. We have never spoken of it since. And because we haven't, it has retained its power. I'm sure he still thinks about it too.

"We were different people back then," he says, as though he might have read my mind. I wonder if he's as convinced by his words as he's making out. "I wasn't asking because of anything like *that*," he says. "Not out of jealousy . . . or anything."

"*Really?* Because it sounds to me like you're a bit jealous."

"I'm not, I—"

"Did I tell you how good he is in bed? That's the sort of thing friends are meant to tell each other, isn't it?" I know I'm pushing it, but I can't help myself.

"Look," Charlie says. "I just want you to be happy."

How bloody patronizing. I lift my head fully away from his shoulder. I feel the distance between us expanding now, metaphorically as well as physically. "I'm perfectly capable of knowing what does and doesn't make me happy," I say. "In case you haven't noticed I'm thirty-four. Not a sixteen-year-old virgin totally in awe of you."

Charlie grimaces. "God, I know. Sorry, I didn't mean it like that. I care, that's all."

Something has suddenly occurred to me. "Charlie?" I ask. "Did you write me a note?"

"A note?"

I hear the answer to my question in his confusion. It wasn't him.

"It's nothing," I say. "Forget it. You know what? I think I'm going to turn in. If I go now, I can get eight hours' sleep before tomorrow."

"OK," he says. I sense that he is relieved I've called it a night and that pisses me off.

"Give me a hug?" I ask.

"Sure."

I lean into him. His body is softer than Will's, so

much less taut than it used to be. But the scent of him is the same. So familiar, somehow, which is strange—considering how long it's been.

It's still there, I think. He must feel it too. But then attraction never really goes away, does it? I'm sure of it: he's jealous.

When I get back to the room Will's getting undressed. He grins at me, I move toward him.

"Shall we pick up where we left off earlier?" he murmurs.

It's one way, I think, to erase the humiliation of that conversation with Charlie.

I tear open the remaining buttons on his shirt, he rips one of the straps of my jumpsuit trying to get it off me. It's always like the first time with him—that haste—only better, now we know exactly what the other wants. We fuck braced against the bed, him entering me from behind. I come, hard. I'm not quiet about it. In a strange way, it feels as though much of the evening since we got interrupted earlier has been a kind of foreplay. Feeling the gaze of the others upon us: envious, awed. Seeing in their reactions to us how good we look together. And yes, the hurt of having crossed a line with Charlie and being rebuffed. Maybe he'll hear us.

Afterward Will goes for a shower. He takes impeccable care of himself—his routine even makes my own look rather slapdash. I remember being a little surprised when I realized his permanently brown face wasn't actually due to the constant exposure to the elements but to Sisley's self-tan, the same one I use.

It's only now, sitting in the armchair in my robe, that I become aware of a strange odor, more powerful than the evanescently marine scent of sex. It is stronger, undeniably the smell of the sea: a briny, fishy, ammoniac tang at the back of the throat. And as I sit here it seems to gather itself from the shadowy corners of the room, gaining texture and depth.

I go to the window and open it. The air outside is pretty icy, now that it's dark. I can hear the slam of the waves against the rocks down below. Farther out the water is silver in the light of the moon, like molten metal, so bright that I can hardly look at it. You can see the swell in it even from here, great muscular movements beneath the surface, full of intent. I can hear a cackling above me, up on the roof, perhaps. It sounds like a gleeful mocking.

Surely, I think, the smell of the sea should be stronger outside than in? Yet the breeze that wafts in is fresh and odorless by comparison. I can't make sense of it. I reach over to the dressing table and light my scented candle. Then I sit in the chair and try for calm. But I can practically hear the beat of my own heart. Too fast, a flutter in my chest. Is it just the aftermath of our exertions? Or something more than that?

I should talk to Will about the note. Now is the moment, if I'm ever going to do it. But I've already had one confrontation this evening—with Charlie—and I can't quite bring myself to face the thing head-on, to plow ahead and raise it. And it's probably nothing. I'm 99 percent sure, anyway. Maybe 98.

The door to the bathroom opens. Will steps into the room, towel knotted around his waist. Even though I have just had him I'm momentarily distracted by the sight of his body: the planes and ridges of it, the muscles corded in stomach, arms and legs like a statue molded by a Renaissance sculptor.

"What are you doing still up?" he asks. "We should get some rest. Big day tomorrow."

I turn my back to him and drop my robe to the floor, sure I can feel his eyes on me. Enjoying the power of it. Then I lift the cover and slip into the bed and as I do my bare legs make contact with something. Solid and cold, the consistency of dead flesh. That seems to yield as I push my feet unwittingly into it and yet at the same time wraps itself around my legs.

"Jesus Christ! Jesus fucking Christ!"

I leap from the bed, trip, half sprawl on the floor.

Will stares at me. "Jules? What is it?"

I can hardly answer him at first, too scared and repulsed by what I just felt. The panic has risen into my throat in a choke. The shock reverberates through me, deep and visceral and animal. It was the stuff of a nightmare—the sort of thing you dream about finding in your bed, only to wake in a chill sweat and realize it was all in your imagination. But this was real. I can still feel the cold imprint of it against my legs.

"Will," I say, finally finding my voice. "There's something—in the bed. Under the covers."

He strides over in two great bounds, takes the duvet in both hands and rips it away. I can't help screaming. There, in the middle of the mattress, sprawls the huge black body of some marine creature, tentacles stretching in all directions.

Will leaps back. "What the fuck?" He sounds more angry than frightened. He says it again, as though the thing on the bed might somehow answer for itself: "What the fuck . . . ?"

The smell of the sea, of briny, rotting things, is overpowering now, emanating from that black mass on the bed.

And then quickly, recovering much more rapidly

than I do, Will moves closer to it again. As he puts out a hand I shout, "Don't touch it!" But he has already grasped the tentacles, given them a yank. They come free, the thing seems to break apart—horribly, sickeningly. It was there while we fucked, waiting for us beneath the covers . . .

Will gives a short, hard laugh, entirely without humor. "Look—it's only seaweed. It's bloody seaweed!"

He holds it aloft. I lean closer. He's right. It's the stuff I've seen strewn along the beaches here, great thick, dark ropes of it washed up by the waves. Will tosses it onto the floor.

Gradually, the whole spectacle loses its macabre, monstrous aspect and is reduced to a horrible mess. I become aware of the indignity of my position, sprawled as I am, naked, upon the floor. I feel my heartbeat slow. I breathe more easily.

Except . . . how did it come to be here in the first place? Why is it here?

Someone has done this to us. Someone has brought this in, hidden it beneath the duvet, knowing that we would only find it once we got into bed.

I turn to Will. "Who could have done this?"

He shrugs. "Well, I have my suspicions."

"What? About who?"

"It was a prank we used to play on the younger boys at school. We'd go down via the cliff path and collect seaweed on the beaches—as much as we could carry. Then we'd hide it in their beds. So my guess is Johnno or Duncan—possibly all of the guys. They probably thought it was funny."

"You'd call this a *prank*? We're not at school, Will, it's the night before our wedding! What the fuck?" In a way, my anger is a relief.

Will shrugs. "It's not a prank for you, it's for me. You know, for old times' sake. They wouldn't have meant you to get upset—"

"I'm going to go and get them all up now, find out which one of them it was. Show them exactly how funny I think it is."

"Jules." Will takes hold of my shoulders. And then, soothingly: "Look, if you were to do that . . . well, you might say things you'd regret. It would spoil things for tomorrow, wouldn't it? It could change the whole dynamic."

I do, sort of, see what he means. God, he's always so reasonable—sometimes infuriatingly so, always taking the measured approach. I look at the black mass, now on the floor. It's hard to believe that some darker message wasn't intended by it.

"Look," Will says gently. "We're both tired. It's

been a long day. Let's not worry about it now. We can get a new sheet from the spare room."

The spare room was intended for Will's parents. They balked at the outlandish idea of actually staying on the island. Will didn't seem surprised: "My father's never been particularly impressed by anything I've done—getting married is undoubtedly no exception." He seemed bitter. He doesn't talk about his father much—which paradoxically gives me the impression that he's a bigger influence upon my husband than he likes to admit.

"Get a new duvet, too," I tell Will now. I'm half-tempted to say I want to swap to the other room. But that would be irrational, and I pride myself on being the opposite.

"Sure." Will gestures to the seaweed. "And I'll sort out this, too—I've dealt with much worse, trust me."

On the program Will has escaped from wolves and been swarmed by vampire bats—though he's never far from the help of the crew—so this must all seem a little pathetic to him. A bit of seaweed on the sheets is hardly a big deal, in the grand scheme of things.

"I'll have a word with the guys tomorrow morning," he says. "Tell them they're fucking idiots."

"OK," I say. He's so good at providing comfort. He's so—well, there's only really one word for it—perfect.

And yet, in this moment, with particularly nasty timing, the words on that horrible little note surface.

Not the man you think he is . . . cheat . . . liar . . .

Don't marry him.

"A good night's sleep," Will says, soothingly. "That's what we need."

I nod.

But I don't think I'm going to sleep a wink.

AOIFE

The Wedding Planner

There's a noise outside. It's a strange noise, a keening. It sounds more human than animal—but at the same time it doesn't sound entirely human either. In our bedroom, Freddy and I look at one another. All the guests have gone to bed too, about half an hour ago now. I thought they would never get tired. We had to wait until the bitter end in case they needed anything of us. We listened to the drumming from the dining room, the chanting. Freddy, who has a little schoolboy Latin, could translate the thing they were chanting: "If I cannot move heaven, I shall raise hell." I felt the gooseflesh rise on my skin at that.

They're like overgrown boys, the ushers. I'd say they lack the innocence of boys: but some boys aren't ever really innocent. What I mean is that as grown men they should know better. And there is a pack feeling about them, like dogs that might behave well on their own but, once all together, don't have their own minds. I'll have to keep my eye on them tomorrow, make sure they don't get carried away. It is my experience that some of the smartest affairs, populated by the most well-heeled and upstanding guests, have been those that have got most out of control. I organized a wedding in Dublin that contained half Ireland's political elite—even the Taoiseach was there—only for things to come to blows between the groom and father-in-law before the first dance.

Here there's the added danger of the whole island. The wildness of this place gets under your skin. These guests will feel themselves far from the normal moral codes of society, safe from the prying eyes of others. These men are ex–public schoolboys. They've spent much of their lives being forced to follow a strict set of rules that probably didn't end with their leaving school: choices around what university to attend, what job to do, what sort of house to live in. In my experience those who have the greatest respect for the rules also take the most enjoyment in breaking them.

"I'll go," I say.

"It's not safe," Freddy says. "I'll come with you." I tell Freddy I'll be fine. To reassure him I tell him I'll pick up the poker from beside the fire on my way out. I'm the braver of the two of us, I know. I don't say this with any great pride. It's simply that when the worst has happened, you rather lose your fear of anything else.

I step into the night, appreciating the quality of the darkness, the velvet black as it folds me into itself. Any light from the Folly makes very little impact upon it, though the kitchen is aglow—and also one of the upstairs windows, the room the soon-to-be-married couple are occupying. Well, I know what's keeping them up. We heard the rhythmic shudder of the bed against the floorboards.

I won't use the flashlight yet. It will make me stupid in the darkness. I stand here, listening intently. All I can make out at first is the slam of the water on the rocks and an unfamiliar, susurrating sound which I finally identify as the marquee, the fabric rustling in the gentle breeze some fifty yards away.

And then the other noise begins again. I'm better able to recognize it, now. It's the sound of someone sobbing. Man or woman, though, it's impossible to tell. I turn in its direction and as I do I think I catch a shimmer of movement out of the corner of my eye, in the direction of the outbuildings behind the Folly. I don't know how I saw it, it being so dark. But it is hardwired into us, I think, into our animal selves. Our eyes are alert to any disturbance, any change in the pattern of the darkness.

It might have been a bat. Sometimes in the early evening you can see them flit above in the twilight, so quick you're not sure you've seen them. But I think it was bigger. I'm sure it was a person, the same person who sits weeping cloaked in darkness. Even when I came here all those years ago, even though the island was inhabited then, there were ghost stories. The grieving women mourning their husbands, brutally slain. The voices from the bog, denied their proper burial. At the time we scared ourselves silly with them. And in spite of myself I feel it now, the sensation of my skin shrinking over my bones.

"Hello?" I call. The sound stops, abruptly. When there is no answer I click my torch on. I swing the beam this way and that.

The beam catches on something as I move it in a slow arc. I train it on the same spot, and guide it up the figure that stares back at me. The beam marks out the dark wild hair, the gleaming eyes. Like a being straight from folklore—the Pooka: the phantom goblin, portent of impending doom.

In spite of myself I take a step back, the torch beam wavering. But gradually, recognition dawns. It's only the best man, slumped against the wall of one of the outbuildings.

"Who's there?" His voice sounds slurred and hoarse.

"It's me," I say. "Aoife."

"Oh, Aoife. Come to tell me it's time for lights out? Time to get into bed like a good little boy?" He gives me a crooked grin. But it's a halfhearted affair, and I think those are tear tracks that catch in the beam.

"It's not safe for you to go wandering around the outbuildings," I say, all practicality. There's old farm machinery in there that could cut a person in half. "Especially without a torch," I add. And especially when you're as drunk as you are, I think. Although, oddly enough, I feel as though I am protecting the island from him—rather than the other way round.

He stands up, walks toward me. He's a big man, drunk and more besides—I catch a sickly sweet vegetable waft of weed. I take another step away from him and realize that I'm gripping the poker hard. Then he grins, showing crooked teeth. "Yeah," he says. "Time for Johnny boy to go to bed. Think I had a bit too much of the old, you know." He mimes drinking from a bottle, then smoking. "Always makes me feel a bit off, having too much of both together. Thought I was fucking seeing things."

I nod, even though he can't see me. *So did I.*

I watch as he turns on his heel and lurches his way toward the Folly. The forced good humor didn't convince me for a second. Despite the grin he seemed caught between miserable and terrified. He looked like a man who had seen a ghost.

EARLIER THAT DAY

HANNAH

The Plus-One

When I wake, my head aches. I think of all that champagne—then the vodka. I check the alarm clock: 7 A.M. Charlie's fast asleep, flat on his back. I heard him come in last night, take his clothes off. I waited for the stumbling, the swearing, but he seemed surprisingly in control of his faculties.

"Han," he whispered to me, as he got into bed. "I left the drinking game. I only did the one shot." That made me feel a bit less hostile toward him. Then I wondered where else he'd been, for all that time. With whom. I remembered his flirting with Jules. I remembered how Johnno had asked if they'd slept together—and how they never answered.

So I didn't reply. I pretended to be asleep.

But I've woken up feeling turned on. I had some

pretty crazy dreams. I think the vodka was partly responsible. But also the memory of Will's eyes on me at the beginning of the evening. Then talking in the cave with Olivia at the end: sitting so close in the dark with the water lapping at our feet and only the candle for light, passing the bottle between us. Secret, somehow sensual. I found myself hanging on her every word, the images she painted for me vivid in the darkness. As though it were me up against the wall, my skirt pushed up over my hips, someone's mouth upon me. The guy might have been a dickhead but the sex sounded pretty hot. And it made me remember the slightly dangerous thrill of sleeping with someone unknown, where you're not anticipating their every move.

I turn to Charlie. Perhaps now is the time to break our sex drought, regain that lost intimacy. I sneak a hand beneath the covers, grazing the springy hair that covers his chest, moving my hand lower—

Charlie makes a sleepy, surprised noise. And then, his voice claggy with sleep: "Not now, Han. Too tired."

I pull my hand away, stung. "Not now": like I'm an irritation. Tired because he stayed up late last night doing God knows what, when on the boat over here he spoke of this as a weekend for *us.* When he knows how raw I feel at the moment. I have a sudden frightening urge to pick up the hardback on the nightstand and hit him over the head with it. It's alarming, the rush of anger. It feels like I might have been harboring it for a while.

Then a sneaking thought. I allow myself to wonder what it must be like for Jules, to wake up next to Will. I heard them, last night—everyone in the Folly must have. I think again of the strength of Will's arms as he lifted me out of the boat yesterday. I think, too, of how I caught him looking at me last night with that strange questioning look. The sense of power, feeling his eyes on me.

Charlie murmurs in his sleep and I catch a waft of sour morning breath. I can't imagine Will having bad breath. Suddenly, I feel it's important to remove myself from this bedroom, from these thoughts.

There's no sound of movement inside the Folly, so I think I'm the first one up.

There must be quite a breeze today, as I can hear it whistling about the old stones of the place as I creep down the stairs, and every so often the windowpanes rattle in their frames as though someone's just smacked a palm against them. I wonder if we had the best of the weather yesterday. Jules won't like that. I tiptoe into the kitchen.

Aoife's standing there in a crisp white shirt and

slacks, a clipboard in her hand, looking as if she's been up for hours. "Morning," she says—and I sense she is scrutinizing my face. "How are you today?" I get the impression Aoife doesn't miss a lot, with those bright, assessing eyes of hers. She's quietly rather beautiful. I sense that she makes an effort to underplay it but it shines through. Beautifully shaped dark eyebrows, gray-green eyes. I'd kill for that sort of natural, Audrey Hepburn–esque elegance, those cheekbones.

"I'm good," I say. "Sorry. Didn't realize anyone else was up."

"We started at the crack of dawn," she says. "With the big day today."

I'd practically forgotten about the actual wedding. I wonder how Jules is feeling this morning. Nervous? I can't imagine her being nervous about anything.

"Of course. I was going to go for a walk. Bit of a sore head."

"Well," she says, with a smile. "Safest to walk to the crest of the island, following the path past the chapel, leaving the marquee on the other side. That should keep you out of the bog. And take some wellies from by the door—you need to be careful to stick to the drier parts, or you'll find yourself in the turf. There's some signal up there too, if you need to make a phone call."

A phone call. Oh God—the kids! With a swoop of

guilt, I realize they have totally slipped my mind. *My own children.* I'm shocked by how much this place has already made me forget myself.

I head outside and find the path, or what remains of it. It's not quite as easy as Aoife made out: you can just about see where it must have been trodden into existence, where the grass hasn't grown quite as well as elsewhere. As I walk the clouds scurry overhead, whirling out toward the open sea. It's definitely breezier today, and more overcast, though every so often the sun bursts dazzlingly through the cloud. The huge marquee, on the left of me, rustles in the wind as I pass it. I could sneak inside and have a look. But I am drawn toward the graveyard, instead, to the right of me beyond the chapel. Maybe this is a reflection of my state of mind at this time of year, the morbid mood that descends on me every June.

Wandering among the markers I see several very distinctive Celtic crosses, but I can also make out faint images of anchors, flowers. Most of the stones are so ancient that you can hardly read the writing on them anymore. Even if you could, it's not in English: Gaelic, I suppose. Some are broken or worn down until they have no real shape at all. Without really thinking what I am doing I touch a hand to the one nearest to me and feel where the rough stone has been smoothed by wind and water over the decades. There are a few that look a bit newer, perhaps from shortly before the islanders left for good. But most are pretty overgrown with weeds and mosses, as though they haven't been tended for a while.

Then I come across one that stands out because there's nothing growing over it. In fact it's in good nick: a little jam jar of wildflowers in front of it. From the dates—I do some quick maths—it must have been a child, a young girl: *Darcey Malone*, the stone reads, *Lost to the sea.* I look toward the sea. Many have drowned in making the crossing, Mattie told us. He didn't actually tell us *when* they drowned, I realize. I had assumed that was hundreds of years ago. But maybe it was more recent. To think: this was someone's child.

I bend down and touch the stone. There's an ache at the back of my throat.

"Hannah!" I turn toward the Folly. Aoife stands there, looking at me. "It's not that way," she says, then points to where the path continues at an angle away from the chapel. "Over there!"

"Thanks!" I call to her. "Sorry!" I feel as though I have been caught trespassing.

As I get farther away from the Folly any sign of the path seems to disappear completely. Patches of earth that look safe and grassy give way beneath my feet, collapsing into a black ooze. Cold bogwater has already seeped into my right welly and my foot squelches inside its soaked sock. The thought of the bodies somewhere beneath me makes me shiver. I wonder if anyone will know tonight how close they're dancing to a burial pit.

I hold up my phone. Full signal, as Aoife promised. I ring home. I can make out the tone at the other end over the wind, then my mum's voice saying: "Hello?"

"It's not too early is it?" I ask.

"Goodness no, love. We've been up for . . . well, it *feels* like hours."

When she passes me to Ben I can hardly make out what he's saying, his voice is so high and reedy.

"What was that, darling?" I press the phone to my ear.

"I said hello, Mum." At the sound of his voice I feel it deep down inside, the powerful tug of my bond to him. When I look for something to compare my love for the kids with it's actually not my love for Charlie. It's animal, powerful, blood-thick. The love of kin. The closest thing I can find to it is my love for Alice, my sister.

"Where are you?" Ben asks. "It sounds like the sea. Are there boats?" He's obsessed with boats.

"Yes, we came over on one."

"A big one?"

"Big-ish."

"Lottie was really sick yesterday, Mum."

"What's wrong with her?" I ask, quickly.

The thing that most worries me is the thought of anything happening to my loved ones. When I was little and woke in the night I'd sometimes creep over to my sister Alice's bed to check that she was definitely breathing, because the worst thing I could imagine was her being taken from me. "I'm OK, Han," she'd whisper, a smile in her voice. "But you can get in if you want to." And I'd lie there, pressed against her back, feeling the reassuring movement of her ribs as she breathed.

Mum comes on to the line. "Nothing to worry about, Han. She overdid herself yesterday afternoon. Your dad—the dolt—left her on her own with the Victoria sponge while I was at the shops. She's fine now, love, she's watching CBeebies on the sofa, ready for her breakfast. Now," she says to me, "go have fun at your glamorous weekend."

I don't feel very glamorous right now, I think, with my soggy sock and the breeze stinging tears from my eyes. "All right, Mum," I say, "I'll try and call tomorrow, on our way home. They're not driving you too crazy?"

"No," Mum says. "To be honest—" The little catch in her voice is unmistakable.

"What?"

"Well, it's a nice distraction. Positive. Looking after the next generation." She stops, and I hear her take a deep breath. "You know . . . it's this time of year."

"Yeah," I say. "I get it, Mum. I feel it too."

"Bye, darling. You take care of yourself."

As I ring off it hits me. Is *that* who Olivia reminds me of? Alice? It's all there: the thinness, the fragility, the deer-in-headlights look. I remember when I first saw my sister after she came home from university for the summer holidays. She had lost about a third of her body weight. She looked like someone with a terrible disease—like something was eating her from the inside out. And the worst part was that she didn't think she could talk to anyone about what had happened to her. Not even me.

I start walking. And then I stop, look about me. I'm not sure I'm going the right way but it's not obvious which way *is* right. I can't see the Folly or even the marquee from here, hidden as they are by the rise of the ground. I'd assumed it would be easier going on my return, because I'd know the route. But now I feel disoriented—my thoughts have been somewhere else completely. I must have taken a different way; it seems even boggier here. I'm having to hop between drier tussocks of grass to avoid soft, wet black patches of peat. I plow on. Then I get a bit stuck and chance a big leap. But I've misjudged it: my footing slips and my left welly lands not on the grassy hillock but on the soft surface of the peat.

I sink—and I keep sinking. It happens so fast. The ground opens up and swallows my foot. I lose my balance, staggering backward, and my other foot goes in with a horrible slurp of suction, quick as the black throat of that cormorant swallowing the fish. Within moments, the peat seems to be over the top of my boots and I'm sinking further. For the first few seconds I'm stupid with surprise, frozen. Then I realize I have to act, to rescue myself. I reach out for the dry patch of land in front of me, and grip hold of two hunks of grass.

I heave. Nothing happens. I seem to be stuck fast. How embarrassing this is going to be, I think, when I get back to the Folly absolutely filthy and have to explain what happened. Then I realize that I'm still sinking. The black earth is inching over my knees, up my lower thighs. Little by little it is drinking me in.

Suddenly I don't care about embarrassment any longer. I'm genuinely terrified. "Help!" I shout. But my words are swallowed by the wind. There's no way my voice is going to carry a few yards, let alone all the way to the Folly. Nevertheless, I try again. I scream it: "Help me!"

I think of the bodies in the bog. I imagine skeletal hands reaching up toward me from deep beneath the earth, ready to drag me down. And I begin to scrabble at the bank, using all my strength to haul myself upward, snorting and growling with the effort like an animal. It feels like nothing's happening but I grit my teeth and try even harder.

And then I am aware of the distinct feeling of being watched. A prickle down the spine.

"You want a hand there?"

I start. I can't quite twist myself round to see who has spoken. Slowly they move around to stand in front of me. It's two of the ushers: Duncan and Pete.

"We were having a little explore," Duncan says. "You know, get the lay of the land."

"Didn't think we'd have the pleasure of rescuing a damsel in distress," Pete says.

Their expressions are almost completely neutral. But there's a twitch at the corner of Duncan's mouth and I get the feeling they were laughing at me. That they might have been observing me for a while as I struggled. I don't want to rely on their help. But I'm also not really in any position to be picky.

They each take one of my hands. With them pulling, I finally manage to yank one foot from the bog's hold. I lose the boot as I pull my foot from the last of the muck and the earth closes over it as quickly as it had opened. I pull my other foot out and scrabble on to the bank, safe. For a moment I'm sprawled upon the ground, trembling with exhaustion and adrenaline, unable to find the energy to rise to my feet. I can't quite believe what just happened. Then I remember the two men looking down at me, each holding one of my hands. I scramble to my feet, thanking them, dropping their hands as quickly as seems polite—the clasp of our fingers suddenly feels oddly intimate. Now that the adrenaline is receding I'm becoming aware of how I must have looked to them as they pulled me out: my top gaping to expose my old bra, cheeks flushed and sweaty. I'm also aware of how isolated we are, here. Two of them, one of me.

"Thanks, guys," I say, hating the wobble in my voice. "I think I'm going to head back to the Folly now."

"Yes," Duncan drawls. "Got to wash all that filth off for later." And I can't work out if I'm reading too much into it or whether there really is something suggestive in the way he says it.

I start back in the direction of the Folly. I'm moving

as fast as I can go in my socked feet, while being careful to pick only the safest crossings. I suddenly want very much to get back inside, and yes, back to Charlie. To put as much space as possible between myself and the bog. And, to be honest, my rescuers.

AOIFE

The Wedding Planner

I sit at my desk going through the plans for today. I like this desk. Its drawers are full of memories. Photographs, postcards, letters—paper yellowed with age, handwriting a childish scrawl.

I tune the radio in to the forecast. We get a few Galway stations here.

"It's likely to get a little windy later today," the weatherman's saying. "We have conflicting evidence about the gale-force number, but we can say that most of Connemara and West Galway will be affected, particularly the islands and coastal areas."

"That doesn't sound good," Freddy says, coming in to stand behind me.

We listen as the man on the radio announces that the winds will hit properly after 5 P.M.

"By that time they'll all be safely inside the marquee," I say. "And it should hold fast, even in a bit of wind. So there will be nothing to worry about."

"What about the electrics?" Freddy asks.

"They're pretty good, aren't they? Unless we have a real storm on our hands. And he didn't say anything about that."

We have been up since dawn this morning. Freddy has even made a trip over to the mainland with Mattie to get a few last-minute supplies, while I am checking everything is in order here. The florist will arrive shortly to arrange the sprays of local wildflowers in the chapel and marquee: speedwell and wild spotted orchids and blue-eyed grass.

Freddy returns to the kitchen to put the finishing touches to whatever food can be prepared in advance: the canapés and hors d'oeuvres, the cold starters of fish from the Connemara Smokehouse. He's passionate about food, is my husband. He can talk about a dish he's thought up in the way that a great musician might rhapsodize about a composition. It stems from his childhood; he claims that it comes from not having any variety in his diet when he was young.

I walk over to the marquee. It occupies the same higher land as the chapel and graveyard, some fifty yards to the east of the Folly along a tract of drier land, with the marshier stuff of the turf bog on either side. I hear frantic scurryings ahead and then in front of me they appear: hares startled out of their "forms," the hollows they make in the heather to bed down in. They sprint in front of me for a while, their white tails bobbing, their powerful legs kicking out, before veering off into the long grasses on either side and disappearing from view. Hares are shape-shifters in Gaelic folklore; sometimes when I see them here I think of all of Inis an Amplóra's departed souls, materializing once more to run amidst the heather.

In the marquee I begin my duties, filling up the space heaters and putting certain finishing touches on the tables: the hand-watercolored menus, the linen napkins in their solid silver rings, each engraved with the name of the guest who will take it home. There'll be a striking contrast later between the refinement of these beautifully dressed tables and the wildness outdoors. Later, when we light them, there'll be the scent of the candles from Cloon Keen Atelier, an exclusive Dublin perfumer, shipped over from the boutique at no small expense.

The marquee shivers around me as I do my checks. It's quite amazing to think that in a few hours this echoing empty space will be filled with people. The light in here is dull and yellow compared to the bright cold light of outside but tonight this whole structure will glow like one of those paper lanterns you send up into the night sky. People on the mainland will be able to look across and see that something exciting is going on, on Inis an Amplóra—the island they all speak about as the dead place, the haunted isle, as though it only exists as history. If I do my job right, this wedding will make sure they'll be talking about it in the present again.

"Knock knock!"

I turn. It's the groom. He's got one hand up and he's pretending to knock on the side of the canvas flap as though it were a real door.

"I'm looking for two errant ushers," he says. "We should be getting into our morning suits. You haven't seen any sign of them?"

"Oh," I say. "Good morning. No, I don't think I have. Did you sleep well?" I still can't believe it's really him, in the flesh: Will Slater. Freddy and I have watched *Survive the Night* since the start. I haven't mentioned this to the bride and groom, though, in case they worry that we're crazed superfans who are going to embarrass ourselves and them.

"Well!" he says. "Very well." He is very good-looking in real life, more so even than he looks on-screen. I reach down to straighten a fork, in case I'm staring. You can tell he's always had these looks. Some people are awkward and unformed as children but grow into attractive adults. But this man wears his beauty with such ease and grace. I suspect he uses it to great effect, is clearly very aware of its power. Every movement is like watching the working of a finely tuned machine, an animal in the peak of its condition.

"I'm pleased you slept well," I say.

"Ah," he says, "although we discovered a slight issue on going to bed."

"Oh?"

"Some seaweed under the duvet. The ushers' little prank."

"Oh my goodness," I say. "I'm very sorry. You should have called Freddy or me. We would have sorted it out for you, remade the bed with new sheets."

"You don't have to apologize," he says—that charming grin again. "Boys will be boys." He shrugs. "Even if Johnno is a somewhat overgrown one." He comes to stand beside me, close enough that I can detect the scent of his cologne. I take a small step back. "It's looking great in here, Aoife. Very impressive. You're doing a wonderful job."

"Thank you." My tone does not invite conversation. But I imagine Will Slater isn't used to people not wanting to talk to him. I realize, when he doesn't move, that it's even possible he sees my curtness as a challenge.

"So what's your story, Aoife?" he asks, his head tilted to one side. "Don't you get lonely, living here, only the two of you?"

Is he really interested, I wonder, or simply feigning it? Why does he want to know about me? I shrug. "No, not really. I'm what you might call a loner anyways. In the winter it just feels like survival, to be honest. The summers are what we stay for."

"But how did you end up here?" He seems genuinely intrigued. He really is one of those people that has you convinced they are fascinated by your every word. It's all part of what makes him so charming, I suppose.

"I used to come here on summer holidays," I say, "when I was little. My family, we all used to come here." I don't often talk about that time. There's a lot I could tell him, though. Of cheap strawberry ice lollies on the white sand beaches, the stain of red food coloring on lips and tongues. Of rock-pooling on the other side of the island, filleting through the contents of our nets with eager fingers to find shrimp and tiny, translucent crabs. Splashing about in the turquoise sea in the sheltered bays until we got used to the freezing temperature. I won't tell him any of this, obviously: it would not be appropriate. I need to maintain that essential boundary between myself and the guests.

"Ah," he says. "I didn't think you had the local accent." I wonder what he expects. *Top o' the morning* and *to be sure, to be sure* and shamrocks and leprechauns?

"No," I say, "I have a Dublin accent, which perhaps sounds less pronounced. But I've also lived in different places. When I was younger we moved around a lot, because of my father's job—he was a university professor. England for a bit—even the States for a while."

"You met Freddy abroad? He's English, isn't he?" Still so interested, so charming. It makes me feel a little uneasy. I wonder exactly what he wants to know.

"Freddy and I met a long long time ago," I tell him.

He smiles that charming, interested smile. "Childhood sweethearts?"

"You could say that." It's not quite right, though. Freddy's several years younger than me and we were friends first, for years before anything else. Or perhaps not even friends, more clinging to one another as each other's life rafts. Not long after my mother became a shell of the woman she had once been. Several years before my father's heart attack. But I'm hardly going to tell the groom all of that. Besides everything else, in this profession it is important to never allow yourself to seem too human, too fallible.

"I see," he says.

"Now," I say, before the next question can form on

his lips, whatever it may have been. "If you don't mind, I'd better be getting on with everything."

"Of course," he says. "We've got some real party animals coming this evening, Aoife," he says. "I only hope they don't cause too much mayhem." He pushes his hand through his hair and grins at me in what I think is probably intended to be a rueful, winning way. His teeth are very white when he smiles. So bright, in fact, that it makes me wonder if he gets them specially lightened.

Then he moves a little closer and puts a hand on my shoulder. "You're doing a fantastic job, Aoife. Thank you." He leaves his hand there a beat too long, so that I can feel the heat of his palm seeping through my shirt. I am suddenly very aware that it is just the two of us in this big echoing space.

I smile—my politest, most professional smile—and take a small step away. I suppose a man like him is very sure of his sexual power. It reads as charm at first, but underneath there is something darker, more complicated. I don't think he is actually attracted to me, nothing like that. He put his hand on my shoulder because he can. Perhaps I'm reading too much into it. But it felt like a reminder that he is the one in charge, that I am working for him. That I must dance to his tune.

NOW

THE WEDDING NIGHT

The search party marches out into the darkness. Instantly the wind assaults them, the screaming rush of it. The flames of the paraffin torches billow and hiss and threaten to extinguish. Their eyes water, their ears ring. They find themselves having to push against the wind as though it were a solid mass, their heads bent low.

The adrenaline is coursing through them, it's them versus the elements. A feeling remembered from boyhood—deep, unnameable, feral—stirring memories of nights not altogether unlike this. Them against the dark.

They move forward, slowly. The longish tract of land between the Folly and the marquee, hemmed in by the peat bog on either side: this is where they will begin their search. They call out: "Is anyone out there?" and "Is anyone hurt?" and "Can you hear us?"

There is no reply. The wind seems to swallow their voices.

"Maybe we should spread out!" Femi shouts. "Speed up the search."

"Are you mad?" Angus replies. "When there's a bog in either direction? None of us knows where it starts. And especially not in the dark. I'm not—I'm not frightened. But I don't fancy finding, you know . . . shit on my own."

So they remain close together, within touching distance.

"She must have screamed pretty loud," Duncan shouts. "That waitress. To be heard over this."

"She must have been terrified," Angus shouts.

"You scared, Angus?"

"No. Fuck off, Duncan. But it's—it's really hard to see—"

His words are lost to a particularly vicious gust. In a shower of sparks, two of the big paraffin torches are snuffed out like birthday candles. Their bearers keep the metal supports anyway, holding them out in front like swords.

"Actually," Angus shouts. "Maybe I am a bit. Is that so shameful? Maybe I'm not enjoying being out here in a bloody gale, or . . . or looking forward to what we might find—"

His words are cut off by a panicked cry. They turn, holding their torches aloft to see Pete grasping at the air, the lower half of one leg submerged.

"Stupid fucker," Duncan shouts, "must have wandered away from the drier part." He's relieved though, they all are. For a moment they thought Pete had found something.

They haul him out.

"Jesus," Duncan shouts, as Pete, freed, sprawls on hands and knees at their feet, "you're the second person we've had to rescue today. Femi and I found Charlie's wife squealing like a stuck pig earlier in this bloody bog."

"The bodies . . . ," Pete moans, "in the bog . . ."

"Oh pack it in, Pete," Duncan shouts angrily. "Don't be an idiot." He swings his torch nearer to Pete's face, turns to the others. "Look at his eyes—he's tripping out of his mind. I knew it. Why did we bring him? He's a bloody liability."

They are all relieved when Pete falls silent. No one mentions the bodies again. It is a piece of folklore, they know this. They can dismiss it—albeit less easily than they might in the light of day, when everything felt more familiar. But they can't dismiss the purpose of their own mission, the possibility of what they may find. There are real dangers out here, the landscape unfamiliar and treacherous in the dark. They are only now beginning to realize it fully. To understand just how unprepared they are.

EARLIER THAT DAY

JULES

The Bride

I open my eyes. The big day.

I didn't sleep well last night and when I did I had a strange dream: the ruined chapel crumbling to dust around me as I walked into it. I woke up feeling off, uneasy. A touch of hungover paranoia from a glass too many, no doubt. And I'm sure I can still detect the lingering stench of the seaweed, even though it's hours since it was removed.

Will moved to the spare room first thing in a nod to tradition, but I find myself rather wishing he were here. No matter. Adrenaline and willpower will carry me through: they'll have to.

I look over at the dress, hanging from its padded hanger. Its wings of protective tissue dance gently to and fro in some mysterious breeze. I've learned by now that there are currents in this place that somehow find their way inside, despite closed doors and shut windows. They eddy and caper through the air, they kiss the back of your neck, they send a prickle down your spine, soft as the touch of fingertips.

Beneath my silk robe I'm wearing the lingerie I picked out for today from Coco de Mer. The most delicate Leavers lace, fine as cobweb, and an appropriately bridal cream. Very traditional, at first glimpse. But the knickers have a row of tiny mother-of-pearl buttons all the way through, so that they can be completely opened. Nice, then very naughty. I know Will will enjoy discovering them, later.

A shiver of movement through the window catches my attention. Below, on the rocks, I see Olivia. She's wearing the same baggy sweater and ripped jeans as yesterday, picking her way in bare feet toward the edge, where the sea smashes up against the granite in huge explosions of white water. Why on earth isn't she getting ready, as she should be? Her head is bent, her shoulders slumped, her hair blowing in a tangled rope behind her. There's a moment when she's so close to the edge, to the violence of the water, that my breath catches in my throat. She could fall and I wouldn't be able to get down from here in time to save her. She could drown right there while I stand here helpless.

I rap on the window, but I think she's ignoring me or—I admit it's likely—can't hear me above the sound of the waves. Luckily, though, she seems to have stepped a little farther away from the drop.

Fine. I'm not going to worry anymore about her. It's time to start getting ready in earnest. I could easily have had a makeup artist shipped over from the mainland, but there is no way in hell I'd hand over control of my appearance to someone else on such an important day. If doing your own makeup is good enough for Kate Middleton, it's good enough for me.

I reach for my makeup bag but a little unexpected tremor of my hand sends the whole thing crashing to the floor. Fuck. I'm *never* clumsy. Am I . . . nervous?

I look down at the spilled contents, shining gold tubes of mascara and lipsticks rolling in a bid for freedom across the floorboards, an overturned compact leaking a trail of bronzing powder.

There, in the middle of it all, lies a tiny folded piece of paper, slightly soot-blackened. The sight of it turns my blood cold. I stare at it, unable to look away. How is it possible that such a small thing could have occupied such a huge space in my mind over the last couple of weeks?

Why on earth did I keep it?

I unfold it even though I don't need to: the words are imprinted on my memory.

Will Slater is not the man you think he is. He's a cheat and a liar. Don't marry him.

I'm sure it's some random weirdo. Will's always getting mail from strangers who think they know him, know all about his life. Sometimes I get included in their wrath. I remember when a couple of pictures emerged of us online. *"Will Slater out shopping with squeeze, Julia Keegan."* It was a slow day at the *Mail Online*, no doubt.

Even though I knew—*knew*—it was a terrible idea, I ended up scrolling down to the comments section underneath. Christ. I've seen that bile on there before, but when it's directed at you it feels particularly poisonous, especially personal. It was like stumbling into an echo chamber of my own worst thoughts about myself.

—God she thinks shes all that doesn't she?

—Looks like a proper b*tch if you ask me.

—Jeez love haven't you heard your never meant to sleep with a man with thighs thinner than your own?

—Will! ILY! Pick me instead!:):):) She doesn't deserve you. . . . . .

—God, I hate her just from looking at her. Snotty cow.

Nearly all of the comments were like this. It was hard to believe that there were that many total strangers out there who felt such vitriol for me. I found myself scrolling down until I found a couple of naysayers:

—He looks happy. She'll be good for him!

—BTW she's behind The Download—favorite site everrrr. They'll make a good match.

Even these kinder voices were as unsettling in their own way—the sense some of them seemed to have of knowing Will—knowing *me*. That they were in a position to comment on what was good for him. Will's not a household name. But at his level of celebrity you get even more of this sort of thing, because you haven't yet risen above people thinking they have ownership of you.

The note is different to those comments online, though. It's more personal. It was dropped through the letterbox without a stamp, meaning it had to have been hand delivered. Whoever wrote it knows where we live. He or she had come to our place in Islington—which was, until Will moved in recently, *my* place. Less likely, surely, to have been a random weirdo. Or it could have been the very worst kind of weirdo.

But it occurs to me it could conceivably be someone we know. It could even be someone who's coming to this island today.

The night the note arrived I threw it into the log burner. Seconds later I snatched it back, burning my wrist in the process. I've still got the mark—a shiny, risen pink seal on the tender skin there. Every time I've caught sight of it I've thought of the note, in its hiding place. Three little words:

Don't marry him.

I rip the note in half. I rip it again, and again, until it is paper confetti. But it isn't enough. I take it into the bathroom and pull the chain, watching intently until all the pieces have disappeared, swirling out of the bowl. I imagine them traveling down through the plumbing, out into the Atlantic, the same ocean that surrounds us. The thought troubles me more than it probably should.

Anyway, it is out of my life now. It is gone. I am not going to think about it anymore. I pick up my hair-brush, my eyelash curler, my mascara: my arsenal of weapons, my quiver.

Today I am getting married and it is going to be bloody brilliant.

NOW
THE WEDDING NIGHT

"Christ, it's hard going in this." Duncan puts up a hand to shelter his face from the stinging wind, waving his torch with the other, letting off a spray of sparks. "Anyone see anything?"

See what, though? This is the question that occupies their thoughts. Each of them is remembering the waitress's words. *A body.* Every lump or divot in the ground is a potential source of horror. The torches that they hold in front of them don't help as much as they might. They only make the rest of the night seem blacker still.

"It's like being back at school," Duncan shouts to the others. "Creeping around in the dark. Anyone for Survival?"

"Don't be a dick, Duncan," Femi shouts. "Have you forgotten what we're supposed to be looking for?"

"Well, yeah. Guess you can't call it Survival, then."

"That's not funny," Femi shouts.

"All right, Femi! Calm down. I was only trying to lighten the mood."

"Yeah, but I don't think now's the time for that either."

Duncan rounds on him. "I'm out here looking, aren't I? Better than those cowardly fucks in the marquee."

"Survival wasn't funny, anyway," Angus shouts. "Was it? I can see that now. I'm—I'm done with pretending it was all some big lark. It was totally messed up. Someone could have died . . . someone did die, actually. And the school let it carry on—"

"That was an accident," Duncan cuts in. "When that kid died. That wasn't because of Survival."

"Oh yeah?" Angus shouts back. "How'd you figure that one? Just because you loved all of that shit. I know you got off on it, when it came to your turn, freaking the younger boys out. Can't go around being a sadistic bully now, can you? I bet you haven't had such a big thrill since—"

"Guys," Femi, ever the peacekeeper, calls to them. "Now is *not* the time."

For a while they fall silent, continuing to trudge through the darkness, alone with their own thoughts. None of them has ever been out in weather like this. The wind comes and goes in squally gusts. Sometimes it drops enough for them to hear themselves think. But it is only gathering itself for the next onslaught: a busy murmuring, like the sound of thousands of insects swarming. At its highest it rises to a howl that sounds horribly like a person shrieking, an echo of the waitress's scream. Their skin is flayed raw by it, their eyes blinded by tears. It sets their teeth on edge—and they are in its teeth.

"It doesn't feel real, does it?"

"What's that, Angus?"

"Well, you know—one minute we're all in the marquee, prancing around, eating wedding cake. Now we're out here looking for . . ." He summons his courage to say it out loud: "A *body*. What do you think could have happened?"

"We still don't know what we're looking for," Duncan answers. "We're going off the word of one kid."

"Yeah, but she seemed pretty sure . . ."

"Well," Femi calls, "there were a lot of drunk people about. It got seriously loose in there. It's not all that difficult to imagine, is it? Someone wandering out of the marquee into the dark, having an accident—"

"What about that Charlie bloke?" Duncan suggests. "He was in a total state."

"Yeah," Femi shouts, "he was definitely the worse for wear. But after what we did to him on the stag—"

"Less said about that the better, Fem."

"Did you see that bridesmaid, earlier, though?" Duncan shouts. "Anyone else think the same thing I did?"

"What?" Angus answers. "That she was trying to . . . you know . . ."

"Top herself?" Duncan shouts. "Yeah, I do. She's been acting funny since we arrived, hasn't she? Clearly a bit of a basket case. Wouldn't put it past her to have done something stup—"

"Someone's coming," Pete shouts, cutting him off, pointing into the darkness behind them, "someone's coming for us—"

"Oh shut *up*, you twat." Duncan rounds on him. "Christ, he's doing my head in. We should take him back to the marquee. Because I swear—"

"No." There's a wobble in Angus's voice. "He's right. There's something there—"

The others turn to look too, moving in a clumsy circle, bumping into each other, fighting down their unease. All of them fall silent as they stare behind them, into the night.

A light bobs toward them through the darkness. They hold out their own torches, strain to see what it is.

"Oh," Duncan shouts, in some relief. "It's just him—that fat bloke, the wedding planner's husband."

"But wait," Angus says. "What's that . . . in his hand?"

EARLIER THAT DAY

OLIVIA

The Bridesmaid

Out of the window I can see the boats carrying the wedding guests to the island, still distant dark shapes out on the water but moving ever closer. It will all be happening soon. I'm supposed to be getting ready, and God knows I've been up since early. I woke with this ache in my chest and a throbbing head, and took myself outside to get some air. But now I'm sitting here in my room in my bra and pants. I can't bring myself to get changed yet, into that dress. I found a little crimson stain on the pale silk where the small cut I'd made on my thigh must have bled a bit yesterday when I was trying it on. Thank God Jules didn't notice. She really might have lost her shit at that. I've scrubbed it in the sink down the hall with some cold water and soap. It's nearly all come out, thank God. Just a tiny darker pink patch was left, as a reminder.

It made me remember the blood, all those months ago. I hadn't known there would be so much. I shut my eyes. But I can see it there, beneath my eyelids.

I glance out of the window again, think about all those people arriving. I've been feeling claustrophobic in this place since we arrived, feeling like there's no escape, nowhere to run to . . . but it's going to get so much worse today. In less than an hour, Jules will call for me and then I'll have to walk down the aisle in front of her, with everyone looking at us. And then all the people—family, strangers—who I'll have to talk to. I don't think I can do it. Suddenly I feel like I can't breathe.

I think about how the only time I've felt a bit better, since I've been here, was last night in the cave, talking with Hannah. I haven't been able to speak to anyone else the way I did with her: not my mates, not anyone. I don't know what it was about her. I guess it was because she seemed like an odd one out, like she was trying to hide from everything too.

I could go and find Hannah. I could talk to her now, I think. Tell her the rest. Get it all out in the open. The thought of it makes me feel dizzy, sick. But maybe I'd feel better too, in a way—less like I can't get any air into my lungs.

My hands shake as I pull on my jeans and my sweater. If I tell her, there'll be no taking it back. But I think I've made up my mind. I think I have to do it, before I go totally mental.

I creep out of my room. My heart feels like it's moved up into my throat, beating so hard I can hardly swallow. I tiptoe through the dining room, up the stairs. I can't bump into anyone else on the way—if I do I know I'll chicken out.

Hannah's room is at the end of the long corridor, I think. As I get closer, I realize I can hear the murmur of voices coming from inside, growing louder.

"Oh for God's sake, Han," I hear. "You're being completely ridiculous—"

The door's open a crack, too. I creep a little closer. Hannah's out of sight but I can see Charlie in just a pair of boxers, gripping onto the edge of the chest of drawers as though he's trying to contain his anger.

I stop short. I feel like I've seen something I shouldn't, like I'm spying on them. I stupidly hadn't thought about Charlie being in there too—Charlie, who I used to have that cringeworthy teenage crush on. I can't do it. I can't go up and knock on their door, ask

Hannah if she'll come for a chat . . . not when they're half-dressed, clearly in the middle of some sort of argument. Then I nearly jump out of my skin as another door opens behind me.

"Oh, hello, Olivia." It's Will. He's wearing suit trousers and a white shirt that hangs open to show his chest, tanned and muscular. I glance quickly away.

"I *thought* I heard someone outside," he says. He frowns at me. "What are you doing up here?"

"N-nothing," I say, or try to say, because hardly any sound comes out of my mouth, just a hoarse whisper. I turn to leave.

Back in my room I sit down on the bed. I've failed. It's too late. I've missed my chance. I should have found a way to tell Hannah last night.

I look out through the window at the boats approaching: closer now. It feels like they are bringing something bad with them to this island. But that's silly. Because it's here already, isn't it? It's me. I'm the bad thing. What I've done.

AOIFE

The Wedding Planner

The guests are arriving. I watch the approach of the boats from the jetty, ready to welcome them. I smile and nod, try to present a front of decorum. I'm wearing a plain, navy dress now, low wedge heels. Smart, but not too smart. It wouldn't be appropriate to look like one of the guests. Though I needn't have worried about that. It's clear they have all made a *big* effort with their outfits: glittering earrings and painfully high heels, tiny handbags and real fur stoles (it might be June, but this is the cool Irish summer, after all). I even see a smattering of top hats. I suppose when your hosts are the owner of a lifestyle magazine and a TV star, you have to step up your game.

The guests disembark in groups of thirty or so. I can see them all taking in the island, and feel a little surge of personal pride as they do. We'll be a hundred and fifty tonight—that's a lot of people to introduce to Inis an Amplóra.

"Where's the nearest loo?" one man asks me urgently, rather green about the gills, plucking at his shirt collar as though it's strangling him. Several of the guests, in fact, are looking worse for wear beneath their finery. And yet it's not too choppy at the moment, the water somewhere between white and silver—so bright with the cold sunlight on it that you can hardly look at it. I shield my eyes and smile graciously and point them on their way. Perhaps I should offer some strong seasickness pills for the return journey, if it's going to get as windy as the forecast suggests.

I remember the first time we came here as kids, stepping off the old ferry. We didn't feel seasick, not that I remember. We stood out at the front and held on to the rail and squealed as we soared over the waves, as the water came up in big arcs and soaked us. I remember pretending we were riding a huge sea serpent.

It was warm for this part of the world that summer, and the sun would soon dry us. And children are tough. I remember running down the beaches into the water like it was nothing. I guess I hadn't yet learned to be wary of the sea.

A smart couple in their sixties get off the final boat.

I somehow know even before they come over and introduce themselves that they are the groom's parents. He must get his looks from his mother and probably his coloring, too, though her hair is gray now. But she doesn't have anything like the groom's easy confidence. She gives the impression of someone trying to hide herself away, even within her own clothes.

The groom's father's features are sharper, harder. You'd never call a man like that good-looking, but I suppose you could imagine seeing a profile like his on the bust of a Roman emperor: the high, arched eyebrows, the hooked nose, the firm, slightly cruel thin-lipped mouth. He has a very strong handshake, I feel the small bones of my hand crushing into one another as he squeezes it. And he has an air of importance about him, like a politician or diplomat. "You must be the wedding planner," he says, with a smile. But his eyes are watchful, assessing.

"I am," I say.

"Good, good," he says. "Got us a seat at the front of the chapel, I hope?" On his son's wedding day it is to be expected. But I think this man would expect a seat at the front of any event.

"Of course," I tell him. "I'll take you up there now."

"You know," he says, as we walk up toward the chapel, "it's a funny thing. I'm a headmaster, at a boys' school. And about a quarter of these guests used to go there, to Trevellyan's. Odd, seeing them all grown up."

I smile, show polite interest: "Do you recognize all of them?"

"Most. But not all, not all. Mainly the larger-than-life characters, as I think you'd call them." He chuckles. "I've seen some of them do a double take already, seeing me. I have a reputation as a bit of a disciplinarian." He seems proud of this. "It's probably put the fear of God in them, catching sight of me here."

I'm sure it has, I think. I feel as though I know this man, though I have never met him before. Instinctively, I do not like him.

Afterward, I go and thank Mattie, who's captained the last boat over.

"Well done," I say. "That all went very smoothly. You've done a great job synchronizing it all."

"And you've done a fine job getting someone to hold their wedding here. He's famous, isn't he?"

"And she has a profile too." I doubt Mattie's up-to-date on women's online magazines, though. "We offered a big discount in the end, but it'll be worth it for the write-up."

He nods. "Put this place on the map, sure it will." He looks out over the water, squinting into the sunlight. "It was easy sailing this morning," he says. "But it will be different later on, to be sure."

"I've been keeping an eye on the forecast," I say. It's hard to imagine the weather turning, with the blustery sunshine we've got now.

"Aye," Mattie says. "The wind's set to get up. This evening is looking quare bad. There's a big one brewing out to sea."

"A storm?" I say, surprised. "I thought it was just a little wind."

He gives me a look that tells me just what he thinks of such Dubliner naïveté—however long we've been here, Freddy and I, we'll forever be the newcomers. "You don't need some forecast fella sitting in a studio in Galway City to tell you," he says. "Use your eyes."

He points and I follow his finger to a stain of darkness, far out, upon the horizon. I'm no seaman like Mattie, but even I can see that it doesn't look good.

"There it is," Mattie says triumphantly. "There's your storm."

JOHNNO

The Best Man

Will and I are getting ready in the spare room. The other guys should be joining us in a sec, so I want to say the thing I've been planning first. I'm bad at stuff like this, speaking about how I feel. But I go for it anyway, turning to Will. "I wanted to tell you, mate . . . well, you know, I'm properly honored to be your best man."

"There was never anyone else in my mind for the job," he says. "You know that."

Yeah, see, I'm not *totally* sure that's true. It was a bit desperate, what I did. Because maybe I was wrong, but I got this impression that, for a while, Will's been trying to cut me out of his life. Since all the TV stuff happened, I've hardly seen the bloke. He hadn't even told me about the engagement—I read about it in the papers. And that stung, I'm not going to pretend it didn't. So I called him up and said I wanted to take him for a drink, to celebrate.

And over drinks I said it. "I accept! I'll be your best man."

Did he look a bit awkward, then? Difficult to tell with Will—he's smooth. After a short pause he nodded and said: "You've read my mind."

It wasn't totally out of the blue. He'd promised it, really. When we were kids, at Trevellyan's.

"You're my best mate, Johnno," he said to me once. "Numero uno. My best man." I didn't forget that. History ties us together, him and me. Really, I think we both knew I was the only person for the job.

I look in the mirror, straighten my tie. Will's spare suit looks like shit on me. Hardly surprising, really, considering it's about three sizes too small. And considering I look like I was up all night, which I was. I'm sweating already in the too-tight wool. Next to Will I look even more shit because his seems to have been sewn onto his body by a host of fucking angels. Which it has, in a way, because he got it made to measure on Savile Row.

"I'm not at my best," I say. Understatement of the century.

"That's your comeuppance," Will says, "for forgetting your suit." He's laughing at me.

"Yeah," I say. "I'm such an idiot." I'm laughing at me, too.

I went to get my suit with Will a few weeks ago. He suggested Paul Smith. Obviously all the shop assistants in there looked at me like I was going to steal something. "It's a good suit," Will told me, "probably the best you can get without going to Savile Row." I did like how I looked in it, no doubt about it. I've never had a good suit before. Haven't worn anything all that smart since school. And I liked how it skimmed my belly. I've let myself go a bit over the last couple of years. "Too much good living!" I'd say, and pat the paunch. But I'm not proud of it. This suit, it hid all that. It made me look like a fucking boss. It made me look like someone I am definitely not.

I turn sideways in the mirror. The buttons on the jacket look like they're about to ping off. Yeah, I miss that belly-skimming Paul Smith wool. Anyway. No point in crying over spilled milk, as my mum would say. And not much use in being vain. I was never much of a looker in the first place.

"Ha—Johnno!" Duncan says, barreling into the room and looking very slick in his own suit, which fits perfectly. "What the fuck is that? Did yours shrink in the wash?"

Pete, Femi and Angus are close behind him. "Morning, morning, chaps," Femi says. "They're all arriving. Just went and accosted a load of old Trevs boys down at the jetty."

Pete lets out a howl. "Johnno—Jesus. Those trousers are so tight I can see what you had for breakfast, mate."

I hold my arms out to the side so my wrists stick out, prance around for them, playing the fool like always.

"Christ and look at you." Femi turns to Will. "Like butter wouldn't fucking melt."

"He was always a bad'un that looked like a good'un though," Duncan says. He leans over to ruffle Will's hair—Will quickly picks up a comb and smooths it flat again. "Wasn't he? That pretty boy face. Never got in trouble with the teachers, did you?"

Will grins at us all, shrugs. "Never did anything wrong."

"Bollocks!" Femi cries. "You got away with murder. You never got caught. Or they turned a blind eye, with your dad being head and all that."

"Nope," Will says. "I was good as gold."

"Well," Angus says, "I'll never understand how you aced those GCSEs when you did no fucking work."

I shoot a look at Will, try to catch his eye—could Angus have guessed? "You're such a jammy bastard," he says now, leaning over to give Will a pinch on the arm. Nah, on second thought he doesn't sound suspicious, just admiring.

"He didn't have any choice," Femi says. "Did you, mate? Your dad would have disowned you." Femi's always been sharp like that, reading people.

"Yeah." Will shrugs. "That's true."

It could have been social leprosy, being the headmaster's kid. But Will survived it. He had tactics. Like that girl he slept with from the local high school, passing those topless Polaroids of her all around our year. After that, he was untouchable. And actually, Will was always the one pushing me to do stuff—because he knew he could get away with it, probably. Whereas I was scared, at least in the beginning, of losing the scholarship. It would have destroyed my parents.

"Remember that trick we used to play with the seaweed?" Duncan says. "That was all your idea, mate." He points at Will.

"No," Will says. "I'm sure it wasn't." It definitely was.

The younger ones, who it had never been done to before, would lose their shit while the rest of us lay there listening to them, cracking up. But that was how it was if you were one of the younger boys. We'd all been there. You had to take the shit that was thrown at you. You knew that in the end you'd get your turn to throw it at someone else.

There was one kid at Trevellyan's who was a pretty cool customer when we put the seaweed in his bed. A first year. He had a weird, effeminate name. Anyway, we called him Loner, because it fit. He was completely obsessed with Will, who was his head of house, maybe even a bit in love with him. Not in a sexual way, at least I don't think so. More in the way little kids sometimes are with older ones. He started doing his hair in the same way. He'd sort of trail around after us. Sometimes we'd find him lurking behind a bush or something, watching us, and he'd come and watch all our rugby matches. He was the smallest boy in the school, spoke with a funny accent and wore these big glasses, so he was a prime candidate for shitting on. But he tried pretty hard to be liked. And I remember actually being quite impressed by the fact that he survived that first term without having some sort of breakdown, like some boys did. Even when we did the seaweed trick he didn't bitch and moan about it like some of the other kids, like that chubby little friend of his—Fatfuck, I think we called him—who ran off to tell Matron. I remember being pretty impressed by that.

I tune back in to the others. I feel like I'm coming up from underwater.

"It was always the rest of us who got hauled up for it," Duncan says, "who ended up having to do the lines."

"Me most of all," Femi says. "Obviously."

"Speaking of seaweed," Will says, "it wasn't funny, by the way. Last night."

"What wasn't funny?" I look at the others, they seem confused.

Will raises his eyebrows. "I think you know. The seaweed in the bed. Jules *freaked* out. She was pretty pissed off about it."

"Well it wasn't me, mate," I say. "Honest." It's not like I'd do anything that would bring back memories of our time at Trevs.

"Not me," Femi says.

"Or me," Duncan says. "Didn't have an opportunity. Georgina and I were otherwise engaged before dinner, if you get what I'm saying . . . certainly had better things to be doing than wandering around collecting seaweed."

Will frowns. "Well, I know it was one of you," he says. He gives me a long look.

There's a knock on the door.

"Saved by the bell!" Femi says.

It's Charlie. "Apparently the buttonholes are in here?" he says. He doesn't look at any of us properly. Poor bloke.

"They're over there," Will says. "Chuck Charlie one, will you, Johnno?"

I pick one up, little sprig of green stuff and white flowers, and toss it to Charlie, but not *quite* hard enough to reach him. Charlie makes a sort of lunge for it and doesn't manage to catch it, fumbles around on the floor.

When he's finally picked it up he leaves as quickly as possible, without saying anything. I catch the others' eyes and we all stifle a laugh. And for a moment it's like we're kids again, like we can't help ourselves.

"Fellas?" Aoife calls. "Johnno? The guests are all here. They're in the chapel."

"Right," Will says, "how do I look?"

"You're an ugly bastard," I say.

"Thanks." He straightens his jacket in the mirror. Then, as the others go ahead, he turns to me. "One other thing, mate," he says, in an undertone. "Before we go down, as I know I won't get a chance to mention it later. The speech. You're not going to totally embarrass me, are you?" He says it with a grin, but I reckon he's serious. I know there's stuff he doesn't want me to get into. But he doesn't need to worry—I don't want to get into it either. It doesn't reflect well on either of us.

"Nah, mate," I say. "I'll do you proud."

JULES

The Bride

I lift the gold crown onto my head, with hands that—I cannot help noticing—betray a telltale tremble. I turn my head, this way and that. It's the one capricious element of my outfit, the one concession to a romantic fantasy. I had it made by a hatmaker's in London. I didn't want to go for a full flower crown, because that would be a bit hippy child, but I felt this would be a stylish solution. A vague nod to a bride from an Irish folktale, say.

The crown gleams nicely against my dark hair, I can see that. I pick my bouquet out of its glass vase, a gathering of local wildflowers: speedwell, spotted orchids and blue-eyed grass.

Then I walk downstairs.

"You look stunning, sweetheart."

Dad stands there in the drawing room, looking very dapper. Yes, my father is going to walk me down the aisle. I considered other possibilities, I really did. Obviously my father is not the best representative of the joys of marriage. But in the end that little girl in me, the one who wants order, who wants things done in the right way, won out. Besides, who else was going to do it? My *mother*?

"The guests are all seated in the chapel," he says. "So everything's just waiting on us now."

In a few minutes we will make the short journey along the gravel drive that divides the chapel from the Folly. The thought makes my stomach do a somersault, which is ridiculous. I can't think of the last time I felt like this. I did a TEDx Talk last year about digital publishing to a room of eight hundred people and I didn't feel like this.

I look at Dad. "So," I say, more to distract myself from the roiling in my stomach than anything else, "you've finally met Will." My voice sounds strange and slightly strangled. I cough. "Better late than never."

"Yep," Dad says. "Sure have."

I try to keep my tone light. "What is that supposed to mean?"

"Nothing, Juju. Just—yep, sure have met him."

I know, even before it crosses my lips, that I should

not ask this next question. But I can't *not* ask it. I need to know his opinion, like it or not. More than anyone else's, I have always sought my dad's approval. When I opened my A-level results in the school car park, his, not Mum's, was the expression of delight I imagined, his the "Nice one, kiddo." So I ask. "*And*?" I say. "And did you *like* him?"

Dad raises his eyebrows. "You really want to have this conversation now, Jules? Half an hour before you get married to the fella?"

He's right, I suppose. It's spectacularly bad timing. But now we've started down this path, there's no going back. And I'm beginning to suspect that his lack of an answer might be an answer in itself.

"Yes," I say. "I want to know. *Do you like him?*"

Dad does a sort of grimace. "He seems like a very charming man, Juju. Very handsome, too. Even I can see that one. A catch, to be sure."

Nothing good can come of this. And yet I can't stop. "But you must have had a stronger first impression," I say. "You've always told me you're good at reading people. That it's such an important skill in business, that you have to be able to do it very quickly . . . yada yada yada."

He makes a noise, a kind of groan, and puts his hands on his knees as though he's bracing himself. And I feel a small, hard kernel of dread, one that's been there ever since I saw the note this morning, beginning to unfurl itself in my belly.

"Tell me," I say. I can hear the blood pounding in my ears. "Tell me what your first impression of him was."

"See, I don't reckon what I think's important," Dad says. "I'm only your old da. What do I know? And you've been with him for what now . . . two years? I should say that's long enough to know."

It's not two years, actually. Nowhere near it. "Yes," I say. "It is long enough to know when it's right." It's what I've said so many times before, to friends, to colleagues. It's what I said last night, effectively, in my toast. And every time before, I meant it. At least . . . I think I did. So why, this time, do my words seem to ring so hollowly? I can't help feeling that I'm saying it not to convince my dad so much as myself. Since finding that note again the old misgivings have reared their heads. I don't want to think about those, so I change tactic. "Anyway," I add. "To be honest, Dad, I probably know him better than I know you—considering we've only spent about six weeks together in my entire life."

It was meant to wound and I see it land: he recoils as though struck by a physical blow. "Well," he says, "there you go. That's all you need to say. You won't be needing my opinion."

"Fine," I say. "Fine, Dad. But you know what? Just this once, you could have come out and told me you thought he was a great guy. Even if you had to lie through your teeth to do it. You know what I needed to hear from you. It's . . . it's selfish."

"Look," Dad says. "I'm sorry. But . . . I can't lie to you, kid. Now I understand if you don't want me to walk you up the aisle." He says it magnanimously, like he's handed me some great gift. And I feel the hurt of it go right through me.

"Of course you're going to walk me up the bloody aisle," I snap. "You've barely been in my life, you were barely free to even attend this wedding. Yes, yes, I know . . . the twins are teething or whatever it is. But I've been your daughter for thirty-four years. You know how important you are to me, even though I wish to God it were otherwise. You are one of the reasons I chose to have my wedding here, in Ireland. Because I know how much you value that heritage, I value it too. I *wish* it didn't matter to me, what you think. But it bloody does. So you're going to walk me up the aisle. That's the very least you can do. You can walk me up that aisle and look bloody delighted for me, every step of the way."

There's a knock on the door. Aoife pops her head round. "All ready to go?"

"No," I say. "I need a moment, actually."

I march upstairs to the bedroom. I'm looking for something, the right shape, the right weight. I'll know it when I see it. There's the scented candle—or, no, the vase that held my bridal bouquet. I pick it up and heft it in my hand, readying myself. Then I hurl it at the wall, watching in satisfaction as the top half of it explodes into shards of glass.

Next I wrap my hand in a T-shirt—I've always been careful to avoid cuts, this is not about self-harm—pick up the unbroken base and slam it into the wall, again and again until I am left with smithereens, panting with the effort, my teeth gritted. I haven't done this for a while, for too long. I haven't wanted Will to see this side of me. I had forgotten how good it feels. The *release* of it. I unclench my teeth. I breathe in, out.

Everything feels a little clearer, calmer, on the other side.

I clean up the mess, as I have always done. I take my time about it. This is my day. They can all bloody well wait.

In the mirror I put my hands up and rearrange the crown on my head where it has slipped to one side. I see that my exertions have lent a rather flattering color to my complexion. Rather appropriate, for the blushing bride. I bring my hands up to my face and massage it, rearranging, remolding my expression into one of blissful, expectant joy.

If Aoife and Dad heard anything, their faces don't belie it when I reemerge. I nod to them both. "Ready to go." Then I yell for Olivia. She emerges, from that little room next to the dining room. She looks even paler than normal, if that's possible. But miraculously she is ready—in her dress and shoes, holding her garland of flowers. I snatch my own bouquet from Aoife. Then I stride out of the door, leaving Olivia and Dad following in my wake. I feel like a warrior queen, walking into battle.

As I walk the length of the aisle my mood changes, my certainty ebbs. I see them all turn to look at me and they seem a blur of faces, each oddly featureless. The Irish folksinger's voice eddies around me and for a moment I am struck by how mournful the notes sound, though it is meant to be a love song. The clouds scud overhead above the ruined spires—too fast, as in a nightmare. The wind has picked up and you can hear it whistling among the stones. For a strange moment I have the feeling that our guests are all strangers, that I'm being observed, silently, by a congregation of people I have never met before. I feel dread rise up through me, as though I've stepped into a tank of cold water. All of them are unknown to me, including the man waiting at the end, who turns his head as I approach. That excruciating conversation with Dad pinballs around in my brain—but loudest of all are the words he didn't say. I loosen my grip on his arm, try to put some distance between the two of us, as though his thoughts might further infect me.

Then suddenly it is as though a mist clears and I can see them properly: friends and family, smiling and waving. None of them, thank God, pointing phones at us. We got round that with a stern note on the wedding invite telling them to refrain from pictures during the ceremony. I manage to unfreeze my face, smile back. And then beyond them all, standing there in the center of the aisle, literally haloed in the light that has momentarily broken through the cloud: my husband-to-be. He looks immaculate in his suit. He is incandescent, as handsome as I have ever seen him. He smiles at me and it is like the sun, now warm upon my cheeks. Around him the ruined chapel rises, starkly beautiful, open to the sky.

It is perfect. It is absolutely as I had planned: better than I had planned. And best of all is my groom—

beautiful, radiant—awaiting me at the altar. Looking at him, stepping toward him, it is impossible to believe that this man is anything other than the one I know him to be.

I smile.

HANNAH

The Plus-One

During the ceremony I've been sitting on my own, crammed onto a bench with some cousins of Jules's—Charlie had a seat reserved at the front, as part of the wedding party. There was a weird moment, as Jules walked up the aisle. She wore an expression I've never seen on her before. She looked almost afraid: her eyes wide, her mouth set in a grim line. I wondered if anyone else noticed it, or even if I'd imagined it, because by the time she joined Will at the front she was smiling, the radiant bride everyone expects to see, greeting her groom. All around me there were sighs, whispers about how wonderful they both looked together.

The whole thing has gone very smoothly since: no fumbles over the vows, like at some weddings I've been to. The two of them speak the words loudly, clearly, as we all look on silently, the only other sound the whistling of the breeze among the stones. I'm not actually looking at Jules and Will, though. I'm trying to get a glimpse of Charlie, instead, all the way down at the front. I want to try and see what expression he wears as Jules says *I will.* But it's impossible: I can see only the back of his head, the set of his shoulders. I give myself a little mental shake: What did I think I was going to see, anyway? What proof am I looking for?

And suddenly it's all over. People are getting up around me with a sudden explosion of noise, laughing and chattering. The same woman who sang while Jules walked into the chapel sings us out, too, the notes of the accompanying fiddle tripping along behind. The words are all in Gaelic, her voice ethereally high and clear, echoing slightly eerily around the ruined walls.

I follow the trail of guests outside, dodging the huge floral arrangements: big sprays of greenery and colorful wildflowers which I suppose are very chic and right for the dramatic surroundings. I think of our wedding, how my mum's friend Karen gave us mates' rates on our flowers. It was all done in rather retro pastel shades. But I wasn't about to complain; we could never have afforded a florist of our choice. I wonder what it must be like to have the money to do exactly what you want.

The other guests are a very well-dressed, well-heeled bunch. When I looked around at the rest of the congregation in the chapel I realized no one else here is wearing a fascinator. Maybe they're not the thing, in circles like this? Every other woman seems to be in an expensive-looking hat, the sort that probably comes in its own specially made box. I feel like I did on the day at school when we hadn't realized it was home clothes day and both Alice and I wore our uniforms. I remember sitting in assembly and wishing I could spontaneously combust, to avoid spending the day feeling everyone's eyes on me.

We're given crushed dried rose petals to throw as Will and Jules step out of the chapel. But the breeze is stiff enough that they're whipped quickly away. I don't see a single petal land on the newlyweds. Instead they're carried off in a big cloud, up and out toward the sea. Charlie's always telling me I'm too superstitious, but I wouldn't like that, if I were Jules.

The bridal party are taken off for photographs, while everyone else pours away to the outside of the marquee where there's a bar set up. I need some Dutch courage, I decide. I pick my way across the grass toward it, my heels sinking in with every couple of steps. A couple of barmen are taking orders, sloshing cocktail shakers. I ask for a gin and tonic, which comes with a big sprig of rosemary in it.

I chat to the barmen for a bit because they seem like the friendliest faces in this crowd. They're a couple of young local guys, home for the summer from university: Eoin and Seán.

"We normally work in the big hotel on the mainland," Seán tells me. "Used to belong to the Guinness family. Big castle on a lough. That's where people usually want to get married. Never heard of a wedding here, other than in the old days. You know this place is meant to be haunted?"

"Yeah." Eoin leans across, dropping his voice. "My gran tells some pretty dark tales about this place."

"The bodies in the turf," Seán says. "No one knows for sure how they died, but they think they were hacked to pieces by the Vikings. They're not buried in hallowed ground, so there's all this talk about them being unquiet souls."

I know they're probably just pulling my leg but I feel a prickle of disquiet all the same.

"And the rumors are that's why the latest folk all left this place in the end," Eoin says. "Because the voices from the bog got too loud for them." He grins at Seán, then at me. "I'm not looking forward to being here after dark tonight, I tell you. It's the island of ghosts."

"Excuse me," a man in aviators and a tweed jacket behind me says, crossly. "This all sounds very bloody interesting, but would you mind making me an old-fashioned?"

I take that as my cue to leave them to their work.

I decide to sneak a peek inside the marquee, via the entranceway lit by flaming torches. Inside there's a delicious floral scent from lots of expensive-looking candles. And yet (I'm not proud to be pleased by this) there's definitely a whiff of damp canvas underneath. I suppose at the end of the day it's still a big tent. But *what* a tent. "Tents" plural, actually: in a smaller one at one end there's a laminate dance floor with a stage set up for a band and at the other end is a tent containing another bar. Jesus. Why have one bar at your wedding when you can have two? In the main tent white-shirted waiters are moving with the grace of ballet dancers, straightening forks and polishing glasses.

In the middle of everything, on a silver stand, sits a huge cake. It's so beautiful that it makes me sad to think that later Jules and Will will take a knife to it. I can't begin to guess how much a cake like that costs. Probably as much as our entire wedding.

I step outside the marquee again and shiver as a gust catches me. The wind's definitely picking up. Out to sea there are white horses on the caps of the waves now.

I look at the crowd. Everyone I know at this wedding is in the bridal party. If I don't pluck up my courage I'll be standing here on my own until Charlie returns—and as soon as he's finished with the photos I suppose he'll be straight into the MC duties. So I take a big swig of my gin and tonic and launch myself into a nearby group.

They're friendly enough on the surface, but I can tell they're a group of friends catching up—and I don't belong. I stand there and sip my drink, trying not to poke myself in the eye with the rosemary. I wonder how everyone else with a gin and tonic is managing it without injuring themselves. Maybe that's a thing you get taught at private school: how to drink cocktails with unwieldy garnishes. Because everyone here, without a shadow of a doubt, went to private school.

"Do you know what the hashtag is?" one woman asks. "You know, for the wedding? I checked the invitation but I couldn't see it."

"I'm not sure there is one," her friend replies. "Anyway, the signal here's so awful you wouldn't be able to upload anything while you're on the island."

"Maybe that's *why* they chose this place for the wedding," the first says, knowingly. "You know, because of Will's profile."

"It's very mysterious," the other woman says. "I have to admit I'd have expected Italy—the Lakes, perhaps. That seems to be a trend, doesn't it?"

"But then Jules is a trend*setter*," a third woman chips in. "Perhaps this is the new thing"—a great gust of wind nearly sends her hat flying and she clamps it down with a firm hand—"weddings on godforsaken islands in the middle of nowhere."

"It's rather romantic, isn't it? All wilderness and ruined glory. Makes you think of that Irish poet. Keats."

"Yeats, darling."

The women have the deep, real tans of summer holidays on Greek islands. I know this because they start talking about them next, comparing the benefits of Hydra over Crete. "God," one of them says now, "why would anyone fly economy with kids? I mean, talk about starting the holiday on a bad note." I wonder what they'd say if I chipped in and started debating the benefits of one New Forest campsite versus another. *Personally I think it's all about which has the best chemical loos*, I could say, in the same tone in which they're comparing which waterfront restaurant has the best views. I'll have to save that one up to tell Charlie later. Though, as proven last night, Charlie always gets a bit funny around posh people—a little unsure of himself and defensive.

The guy on my right turns to me: an overgrown schoolboy, one of those very round, pink-and-white faces at odds with a receding hairline. "So," he says, "Hannah, is it? Bride or groom?"

I'm so relieved that someone's actually deigned to talk to me I could kiss him.

"Er—bride."

"I'm groom. Went to school with the bastard." He sticks out his hand, I shake it. I feel like I've walked into his office for an interview. "And you know Julia, how . . . ?"

"Oh," I say. "I'm married to Charlie—he's Jules's mate? He's one of the ushers."

"And where's that accent from then?"

"Um, Manchester. Well—the outskirts." Though I always feel like I've lost a lot of it, having lived down south for so long.

"Support United, do you? You know, I went up for a corporate thing a few years ago. OK match. Southampton I think it was. Two-one, one-nil—not a draw, anyway, which would have been fucking boring. Dreadful food, though. Fucking inedible."

"Oh," I say. "Well, my dad supports—"

But he's turned away, bored already, and is in conversation with the guy next to him.

So I introduce myself to an older couple, mainly because they don't seem to be in conversation with anyone else.

"I'm the groom's father," the man says. This strikes me as an odd way to phrase it. Why not just say: "I'm

Will's dad"? He indicates the woman next to him with one long-fingered hand: "and this is my wife."

"Hello," she says, and looks at her feet.

"You must be very proud," I say.

"Proud?" He frowns at me, inquiringly. He's tall, with no stoop, so I find myself having to crane my neck slightly to look up at him. And maybe it's the long, hooked shape of it, but I feel that he is looking down his nose at me. I'm aware of a slight tightness in my stomach which most reminds me of being told off by a teacher at school.

"Well, yes," I say, flustered. I didn't think I'd have to explain myself. "Mainly because of the wedding, I suppose, but also because of *Survive the Night*."

"Mm." He seems to be considering this. "But it's not a *profession*, is it?"

"Well, um—I suppose not in the traditional sense—"

"He wasn't always the best student. Got himself into a few scrapes, you know—but he's a bright enough boy, all told. He managed to get into a fairly good university. Could have gone into politics or law. Perhaps not of the first rank in those, but respectable."

Jesus Christ. I've remembered that Will's dad is a headmaster. Right now it sounds as though he could be talking about any random boy, not his own son. I'd never have thought I'd feel pity for Will, who seems to have everything going for him—but right now I think I do.

"Do you have children?" he asks me. "Any sons?"

"Yes, Ben, he's—"

"You could do worse than to think of Trevellyan's. I know our methods may be considered a little . . . severe by some, but they have made great men out of some unpromising raw materials."

The idea of handing Ben into the clutches of this profoundly cold man fills me with horror. I want to tell him that even could I afford it and even if Ben were anywhere near senior school age there'd be no way I'd send my son to a place run by him. But I smile politely and excuse myself. If Will's parents are here, the bridal party must have returned from having their photos taken. And if so, why hasn't Charlie come to find me? I search the crowd, finally spotting him in a big group with the rest of the ushers and several other men. I feel a little dart of anger and move toward him as quickly as my heels will let me.

"Charlie," I say, trying not to sound hectoring. "God, it feels like you've been gone hours. I had the weirdest conversation—"

"Hey, Han," he says, a bit absently. By the slight squint he gives me, and perhaps some other subtle change in his features, I'm certain he's already had a bit to drink. There's a full glass of champagne in one of his hands, but I don't think it's his first. I remind myself that he's always in control, that he knows what his limit is. He's a grown-up. "Oh," he says. "By the way. You can probably take that thing off your head now."

He means the fascinator. I feel my cheeks grow hot as I lift it off. Is he ashamed of me?

One of the men Charlie has been talking to walks over and claps Charlie on the shoulder. "This your old lady, Charlie?"

"Yeah," Charlie says. "Rory, this is my wife, Hannah. Hannah, this is Rory. He was on the stag."

"Lovely to meet you, Hannah," Rory says, with a flash of teeth. So much *charm*, all these public schoolboys. I think of the ushers outside the chapel: *Can I offer you a program? Would you like some dried rose petals?* Butter wouldn't melt. But I saw how they got last night. I wouldn't trust any of them further than I could throw them.

"Hannah," Rory says, "I think I should apologize for the state we sent your boy back in after the stag do. But it was all fun and games, wasn't it, Charlie, mate? Last one in and all that."

I don't know what that means, exactly. I'm watching Charlie. And I see it as it happens, the transformation of my husband's face. The tightening of the features, lips disappearing into a taut line, until he wears the very same expression he did when I collected him from the airport after that weekend.

"What on earth *did* you all get up to?" I ask Rory, keeping my tone playful. "Charlie definitely won't tell me."

Rory seems relieved. "Good man," he says, clapping Charlie on the shoulder again. "What happens on the stag stays on the stag and all that." He winks at me. "All good fun, anyhow. Boys will be boys."

"Charlie?" I ask, as Rory peels away and we have a moment alone together. "Have you been drinking?"

"Only a sip," he says. I don't *think* he's slurring. "You know, to lubricate things."

"Charlie—"

"Han," he says, firmly. "A couple of glasses aren't going to derail me."

"And—" I think of him emerging from Stansted airport, looking hollow-eyed and shell-shocked. "What *happened* on the stag do? What was he talking about?"

"Ah, God." Charlie runs a hand through his hair, screws up his face. "I don't know why it got to me so much. It's—well it's because I'm not one of them, I suppose. But it was pretty horrible at the same time."

"Charlie," I say, feeling disquiet curl through my stomach. "What did they do?"

And then my husband turns to me and hisses, between his teeth, that nasty little trace of something—someone—else creeping into his words. "I don't want to *fucking* talk about it, Hannah."

There it is. Oh God. Charlie *has* been drinking.

JOHNNO

The Best Man

I down my glass of champagne and take another off a passing waitress. I'll drink this one quickly, too, then maybe I'll feel more—I dunno, myself. This morning, seeing all of this, seeing everything Will has . . . well, it's made me feel a little shitty. I'm not proud of that. I feel bad about it, of course I do. Will's my best mate. I'd like to just be happy for him. But it's dredged it all up, being with the boys again. It's like none of it affected him, none of it held him back. Whereas I've always felt, I don't know, like I don't deserve to be happy.

There are so many familiar faces in the crowd outside the chapel: blokes from the stag and others who didn't go but who were at school with us. "No plus-one, Johnno?" they ask me. And, "Gonna be putting the moves on some lucky lady tonight then?"

"Maybe," I say. "Maybe."

There's a bit of betting about who I'm going to try to crack on with. Then they're off talking about their jobs, their houses. Share options and portfolios. Some story about the latest politician who's made an arse of himself—or herself. Not much I can add to this conversation as I can't catch the name and even if I could I probably wouldn't know it. I stand here feeling stupid, feeling like I don't belong. I never really have.

They all have high-powered jobs now, this lot. Even the ones that I don't remember as being all that bright. And they all look pretty different to how they did at school. Not surprising, considering it's not all that far off twenty years ago. But it doesn't feel that way. Not to me. Not right now, standing here, in this place. Looking at each face, it doesn't matter how much time has passed, or that there are bald spots where there was once hair, or dark where there was once blond, or contacts now, instead of glasses. I can place them all.

See, even now, even though I've been such a fucking disappointment, my folks have still got the school photo in pride of place on the mantelpiece in our living room. I've never seen it with a speck of dust on it. They're so proud of that photo. *Look at our boy, at his big posh school. One of them.* The whole school out on the pitches in front of the main building, with the cliffs on the other side. All of us perched on one of those metal stands, looking good as gold, with our hair brushed into side-partings by Matron and big, stupid grins: *Smile for the cameras, boys!*

I'm grinning at them all now, like I did in that photo. I wonder if they're secretly all looking at me and thinking the same old thoughts. Johnno: the waster. The fuckup. Always good for a laugh—not much more. Turned out exactly how they thought. Well, that's where I'll prove them wrong. Because I've got the whiskey business to talk about, haven't I?

"Johnno, mate. Can't believe how long it's been." Greg Hastings—third row, second from the left. Had a hot mum, whose looks he definitely didn't inherit.

"Ha, trust you, Johnno, to forget your bloody suit!" Miles Locke—fifth row, somewhere in the middle. Bit of a genius, but not too much of a geek about it, so he got by.

"Didn't forget the rings at least! Wish you had done, that would have been the *ultimate.*" Jeremy Swift—up in the far-right-hand corner. Swallowed a fifty-pence piece in a dare and had to go to hospital.

"Johnno, big fella—you know, I have to tell you, I'm still recovering from the stag. You did a number on me. Christ and that poor bloke! We *really* did a number on him. He's here, isn't he?" Curtis Lowe—fourth row, fifth from the right. Nearly played tennis professionally but ended up an accountant.

See? They call me thick. But I've got a pretty good memory, when it comes down to it.

There's one face in that photo I can't ever bring myself to look at. Bottom row, with the smallest kids, out to the right. *Loner,* the little kid who worshipped Will, would do anything to please him. Anything we asked. He'd steal extra rolls and butter from the kitchens for us, brush the mud off our rugby boots, clean our dorm. All stuff we didn't actually *need* or could've done ourselves. But it was fun, in a way, to think up things for him to do.

We'd find ourselves asking for more and more stupid things. One time we told him to climb up onto the school roof and hoot like an owl, and he did it. Another time we got him to set off all the fire alarms. It was hard not to keep pushing, to see how far he would go. Sometimes we'd go through his stuff, eat the sweets his mum had sent him or pretend to get off from the photo of his hot older sister on the beach. Or we'd find the letters he'd written to send home and read them aloud in a whiny voice: *I miss you all so much.* And sometimes we'd even knock him about a bit. If he hadn't cleaned our rugby boots well enough, say—or what we *said* wasn't clean enough, because he always did a pretty good job. I'd get him to stand there while I hit him on his arse with the studded side of the boot as an "incentive." Seeing what we could get away with. And he'd have let us get away with anything.

I grab another glass of champagne, down it. This one hits home, finally; I feel myself float a little higher. I move into the big group of Old Trevellyans. I want to tell them all about the whiskey business. Just for the next half an hour or so. Just so they might finally realize I'm as good as any of them. But the conversation has moved on and I can't think of a way to get it back.

Someone taps me on the shoulder, hard. I turn round and I'm face-to-face with him: Mr. Slater. Will's dad—but first and foremost, always, headmaster of Trevellyan's.

"Jonathan Briggs," he says. "You haven't changed one bit." He doesn't mean this as a compliment.

Shit, I'd been hoping to give him a wide berth. The sight of him has the same effect on me it always did. Would have thought now, my being an adult, it might be different. But I'm as shit-scared of him as ever. Funny, considering he was the one that once saved my bacon, really.

"Hello, sir," I say. My tongue feels like it's stuck in my throat. "I mean, Mr. Slater." I think he'd prefer it if I called him "sir." I glance over my shoulder. The group I was in before has closed up, so we're stuck on the outside of it now: just him and I. No escape.

He's looking me up and down. "I see you're dressed in the same unusual way. That blazer you had at Trevellyan's: too large at the beginning and far too small at the end."

Yeah, because my folks could only afford the one.

"And I see you're still hanging around my son," he says. He never liked me. But then I can't imagine him liking anyone much, not even his own child.

"Yeah," I say. "We're best mates."

"Oh is that what you are? I was always rather under the impression you simply did his dirty work for him. Like when you broke into my office to steal those GCSE papers."

For a moment everything around me goes still and quiet. I'm so surprised I can't even get a word out.

"Oh yes," Mr. Slater continues, unfazed by my silence. "I know. You think that simply because it wasn't reported you'd got away with it? It would have been a disgrace on the school, on my name, if it had got out."

"No," I say, "I dunno what you're talking about." But what I think is: You don't know the half of it. Or maybe you do and you've got an even better poker face than I realized.

I manage to get away after this. I go and search for

more drink. Something stronger. There's a bar they've set up, near the marquee. They can't pour the stuff fast enough. People are asking for two, three drinks, pretending they're for friends and plus-ones when really I can see them necking them as they walk away. It's going to get loose, this evening, especially with the gear Peter Ramsay's brought. When I pick up my whiskey—the stuff I brought—I notice that my hand is trembling.

Then I see this bloke I recognize, across the crowd of people. He looks at me, frowning. But he's *not* from Trevellyan's. He's about fifty, anyway, way too old to be in that photo. And it annoys me at first, because I can't work out where I know him from.

He has a too-fashionable hipster haircut, even though he's gray and going a bit bald and wears a suit with sneakers. He looks like he's stepped out of some wanky Soho office and isn't quite sure how he ended up here in the middle of nowhere on some random island.

For a few minutes, genuinely, I haven't got a single clue where I could have met someone like him. Then I think we both work it out at the same time. Shit. It's the producer of *Survive the Night.* Something French and fancy-sounding. *Piers.* That's it.

He walks toward me. "Johnno," he says. "It's good to see you."

I'm kind of flattered that he remembers my name,

that he recognizes my face. Then I remember that he hadn't liked my face enough to put me on his TV show, so I dial down my enthusiasm. "Piers," I say, sticking out a hand. I have no fucking idea why he wants to come and speak to me. We only met the once, when I came to do the screen test with Will. Surely it would be less embarrassing if we just raised a glass to each other over everyone's heads and left it at that?

"Long time no see, Johnno," he says, rocking back and forth on his heels. "I hardly recognized you . . . with all that hair." He's being polite. My hair's not that much longer. But I probably look about fifteen years older than the last time we met. It's all the drinking, I guess. "And what have you been up to?" he asks. "I know there must have been something very worthwhile keeping you busy."

I feel like there's something strange about how he put that, but I gloss over it. "Well." I puff myself up. "I've been making whiskey, Piers." I try hard to do the big spiel, but to be honest I can't stop thinking about the way this bloke rejected me with a few lines in an email.

Not quite the right fit for the show.

People don't realize this about me, you see. They see old Johnno, the wild one, the crazy one . . . without much going on backstage. And of course I like them thinking that, I play up to it. But I do feel stuff too, and I am embarrassed by this conversation, just like I was when the production company dropped me. At least I got paid a couple of grand for the concept, I guess.

See, the idea for the show was mine. I'm not saying I thought up the whole thing. But I know it was me who planted the seed. A while ago Will and I were sitting in a pub, having a drink. It had always been me who suggested we meet up. Will was always too busy, even though he didn't have much of a TV career to speak of in those days, just an agent. But even if he puts me off a couple of times he never cancels. There's too much of a bond between us for this friendship to die. He knows that too.

I must have got pretty drunk, because I even brought up the game we used to play at school: Survival. I remember Will giving me this look. I think he was afraid of what I might say next. But I wasn't going to go into any of that. We never do. I'd been watching this show the night before with some adventurer guy and it seemed so soft. So I said, "That would have made a much better idea for a TV program than most of the so-called survival stuff you see, wouldn't it?"

He had looked at me differently, then.

"What?" I asked.

"Johnno," he said. "That might be the best idea you've ever come up with."

"Yeah, but you couldn't actually do it. You know . . . because of what happened."

"That was a million years ago," he said. "And it was an accident, remember?" And then, when I didn't respond: "Remember?"

I looked at him. Did he really believe that? He was waiting for an answer.

"Yeah," I said. "Yeah it was."

Next thing I knew, he'd got us both the screen test. And the rest, you could say, was history. For him, anyway. Obviously they didn't want my ugly mug in the end.

I realize that Piers is looking at me a bit funny. I think he's just asked me something. "Sorry," I say. "What was that?"

"I was saying that it sounds like you've got your work cut out for you. I suppose at least our loss is whiskey's gain."

Our *loss*? But it wasn't their loss: they didn't want me, full stop.

I take a big swig of my drink. "Piers," I say. "You didn't *want* me on the show. So, with the greatest possible respect, what the fuck are you talking about?"

AOIFE

The Wedding Planner

On the horizon the stain of bad weather is already spreading, darkening. The breeze has stiffened. Silk dresses flap in the wind, a couple of hats cartwheel away, cocktail garnishes are whisked into the air.

But over the growing sound of the wind the voice of the singer rises:

is tusa ceol mo chroí,
Mo mhuirnín
is tusa ceol mo chroí.
You're the music of my heart,
My darling,
You're the music of my heart.

For a moment it is as though I have forgotten how to breathe. That song. My mother sang it to us when we were little. I force myself to inhale, exhale. Focus, Aoife. You have too much to be getting on with.

The guests are already crowding about me with demands:

"Are there any gluten-free canapés?"

"Where's the best signal here?"

"Will you ask the photographer to take some photos of us?"

"Can you change my seat on the table plan?"

I move among them, reassuring, answering their questions, pointing them in the right direction for the lavatories, the cloakroom, the bar. There seem to be so many more than a hundred and fifty of them: they are everywhere, streaming in and out of the fluttering doors of the marquee, thronging in front of the bar, swarming across the grass, posing for smartphone pictures, kissing and laughing and eating canapés from the army of waiters. I've already corralled several guests away from the bog before they can begin to get in trouble.

"Please," I say, heading off another group who are trying to enter the graveyard, clutching their drinks, as though they're looking around some fairground attraction. "Some of these stones are very old and very fragile."

"It doesn't look as though anyone's visited them in a

while," says one of the men in a calm-down-dear sort of voice as they leave, a little begrudgingly. "It's a deserted island, isn't it? So I don't *think* anyone's going to mind." Evidently he hasn't spotted my own family's little patch yet and I am glad of that. I don't want them milling about among the stones, spilling their drinks and treading upon the hallowed ground in their spike heels and shiny brogues, reading the inscriptions aloud. My own tragedy written there for them all to pore over.

I had prepared myself for how strange it would feel, having all these people, here. It is a necessary evil: This is what I have wanted, after all. To bring people to the island again. And yet I hadn't realized quite how much of a trespass it would seem.

OLIVIA

The Bridesmaid

The ceremony went on for hours—or that's how it felt. In my thin dress I couldn't stop shivering. I held my bouquet so tightly that the thorns of the rose stems bit through the white silk ribbon into my hands. I had to suck the little drops of blood from my palms while no one was watching.

Eventually, though, it was over.

But after the ceremony there were photos. My face hurts from trying to smile. My cheeks *ache*. The photographer kept singling me out, telling me I need to "turn that frown upside down, darling!" I tried. I know it can't have seemed like a smile on the other side—I know it must have looked like I was baring my teeth, because that's how it felt. I could tell Jules was getting annoyed with me, but I didn't know how to do anything about it. I couldn't remember how to smile properly. Mum put a hand on my shoulder. "Are you all right, Livvy?" She could see something was up, I guess. That I'm not all right, not at all.

People crowd around: aunts and uncles and cousins I haven't seen for ages.

"Livvy," my cousin Beth asks, "you still with that boyfriend? What was his name?" She's a few years younger than me: fifteen. And I've always felt like she's kind of looked up to me. I remember telling her all about Callum last year, at my aunt's fiftieth, and feeling proud as she hung on my words.

"Callum," I say. "No . . . not anymore."

"And you've finished your first year at Exeter now?" my aunt Meg asks. Mum hasn't told her about me leaving, then. When I try to nod my head it feels too heavy for my neck. "Yeah," I say, "because it's easier to pretend, "yeah, it's good."

I try to answer all their questions but it's even more exhausting than the smiling. I want to scream . . . inside I *am* screaming. I can see some of them looking at me in confusion—I even see them glancing at each other, like: "What's up with her?" *Concerned looks.* I suppose I don't seem like the Olivia they remember. That girl was chatty and outgoing and she laughed a lot. But then I'm not the Olivia *I* remember. I'm not sure if or how I'll ever get back to her. And I can't act out a role for them. I'm not like Mum.

Suddenly I feel like I can't breathe again, like I can't get the air into my lungs properly. I want to get away from their questions and their kind, concerned faces. I tell them I'm going off to find the loo. They don't seem bothered. Maybe they're relieved. I peel away from the group. I think I hear Mum call my name but I keep on walking and she doesn't call again, probably because she's got distracted talking to someone. Mum loves an audience. I go a little faster. I take off my stupid heels, which have already got covered in dirt. I'm not sure where I'm going exactly, other than in the opposite direction to everyone else.

On my left are cliffs of black stone, shining wet from the water spray. The land drops away in places, like a big chunk of it has suddenly disappeared into the sea, leaving a jagged line behind. I wonder what it would feel like to have the ground suddenly fall away under me, suddenly disappear, so I'd have no choice but to go down with it. For a moment I realize I'm standing here almost hoping for it to happen.

Below the track I'm following I see little pockets in between the cliffs with beaches of white sand. The waves are big, whitecapped far out. I let the wind blow over me, till my hair feels like it's being ripped from my head, till my eyelids feel like they're trying to turn inside out, the wind pushing at me like it's trying its best to shove me over. There's a sting of salt on my face.

The water out there is a bright blue, like the color of the sea in a photo of a Caribbean island, like the one where my mate Jess went last year with her family and from which she posted about fifty thousand photos on Instagram of herself in a bikini (all totally Facetuned, of course, so her legs looked longer and her waist looked smaller and her boobs looked bigger). I suppose that it's all quite beautiful, what I am looking at, but I can't *feel* it being beautiful. I can't properly feel any good things anymore: like the taste of food, or the sun on my face or a song I like on the radio. Looking out at the sea all I feel is a dull pain, somewhere under my ribs, like an old injury.

I find a way down where it's not so steep, where the ground meets the beach in a slope, not a cliff. I have to fight my way through bushes that are growing on the slope, small and tough and thorny. They snag at my dress as I go past and then I trip on a root, and I'm falling down the bank, tripping, tumbling forward. I can feel the silk tear—Jules will flip—and then I'm down on my knees—bam! And my knees are stinging and all I can think is that the last time I fell like this I was a kid, at school, maybe nine years ago. I want to cry like a kid as I stumble down to the beach, because it should hurt, my whole body should hurt, but no tears will come—I haven't been able to make them come for a long time. If I could cry it might all be better, but I can't. It's like an ability I've lost, like a language I've forgotten.

I sit on the wet sand, and I can feel it soaking through my dress. My knees are covered with proper playground grazes, pink and raw and gravelly. I open my little beaded bag and carefully take out the razor blade. I lift up the fabric of my dress and press the razor to my skin. Watch the tiny bright red beads of blood come up—slow at first, then faster. Even though I can feel the pain it doesn't feel like my blood, my leg. So I squeeze the cut, bringing more blood to the surface, waiting to feel like it belongs to me.

The blood is bright red, so bright, kind of beautiful. I put a finger to it and then taste my finger, taste the metal of it. I remember the blood after the "procedure," which is what they called it. They said that "a little light spotting" would be totally normal. But it went on for weeks, it felt like; the dark brown stain appearing in my knickers, like something inside me was rusting away.

I remember exactly where I was when I realized I hadn't had my period. I was with my friend Jess, at a house party some second years were holding at their place, and she'd been telling me she'd had to raid the cupboards in the bathroom for tampons, as hers had come early. I remember how when she told me I felt this odd feeling, like indigestion in my chest, like I couldn't draw a breath—a little like now. I realized I couldn't think of the last time I had to use a tampon, to use anything. And I'd felt strange, kind of bloated and gross and tired, but I thought that was the crap food I ate and feeling shitty over things with Steven. It had been a while. Some months, my periods are really light, so they hardly bother me at all. But they're always there. They're still regular.

It was halfway through the new term. I went to the uni doctor and took a pregnancy test with her, because I didn't trust myself to do it properly. She told me it was positive. I sat there, staring at her, like I wasn't going to fall for it, like I was waiting for her to tell me she was joking. I didn't really believe it could be true. And then she started talking about what my options were, and did I have anyone I could talk to about it? I couldn't say anything. I remember how I opened my mouth a couple of times and nothing came out, not even air, because again I could hardly breathe. I felt like I was suffocating. She sat there, looking sympathetic, but of course she couldn't come and give me a hug because of all that legal stuff. And right then I really, really needed a hug.

I got out of there and I was all shaky and weird, I couldn't walk properly—I felt like a car had slammed into me. My body didn't feel like mine. All this time it had been doing this secret, strange thing . . . without me knowing about it.

I couldn't even make my fingers work on my phone. But eventually I unlocked it. I WhatsApped him. I saw that he'd read it straightaway. I saw the three little dots appear—it told me that he was "typing," at the top. Then they disappeared. Then they appeared again, and he was "typing" for about a minute. Then nothing again.

I called him, because clearly he had his phone right there, in his hand. He didn't answer. I called him again, it rang out. The third time, it went straight to the voice mail message. He'd declined it. So I left him a voice mail—though I'm not sure he would have been able to work out what I was actually saying, my voice was wobbling so much.

Mum took me to the clinic to have it done. She drove all the way from London to Exeter, nearly four hours door to door, and waited for me while I had it done and then drove me home afterward.

"It's the best thing," she told me. "It's the best

thing, Livvy darling. I had a baby when I was your age. I didn't think I had any other choice. I was at the beginning of my life, of my career. It ruined everything."

I knew Jules would like hearing that one. I heard an argument with them once, when Jules had screamed at Mum: "You never wanted me! I know I was your biggest mistake . . ."

It was the only thing I could have done. But it would have been so much easier if he'd answered, if he'd let me know he understood, felt it too. Just a line—that's all it would have taken.

"He's a little bastard," Mum told me. "For leaving you to go through all of this on your own."

"Mum," I told her—in case through some freak chance she happened to bump into Callum and go off on a tirade against him, "he doesn't know. I don't want him to know."

I don't know why I didn't tell her it wasn't Callum. It's not like Mum's a prude, like she would judge me for the whole thing with Steven. But I suppose I knew how much worse it would make me feel, reliving it all, feeling that rejection all over again.

I remember everything about that drive back from the clinic. I remember how Mum seemed so different to usual, how I'd never really seen her like that before.

I saw how her hands gripped the steering wheel, hard enough that the skin went white. She kept swearing, under her breath. Her driving was even worse than normal.

She told me, when we got home, to go and lie on the sofa, and she brought me biscuits and made me tea and arranged a rug over me, even though it was pretty warm. Then she sat down next to me, with her own cup of tea, even though I'm not sure I'd ever seen her drink tea before. She didn't drink it, actually, she just sat there with her hands clenched around her mug as tight as they had been on the steering wheel.

"I could kill him," she said again. Her voice didn't even sound like her own; it was low and rough. "He should have been there with you, today," she said, in that same strange voice. "It's probably a good thing I don't know his full name. The things I would do to him if I did."

I stare out into the waves. I think being in the sea will make me feel better. I think it's the only thing that will work, all of a sudden. It looks so clean and beautiful and flawless, like being inside it would be like being inside a precious stone. I stand up, brush the sand off my dress. Shit . . . it's cold in the wind. But actually it's kind of a good cold—not like the cold in the chapel. Like it's blowing every other thought out of my head.

I leave my shoes in the wet sand. I don't bother stepping out of my dress. I walk into the water and it's ten degrees cooler than the air, absolutely freezing freezing cold, it makes my breath come all fast and I can only take in little gulps of air. I feel the sting of the cut on my leg as the salt gets in it. And I push farther into it, so that the water comes up to my chest, then my shoulders and now I really can't breathe properly, like I'm wearing a corset. I feel tiny fireworks explode in my head and on the surface of my skin and all the bad thoughts loosen, so I can look at them more easily.

I put my head under, shaking it to encourage the bad thoughts to float away. A wave comes, and the water fills my mouth. It's so salty it makes me gag and when I gag I swallow more water and don't manage to breathe and more water goes in, and it's in my nose too and each time I open my mouth for air more water comes in instead, great big salty gulps of it. I can feel the movement of the water under my feet and it feels like it's tugging me somewhere, trying to take me with it. It's like my body knows something I don't because it's fighting for me, my arms and legs thrashing out. I wonder if this is a bit what drowning is like. Then I wonder if I *am* drowning.

JULES

The Bride

Will and I have been away from the melee, having our photos taken beside the cliffs. The wind has definitely picked up. It did so as soon as we stepped outside the protection of the chapel and the handfuls of thrown rose petals were whipped away and out to sea before they could even touch us. Thank goodness I decided to wear my hair down, so the elements can only do so much damage. I feel it rippling out behind me, and the train of my skirt lifts in a stream of silk. The photographer loves this. "You look like an ancient Gaelic queen, with that crown—and your coloring!" he calls. Will grins. "*My* Gaelic queen," he mouths. I smile back at him. My husband.

When the photographer asks us to kiss I slip my tongue into his mouth and he responds in kind, until the photographer—somewhat flustered—suggests that these photos might be a little "racy" for the official records.

Now we return to our guests. The faces that turn toward us as we walk among them are already flushed with warmth and booze. In front of them I feel oddly stripped bare, as though the stress of earlier might be visible on my face. I try to remind myself of the pleasure of friends and loved ones being here together in one place, clearly enjoying themselves. And that it's worked: I have created an event that people will remember, will talk about, will try—and probably fail—to replicate.

On the horizon, darker clouds mass ominously. Women clasp their hats to their heads, their skirts to their thighs, with small shrieks of hilarity. I can feel the wind tugging at my outfit, too, flinging up the heavy silk skirt of my dress as though it were light as tissue, whistling through the metal spokes of my crown as if it would quite like to rip it from my head and hurl it out to sea.

I glance across at Will, to see if he's noticed. He's surrounded by a gaggle of well-wishers and is being his usual, charming self. But I sense that he's not fully engaged. He keeps glancing distractedly over the shoulders of the various relatives and friends who come up to greet us as though he's searching for someone, or looking at something.

"What is it?" I ask. I take his hand. It looks different to me now, foreign, with its plain band of gold.

"Is that—Piers—over there?" he says. "Talking to Johnno?"

I follow his gaze. There, indeed, is Piers Whiteley, producer of *Survive the Night,* balding head bent earnestly as he listens to whatever Johnno has to say.

"Yes," I say, "that's him. What's the matter?" Because *something* is the matter, I'm sure of it—I can see it from Will's frown. It's an expression I rarely see him wear, this look of slightly anxious distraction.

"Nothing—in particular," he says. "I—well, it's just a little awkward, you know. Because Johnno was turned down for the TV stuff. Not sure who it's more awkward for, to be honest. Perhaps I should go over and rescue one of them."

"They're grown men," I say. "I'm sure they can handle themselves."

Will hardly seems to have heard me. In fact, he's dropped my hand and is making his way across the grass toward them, pushing politely but decisively past the guests who turn to greet him as he goes.

It's very out of character. I look after him, wondering. I'd thought the sense of unease would leave me, after the ceremony, after we'd said those all-important vows. But it's still with me, sitting like sickness in the pit of my stomach. I have the sense that there's something malign stalking me, as though at the very edge of my vision, of which I can never get a proper glimpse. But that's crazy. I just need a moment to myself, I decide, away from the fray.

I move quickly past the guests on the outskirts of the crowd, head down, stride purposeful, in case one of them tries to stop me. I enter the Folly via the kitchen. It's blissfully quiet inside. I close my eyes for a long moment, in relief. On the butcher's block in the center of the kitchen, something—part of the meal for later, no doubt—is covered with a large cloth. I find a glass, run myself a cold drink of water, listen to the soothing tick of the clock on the wall. I stand there facing the sink and as I sip my water I count to ten and back down again. *You're being ridiculous, Jules. It's all in your head.*

I'm not sure what it is that makes me aware I am not alone. Some animal sense, maybe. I turn and in the doorway I see—

Oh God. I gasp, stumble backward, my heart hammering. It's a man holding a huge knife, his front smeared with blood.

"Jesus Christ," I whisper. I shrink away from him,

just managing not to drop my glass. A beat of pure fear, of racing adrenaline . . . then logic reasserts itself. It's Freddy, Aoife's husband. He's holding a carving knife, and the blood smears are on the butcher's apron he wears tied about his waist.

"Sorry," he says, in that awkward way of his. "Didn't mean to give you a fright. I'm carving the lamb in here—there's a better surface than in the catering tent."

As if to demonstrate, he lifts the cloth from the butcher's block and beneath I see all the clustered racks of lamb: the crimson, glistening meat, the upthrust white bones.

As my heartbeat returns to normal, I'm humiliated to think how naked the fear must have been on my face. "Well," I say, trying to inject a note of authority. "I'm sure it will be delicious. Thank you." And I walk quickly—but careful not to hurry—out of the kitchen.

As I rejoin my milling guests I become aware of a change in the energy of the crowd. There's a new hum of interest. It seems that something's going on out to sea. Everyone is beginning to turn and look, caught by whatever's happening.

"What is it?" I ask, craning to see over heads, unable to make out anything at all. The crowd is thinning around me, people drifting away wordlessly, toward the sea, trying to get a better view of whatever is going on.

Maybe some sea creature. They see dolphins from here regularly, Aoife told me. More rarely, a whale. That would be quite a spectacle, even a nice bit of atmospheric detail. But the noises coming from those at the front of the crowd of guests don't seem the right pitch for that. I'd expect shrieks and exclamations, excited gesturing. They're watching whatever it is, intently, but they're not making very much noise. That makes me uneasy. It suggests it's something bad.

I press forward. People have become pushy, clustering for position as though they're vying for the best view at a gig. Before, as the bride, I was like a queen among them, cutting a swath through the crowd wherever I walked. Now they have forgotten themselves, too intent on whatever it is that is going on.

"Let me through!" I shout. "I want to see."

Finally, they part for me and I move forward, up to the front.

There is something out there. Squinting, eyes shielded against the light, I can make out the dark shape of a head. It could be a seal or some other sea creature, save for the occasional appearance of a white hand.

There is *someone* in the water. It's difficult to get a proper glimpse of him or her from here. It must be one of the guests; it's not like anyone could swim here from the mainland. I wouldn't be surprised if it were Johnno—although it can't be, he was chatting to Piers moments ago. So if it's not him, perhaps it's one of the other exhibitionists in our number, one of the ushers, showing off. But as I look more closely I realize the swimmer isn't facing the shore, but out to sea. And they aren't swimming, I see now. In fact—

"They're drowning!" a woman is shouting—Hannah, I think. "They're caught in the current—look!"

I'm moving forward, trying to get a better look, pushing through the watching crowd of guests. And then finally I'm at the front and I can see more clearly. Or perhaps it's simply that strange deep knowledge, the way we know those closest to us from a long distance, even if we only see the back of a head.

"Olivia!" I shout. "It's Olivia! Oh my God, it's Olivia." I'm trying to run, my skirt catching under my heels and hampering me. I hear the sound of tearing silk and ignore it, kick off my shoes, keep running, losing my footing as my feet sink into wet, marshy patches of ground. I've never been a runner, and it's a whole other issue in a wedding dress. I seem to be moving unbelievably slowly. Will, thank God, doesn't seem to have the same problem—he tears past me, followed by Charlie and several others.

When I finally get to the beach it takes a few moments for me to work out what's going on, to understand the scene in front of me. Hannah, who must have started running too, arrives next to me, breathing hard. Charlie and Johnno stand thigh-deep in the water, with several other men behind them, on the water's edge—Femi, Duncan and others. And beyond them, emerging from the depths, is Will, with Olivia in his arms. She seems to be struggling, fighting him, her arms windmilling, her legs kicking out desperately. He holds on tight. Her hair is a black slick. Her dress is absolutely translucent. She looks so pale, her skin tinged with blue.

"She could have drowned," Johnno says, as he returns to the beach. He looks distraught. For the first time I feel more warmly toward him. "Lucky we spotted her. Crazy kid, anyone could see it's not sheltered here. Could have got swept straight out to the open sea."

Will gets to shore and lets Olivia go. She launches herself away from him and stands staring at us all. Her eyes are black and impenetrable. You can see her near-naked body through the soaked dress: the dark points of her nipples, the small pit of her navel. She looks primeval. Like a wild animal.

I see that Will's face and throat are scratched, red marks springing up livid on his skin. And at the sight of these a switch is flicked. Where a second ago I had been full of fear for her, now I feel a violent, red-hot solar flare of rage.

"The crazy little *bitch,*" I say.

"Jules," Hannah says gently—but not so gently that I can't hear the note of opprobrium in her voice. "You know, I don't think Olivia's OK. I—I think she might need help—"

"Oh for God's sake, Hannah." I spin toward her. "Look, I get how kind and maternal you are, and whatever. But Olivia doesn't need a fucking mother. She's already got one—who gives her a lot more attention, let me tell you, than I ever got. Olivia doesn't need help. She needs to get her fucking act together. I'm not going to have her ruining my wedding. So . . . back off, OK?"

I see her step, almost stumble, backward. I'm dimly aware of her expression of hurt, of shock. I've gone beyond the pale: there, it's done. But, right now, I don't care. I turn back to Olivia. "What the *hell* were you doing?" I scream at her.

Olivia merely gazes back at me, dully, mute. She looks like she's drunk. I grab hold of her shoulders.

Her skin is freezing to the touch. I want to shake her, slap her, pull her hair, demand answers. And then her mouth opens and closes, open and closes. I stare at her, trying to work it out. It is as though she is attempting to form words but her voice won't come. The expression in her eyes is intent, pleading. It sends a chill through me. For a moment I feel as though she is trying hard to semaphore a message I don't have the means to decipher. Is it an apology? An explanation?

Before I have a chance to ask her to try again, my mother is upon us. "Oh my girls, my girls." She clasps us both in her bony embrace. Beneath the billowing cloud of Shalimar I smell the sharp, acrid tang of her sweat, her fear. It is Olivia she's really reaching for, of course. But for a moment I allow myself to yield to her embrace.

Then I glance behind me. The other guests are catching up with us. I can hear the murmur of their voices, sense the excitement coming off them. I need to defuse this whole situation.

"Anyone else fancy a swim?" I call. No one laughs. The silence seems to stretch out. They all seem to be waiting, now the show is over, for some cue as to where to go now. How to behave. I don't know what to do. This is not in my playbook. So I stand, staring back at them, feeling the dampness of the beach soaking into the skirt of my dress.

Thank God for Aoife, who appears among them, neat in her sensible navy dress and wedge shoes, absolutely unflustered. I see them turn to her, as though recognizing her authority.

"Everyone," she calls. "Listen up." For a small, quiet woman, her voice is impressively resonant. "If you'll follow me back this way. The wedding breakfast will be served soon. The marquee awaits!"

JOHNNO

The Best Man

Look at him. Playing the hero, carrying Jules's sister out of the water. Just fucking look at him. He's always been so good at getting people to see exactly what he wants them to see.

I know Will better than other people, maybe better than anyone in the world. I'll bet I know him a lot better than Jules does, or probably ever will. With her he's put on the mask, put up the screen. But I have kept his secrets for him, because they are both of ours to keep.

I always knew he was a ruthless fucker. I've known it since school, when he stole those exam papers. But I thought I was safe from that side of his character. I'm his best friend.

That's what I thought until about half an hour ago, anyway.

"It was such a shame," Piers said, "when we heard you didn't want to do it. I mean, Will goes down an absolute storm with the ladies, of course. He's made for TV. But he can be a bit too . . . smooth. And between you and me, I don't think male viewers like him all that much. The consumer research we've done has suggested they find him a bit—well, I think the expression one participant used was 'a bit of an arse.' Some viewers, the men, especially, are turned off by a host who they see as a bit too good-looking. You'd have balanced all that."

"Hang on, mate," I said. "Why did you think I *didn't* want to do it?"

Piers looked a bit put out at first—I don't think he's the sort of bloke who likes to be cut off in full flow when he's talking about demographics. Then he frowned, registering what I'd said.

"Why did we think—" He stopped, shook his head. "Well, you never turned up at the meeting, that's why."

I didn't have a clue what he was talking about. "What meeting?"

"The meeting we had to discuss how everything would progress. Will turned up with his agent and said unfortunately you and he had had a long discussion, and you'd decided it wasn't for you after all. That you weren't 'a TV sort of bloke.'"

All the stuff I've been saying to everyone these past four years. Except I never said it to Will. Not then, anyway. Not before some sort of important meeting. "I never heard of any meeting," I said. "I got an email saying you didn't want me."

It seemed to take a while for the penny to drop. Then Piers's mouth opened and closed gormlessly, silently, like a fish: bloop bloop bloop. Finally he said, "That's impossible."

"Nope," I told him. "No, it isn't. And I can tell you that for certain—because I never heard about a meeting."

"But we emailed—"

"Yeah. You never had *my* email, though, did you? It all went through Will, and his agent. They sorted everything like that."

"Well," Piers said. I think he'd just worked out that he'd opened up a massive can of worms. "Well," he went on, like he might as well say it all now. "He definitely told us that you weren't interested. That you'd had this whole period of soul searching and told him you'd decided against it. And it was such a shame, because you and Will, as we'd always planned . . . the rough and the smooth. Now, that could be TV dynamite."

There was no point in saying any more to Piers about

it. He already looked like he wished he could teleport to anywhere else. *We're on a small island, mate,* I nearly told him. *Nowhere to go.* I wasn't surprised he felt like that, though. I could see him glancing over my shoulder, searching for someone to save him.

But my beef wasn't with him. It was with the bloke I thought was my best friend.

Speak of the devil. Will had started striding toward us, grinning at us both, looking so fucking handsome with not a hair out of place, despite the wind. "What are you two over here gossiping about?" he asked. He was close enough that I could see the beads of sweat on his forehead. See, Will is the sort of bloke who hardly ever sweats. Even on the rugby pitch, I barely saw him break much of one. But he was sweating now.

Too late, *mate*, I thought. *Too fucking late.*

I think I get it. He was too clever to cut me off at the beginning. The idea for *Survive the Night* was mine and we both knew it. If he'd done that, I could have spilled the beans, told everyone about what had happened when we were kids. I didn't have nearly so much to lose as him. So he brought me in, made me feel a part of it, and then he made it look like it was down to someone else that I was chucked out. Not his fault at all. *Sorry about that, mate. Such a shame. Would have loved working with you.*

I remember how much I liked doing the screen test. I felt natural, talking about all that stuff, stuff I knew. I felt like I had something to say—something people would listen to. If they'd asked me to recite my times tables, or talk about politics, I would have been fucked. But climbing and abseiling and all that: I taught those skills at the adventure center. I didn't even think about the camera, after the first bit.

The most fucking offensive thing about it is how simple it all must have felt to Will. Stupid Johnno . . . so easy to pull the wool over his eyes. Now I understand why he's been so hard to get hold of recently. Why I've felt like he's pushed me away. Why I practically had to beg to be his best man. When he agreed he must have thought of it as a consolation prize, a Band-Aid. But being best man doesn't pay the bills. It's not a big enough Band-Aid. He's used me, the whole time, ever since school. I've been there to do his dirty work for him. But he didn't want to share the spotlight with me, oh no. When it came to it he threw me under the bus.

I swallow my whiskey in one long gulp. That double-crossing motherfucker. I'll have to find a way to get my own back.

HANNAH

The Plus-One

Olivia is someone else's sister, someone else's daughter. Perhaps I should back off, as Jules told me to. And yet I can't. As the others are streaming into the marquee I find myself walking in the other direction, toward the Folly.

"Olivia?" I call, once I've stepped inside. There's no answer. My voice is echoed back to me by the stone walls. The Folly seems so silent and dark and empty now. It's hard to believe that there's anyone else in here. I know where Olivia's room is, the door that leads off the dining room—I'll try that first, I decide. I knock on the door.

"Olivia?"

"Yeah?" I think I hear a small voice from inside. I take it as my cue to push open the door. Olivia's sitting there on the bed, a towel wrapped around her shoulders.

"I'm fine," she says, without looking up at me. "I'm coming back to the marquee in a minute. I've just got to change first. I'm fine." The second time doesn't make it sound any more convincing.

"You don't really *seem* fine," I say.

She shrugs but doesn't say anything.

"Look," I say. "I know it's not my business. I know we hardly know each other. But when we talked yesterday, I got the sense that you've been going through some pretty major stuff . . . I imagine it must be hard to put on a happy face over all that."

Olivia remains silent, not looking at me.

"So," I say, "I guess I wanted to ask—what were you doing in the water?"

Olivia shrugs again. "I dunno," she says. A pause. "I—it all got a bit much. The wedding, all the people. Saying I must be so happy for Jules. Asking me how I was doing. About uni . . . " She trails off, looks at her hands. I see how the nails are bitten down as a child's, the cuticles red and raw-looking against the pale skin. "I just wanted to get away from all of it."

Jules had made out that it was all a stunt, that Olivia was being a drama queen. I suspect it was the opposite. I think she was trying to disappear.

"Can I tell you something?" I ask her.

She doesn't say no, so I go on.

"You know how I mentioned my sister, Alice, last night?"

"Yeah."

"Well, I . . . I suppose you remind me of her a little bit. I hope you don't mind me saying that. I *promise* it's a compliment. She was the first one in our family to go to university. She got the best GCSEs, straight A's for her A-levels."

"I'm not all that clever," Olivia mumbles.

"Yeah? I think you're cleverer than you like to let on. You did English lit at Exeter. That's a good course, isn't it?"

She shrugs.

"Alice wanted to work in politics," I say. "She knew that she had to have an impeccable record and to get the right grades for it. She got them, of course, she was accepted into one of the UK's top universities. And then in her first year, after she'd realized that she was easily knocking off Firsts for every essay she turned in, she relaxed a bit and got her first boyfriend. We all found it quite funny, me and Mum and Dad, because she was suddenly *so* into him."

Alice told me all about this new guy when she came home for the Christmas holidays. She'd met him at the Reeling Society, which was some posh club she'd joined because they had a fancy ball at the end of term. I remember thinking she brought the same intensity to this new relationship as she brought to her studies. "He's dead fit, Han," she told me. "And everyone fancies him. I can't believe he'd even *look* at me." She told me, swearing me to secrecy, that they'd slept together. He was the first boy she'd ever slept with. She told me that she felt so close to him, that she hadn't realized it could be like that. But I remember she qualified this, said it was probably the hormones and all the sociocultural idealization of young love. My beautiful, brainy sister, trying to rationalize away her feelings . . . classic Alice.

"But then she started going off him," I tell Olivia.

Olivia raises her eyebrows. "She got the ick?" She seems a bit more engaged now.

"I think so. By the Easter holiday she'd stopped talking about him so much. When I asked her she told me that she realized he wasn't quite the guy she thought he was. And that she'd spent too much time wrapped up in him, that she really needed to get her head down and focus on her studies. She'd got a low 2.1 in an essay she'd handed in and that had been her wake-up call."

"Jeez," Olivia says, rolling her eyes. "She sounds

like a massive geek." And then she catches herself. "Sorry."

I smile. "I told her exactly the same thing. But that was Alice, all over. Anyway, she wanted to make sure that she did the decent thing by him, told him in person." That was Alice all over too.

"How did he take it?" Olivia asks.

"It didn't go that well," I say. "He was pretty horrible about it all, said he wouldn't let her humiliate him. That she would pay for it." I remember that because I remember wondering what he could possibly do. How do you make someone "pay" for a breakup?

"She didn't tell me what he did, to get her back," I tell Olivia. "She didn't tell me or Mum or Dad. She was too ashamed."

"But you found out?"

"Later," I say. "I found out later. He'd taken this video of her."

A video of Alice had been uploaded to the university's intranet. It was a video she had let him take, after the fancy Reeling Society ball. It was taken down from the server the second the university found out about it. But by then the news had spread, the damage was done. Other versions of it had been saved on computers around campus. It was posted to Facebook. It was taken down. It was posted again.

"So, like . . . revenge porn?" Olivia asks.

I nod. "That's what we'd call it now. But then it was this, you know, more innocent time. Now you're warned to be careful, aren't you? Everyone knows that if you let someone take photos or a video of you it could end up on the internet."

"I guess," Olivia says. "But people forget. In the moment. Or you know, if you really like someone and they ask you. So I suppose everyone at uni saw it, right?"

"Yes," I say. "But the worst part is we didn't know at the time, she didn't tell us. She was too ashamed. I think maybe she thought it would spoil our image of her. She'd always been so perfect, though of course that wasn't why we loved her."

The fact that she didn't even tell *me*. That's the part that still hurts so much.

"Sometimes," I say, "I think it's too difficult to tell the people closest to you. The ones you love. Does that sound familiar?"

Olivia nods.

"So. I want you to know: you can tell me. Yeah? Because here's the thing. It's always better to get it out in the open—even if it seems shameful, even if you feel like people won't understand. I wish Alice had been able to talk to me about it. I think she might have got some perspective she couldn't see herself."

Olivia looks up at me, then away. It comes out as little more than a whisper. "Yeah."

And then the tinny sound of an announcement comes from the direction of the marquee. "Ladies and gents"—it's Charlie's voice, I realize, he must be doing his MC bit—"Please take your seats for the wedding breakfast."

I don't have time to tell Olivia the rest—and perhaps that's for the best. So I don't tell her how the whole thing was like a huge stain upon Alice's life, on her person—like it was tattooed there. None of us had realized quite how fragile Alice was. She had always seemed so capable, so in control: getting all those amazing grades, playing on the sports teams, getting her place at university, never missing a trick. But underneath that, fueling all this success, was a tangled mass of anxiety that none of us saw until it was too late. She couldn't cope with the shame of it all. She realized she would never—*could* never—work in politics as she had dreamt. It wasn't just that she didn't have her B.A., because she'd dropped out. There was a video of her giving some guy a blow job—and more—on the internet, now. It was indelible.

So I didn't tell Olivia how one June, two months after she came home from uni, Alice took a cocktail of painkillers and pretty much anything else she could find from the medicine cabinet in the bathroom while my mum was collecting me from netball practice. How, seventeen years ago this month, my beautiful, clever sister killed herself.

AOIFE

The Wedding Planner

It's my fault, what just happened, with the bridesmaid. I should have seen it coming. I *did* see it coming: I knew there was trouble brewing with that girl. I knew it when I gave her her breakfast this morning. She held it together during the ceremony, even though she looked like she wanted to turn and bolt out of there. Afterward, of course, I tried to keep my eye on her. But there have been so many other demands on me: the guests were so insistent, so rabid, that the waiting staff—all mostly older schoolkids and students on their summer holidays—could hardly cope.

The next thing I knew, there was the commotion, and she was in the water. Seeing her I was suddenly transported back to a different day. Powerless to help. Having seen the signs, but ignoring them until it was too late. Those insistent images in my dreams: the water rising, my hands reaching out as though I might be able to do something . . .

This time rescue was possible. I think of the groom walking out of the water with her, savior of the day. But maybe I could have prevented it from happening at all, if I had paid more attention at the right time. I am angry with myself for having been so lax. I managed to keep a veneer of cool professionalism in front of the guests, for the time it took to marshal them all into the marquee for the wedding breakfast. Even if I hadn't kept such a firm hold of myself, I doubt anyone would have noticed anything was amiss. After all, it is my job to be invisible.

I need Freddy. Freddy always makes me feel better.

I find him out of sight of the guests, in the catering area of the back of the marquee: plating up with a small army of helpers. I get him to step outside with me, away from the curious gaze of his kitchen aides.

"The girl could have drowned, out there," I say. When I think about it, I can hardly breathe. I'm seeing it all, how it could have happened, playing out before my eyes. It is as though I've been transported back to a different day, when there was no happy ending. "Oh God—Freddy, she could have drowned. I wasn't paying enough attention." It is the past, all over again. All my fault.

"Aoife," he says. He takes a firm hold of my shoulders. "She didn't drown. It's all OK."

"No," I say. "He saved her. But what if—"

"No what-ifs. The guests are in the marquee, now. Everything is going to go perfectly, trust me. Go back out there and do what you do best." Freddy has always been good at soothing me. "It's a minor blip. Otherwise everything is going beautifully."

"But it's all different to how I imagined," I say. "Harder, having them all here, wandering about all over the place. Those men, with their horrible games last night. And now this—bringing it all back . . ."

"It's nearly done," Freddy says, firmly. "All you have to do is get through the next few hours."

I nod. He's right. And I know I need to get a grip on myself. I can't afford to fall apart, not today.

NOW

THE WEDDING NIGHT

Now they can make him out, the man, Freddy, hurrying toward them as quickly as he is able. He holds a torch in his hand: nothing more sinister than that. The light of their own torches picks out the sheen of sweat on his pale forehead as he draws near. "You should come back to the marquee," he shouts, between gasps of breath. "We've called the Gardaí."

"What? Why?"

"The waitress has come round a little. She says she thinks she saw someone else out there, in the dark."

"We should listen to him," Angus shouts to the others, once Freddy has left them. "Wait for the police. It's not safe."

"Nah," Femi shouts. "We've come too far."

"You really think they're going to be here *soon* do you, Angus?" Duncan asks. "The police? In this weather? No fucking way, mate. We're all alone out here."

"Well, all the more reason. It's not safe—"

"Aren't we jumping to conclusions?" Femi shouts.

"What do you mean?"

"He only said she *might* have seen someone."

"But if she did," Angus calls, "that means—"

"What?"

"Well, if someone else was involved. It means it might not—it might not have been an accident."

He doesn't go so far as to spell it out but they hear it, all the same, behind his words. *Murder.*

They grip their torches a little tighter. "These would make good weapons," Duncan shouts. "If it comes down to it."

"Yeah," Femi shouts, straightening his shoulders a little. "It's us against them. Four of us, one of them."

"Wait, has anyone seen Pete?" Angus says, suddenly.

"What? Shit—no."

"Maybe he went with that Freddy bloke?"

"He didn't, Fem," Angus replies. "And he was really out of it. Shit—"

They call for him: "Pete!"

"Pete, mate—you out there?" There is no answer.

"Christ . . . well, I'm not going to wander around looking for him, too," Duncan shouts, a faint but telling tremor in his voice. "It's not the first time he's been in that state, is it? He can look after himself. He'll be fine." The others suspect he's made an effort to sound more certain than he really is. But they aren't going to question it. They want to believe it too.

EARLIER THAT DAY

JULES

The Bride

Inside the marquee, Aoife has conjured something magical. It's warm in here, a respite from the increasingly cool wind outside. Through the entrance I can see the lighted torches flicker and dip and every so often the roof of the marquee billows and deflates gently, flexing against the wind outside. But in a way it only adds to the sense of coziness inside. The whole place is scented by the candles, and the faces clustered about the candlelight appear rosy, flushed with health and youth—even if the true cause is an afternoon of drinking in the penetrating Irish wind. It's everything I could have wanted. I look around at the guests and see it in their faces: the awe at their surroundings. And yet . . . why am I left feeling so hollow?

Everyone already seems to have forgotten about

Olivia's crazy stunt; it could have happened on another day entirely. They are throwing back the wine, guzzling it down . . . growing increasingly loud and animated. The atmosphere of the day has been recaptured and is following its prescribed track. But I can't forget. When I think about Olivia's expression, about that pleading look in her eyes when she tried to speak, all the little hairs on the back of my neck prickle to attention.

The plates are cleared away, every one practically licked clean. Alcohol has given the guests a real hunger and Freddy is a great talent. I've been to so many weddings where I've had to force down mouthfuls of rubbery chicken breast, school canteen–style vegetables. This was the most tender rack of lamb, velvet on the tongue, crushed potatoes scented with rosemary. It was perfect.

It's time for the speeches. The waiters fan out about the room, carrying trays of Bollinger, ready for toasts. There's a sourness in the pit of my stomach and the thought of yet more champagne makes me feel slightly queasy. I've drunk too much already, in an effort to match the bonhomie of my guests, and feel strange, untethered. The image of that dark cloud on the horizon during the reception drinks keeps playing upon my mind.

There's the sound of a spoon on a glass: *ding ding ding*!

The chatter in the marquee subsides, replaced by an obedient hush. I feel the attention of the room shift. Faces swivel toward us, to the top table. The show is about to begin. I rearrange my expression into one of joyful anticipation.

Then the lights in the marquee shiver, going out. We are plunged into a twilit gloom that matches the fading light outside.

"Apologies," calls Aoife, from the back of the marquee. "It's the wind, outside. The electricity's a bit temperamental here."

Someone, one of the ushers, I think, lets out a long, lupine howl. And then others join in, until it sounds as though there is a whole pack of wolves in here. They're all drunk by now, all getting looser and more wild. I want to scream at them all to shut up.

"Will," I hiss, "can we ask them to stop?"

"It'll only encourage them," he says soothingly. His hand closes over mine. "I'm sure the lights will come on again in a second."

Just when I think I can't bear it any longer, that I really will scream, the lights flicker on again. The guests cheer.

Dad stands, first, to give his speech. Perhaps I

should have banished him at the last minute as a punishment for his earlier behavior. But that would look odd, wouldn't it? And so much of this whole wedding business, I have realized, is about how things *appear*. As long as we can make it through with all seeming joyful, jubilant . . . well, perhaps then we can suppress any darker forces stirring beneath the surface of the day. I bet most people would guess that this wedding is all down to my dad's generosity. Not quite.

Everyone's been asking me what made me decide to hold the wedding here. I put a shout-out on social media: "Pitch me your wedding venue." All part of a feature for *The Download.* Aoife answered the call. I admired the level of planning in her pitch, the consideration of practicalities. She seemed so much hungrier than all the rest. It knocked spots off the competition, really. But that's not why this place won our business. The whole unvarnished truth of why I decided to hold my wedding here was because it was nice and cheap.

Because Daddy dearest, standing up there looking all proud, turned off the tap. Or Séverine did it for him.

No one's going to guess that one, are they? Not when I've got a cake that cost three grand, or solid silver engraved napkin rings, or Cloon Keen Atelier's entire year's output of candles. But those were exactly the sort of things my guests expected from me. And

I could only afford them—and a wedding in the style to which I am accustomed—because Aoife also offered a 50 percent discount if I held it here. She might look dowdy but she's savvy. That's how she clinched it. She knows I'll feature it in the magazine now, knows it'll get press because of Will. It'll pay dividends in the end.

"I'm honored to be here," Dad says, now. "At the wedding of my little girl."

His little girl. *Really.* I feel my smile harden.

Dad raises aloft his glass. He's drinking Guinness, I see—he's always made a point of not drinking champagne, keeping true to his roots. I know that I should be gazing back adoringly but I'm still so cross about what he said earlier that I can barely bring myself to look at him.

"But then Julia has never really been my little girl," Dad says. His accent is the strongest I've heard it in years. It always gets more pronounced at times of heightened emotion . . . or when he's had a fair amount to drink. "She's always known her own mind. Even at the age of nine, always knew exactly what she wanted. Even if I . . ." He gives a meaningful cough, "tried to persuade her otherwise." There's a ripple of amusement from the guests. "She went after whatever she wanted with a single-minded ambition." He smiles, ruefully.

"If I were to flatter myself I might try to say that she takes after me in that respect. But I'm not the same. I'm not nearly so strong. I pretend to know what I want but really it's whatever has taken my fancy. Jules is absolutely her own person, and woe betide anyone who gets in her way. I'm sure any employees of hers will agree." There's some slightly nervous laughter from the table of *The Download* crowd. I smile at them beatifically: None of you are going to get in trouble. Not today.

"Look," Dad says, "sure, I'm not the best role model for this wedding stuff, I'll be totally honest. I believe I have wife number one and number five here this evening. So I suppose you could say I'm a card-carrying member of the club . . . though not a very good one." Not very funny—though there are some dutiful titters from the spectators. "Jules was—ahem—quick to point that out to me earlier today when I attempted to offer some words of fatherly advice."

Fatherly advice. Ha.

"But I would say that I've learned a thing or two over the years, about how to get it right. Marriage is about finding that person you know best in the world. Not how they take their coffee or what their favorite film is or the name of their first cat. It's knowing on a deeper level. It's knowing their soul." He grins at Séverine, who positively preens.

"Besides, I hardly felt qualified to give that advice. I know I haven't always been around. Scratch that. I have hardly ever been around. Neither of us have been. I think Araminta will probably agree with me on that."

Wow. I look toward Mum. She wears a rictus smile that I think might well be as taut as my own. She won't have enjoyed the first wife bit because it'll make her feel old and she'll be livid at the suggestion of parental neglectfulness, considering how much she's been enjoying playing the gracious mother of the bride today.

"So in our absence, Julia has always had to forge her own path. And what a path she has forged. I know I haven't always been very good at showing it, but I am so proud of you, Juju, of all that you have achieved." I think of the school prize-giving ceremony. My graduation. The launch for *The Download*—none of which my father attended. I think about how often I have wanted to hear those words, and now, here they are—right when I'm most furious at him. I feel my eyes fill with tears. Shit. That really caught me unawares. I never cry.

Dad turns to me. "I love you so much . . . clever, complicated, fierce daughter of mine." Oh God. They aren't pretty tears, either, a subtle glistening of the eyes. They spill over onto my cheeks and I have to put up the heel of a hand, then my napkin, to try and staunch them. What is *happening* to me?

"And here's the thing," Dad says, to the crowd. "Even though Jules is this incredible, independent person, I like to flatter myself that she is my little girl. Because there are certain emotions, as a parent, that you can't escape . . . no matter what a shite one you've been, no matter how little right you have to them. And one of those is the instinct to protect." He turns to me again. I have to look at him now. He wears an expression of genuine tenderness. My chest hurts.

And then he turns to Will. "William, you seem like . . . a great guy." Was it just me, or was there a dangerous emphasis on the "seem"? "But," Dad grins—I know that grin. It isn't a smile at all. It's a baring of teeth. "You better look after my daughter. You better not feck this up. And if you do anything to hurt my girl—well, it's simple." He raises his glass, in a silent toast. "I'll come for you."

There's a strained silence. I force out a laugh, though it seems to come out more like a sob. There's a ripple in its wake, other guests following suit—relieved, perhaps, to know how to take it. *Ah, it's a joke.* Only it wasn't a joke. I know it, Dad knows it—and I suspect, from the look on Will's face, he knows it too.

OLIVIA

The Bridesmaid

Jules's dad sits down. Jules looks a wreck: her face blotchy and red. I saw her dabbing her eyes with her napkin. She does feel stuff, my half sister, even if she does a good impression of being so tough all the time. I feel bad about earlier, honestly. I know Jules wouldn't believe it if I told her, but I *am* sorry. I still feel cold, like the chill from the sea got deep under my skin. I've changed into the dress I wore last night, because I thought that would piss Jules off the least, but I wish I could have got into my normal clothes. I'm keeping my arms wrapped around myself to try and stay warm but it doesn't stop my teeth chattering together.

Will gets to his feet to hollers and whistles, a few catcalls. Then the room falls silent. He has their total attention. He has that sort of effect on people. I guess it's how he looks and how he is; his confidence. How he's always totally in control.

"On behalf of my new wife and I," he says—and is almost drowned out by the whoops and cheers, the drumming on the tables, the stamping of feet. He smiles around until everyone settles down. "On behalf of my new wife and I, thank you so much for coming today," he says. "I know Jules will agree with me when I say that it is a wonderful thing to celebrate with all of our most cherished loved ones, our nearest and dearest." He turns to Jules. "I feel like the luckiest man in the world."

Jules has dried her eyes now. And when she looks up at Will her expression is totally different, transformed. She seems suddenly happy enough that it is hard to look at her, like staring at a lightbulb. Will beams back at her.

"Oh my God," I hear a woman whisper, at the next table. "They're just *too* perfect."

Will's grinning around at everyone. "And it really *was* luck," he says. "Our first meeting. If I hadn't been in the right place at the right time. As Jules likes to say, it was our sliding doors moment." He raises his glass: "So: to luck. And to making your own luck . . . or giving it a little helping hand, when it needs it."

He winks. The guests laugh.

"First of all," he says, "it's customary to tell the bridesmaids how beautiful they're looking, isn't it? We only have one, but I think you'll agree she's beautiful enough for seven. So a toast to Olivia! My new sister."

The whole room turns toward me, raising their glasses. I can't bear it. I look at the floor until the cheers die down and Will begins to speak again.

"And next, to my new wife. My beautiful, clever Jules . . ."—the guests go wild again—"Without you, life would be very dull indeed. Without you, there would be no joy, no love. You are my equal, my counterpart. So, please be upstanding to raise a toast to Jules!"

The guests all rise to their feet around me. "To Jules!" they echo, grinning. They're all smiling at Will, the women especially, their eyes not leaving his face. I know what they're seeing. Will Slater: TV star. Husband, now, to my half sister. Hero: look how he rescued me earlier, from the water. All-round good guy.

"Do you know how Jules and I met?" Will asks, when they've all sat down. "It was the work of Fate. She threw a party at the V&A museum, for *The Download.* I was just a plus-one: I had come along with a friend. Anyway, my friend had to leave the party and I was left behind. I was just deciding whether to leave myself. So it was a total spur-of-the-moment decision, to go back inside. So who knows what would have happened, if I hadn't? Would we ever have met? So—even though Jules works so hard that I sometimes feel it's the third person in our relationship, I'd also like to thank it for bringing us together. To *The Download*!"

The guests get to their feet. "To *The Download*!" they parrot.

I didn't meet Jules's new fiancé until after they were engaged. She had been very hush-hush about him. It was like she hadn't wanted to bring him home before she got the ring on her finger, in case we put him off. Maybe I sound like a bitch for saying that, but Jules has always been pretty ruthless about some things. I suppose I don't blame her, exactly. Mum *can* be a bit much.

Jules being Jules, she'd stage-managed the whole thing. They were going to arrive at Mum's for coffee, stay for half an hour, then we'd all head off to the River Café for lunch (their favorite place, Jules told us; she had booked). Her instructions to Mum and me were pretty clear: do not fuck this up for me.

I honestly didn't mean to fuck it up, that first meeting with Jules's fiancé. But when the two of them arrived, and they first walked in through the door,

I had to run to the bathroom and throw up. Then I found I couldn't move. I sank down next to the loo and sat on the floor for what felt like a very long time. I felt winded, like someone had punched me in the stomach.

I saw exactly how it had happened. He'd gone back into the V&A, after he put me in that taxi. There he'd met my sister, belle of the ball—so much better suited to him. Fate. And I remember what he'd said when we first met: "If you were ten years older, you'd be my ideal woman." I saw it all.

After a little while—because she had her important schedule, I suppose—Jules came upstairs. "Olivia," she said, "we need to go off for lunch now. Of course, I'd love you to join us, but if you're not feeling well enough then, well, I suppose that's fine." I could hear that it wasn't fine, not at all, but that was the least of my worries.

Somehow I managed to find my voice. "I—I can't come," I said, through the door. "I'm . . . ill." It seemed the easiest thing to do, right then, to go along with what she'd said. And anyway, I wasn't feeling well—I was sick to my stomach, like I'd swallowed something poisonous.

I've thought about it since, though. What if right then I'd had the balls to open that door and tell her the truth, right then and there to her face? Rather than waiting and hiding, until it was way too late?

"OK," she said. "Fine, then. I'm very sorry you can't come." She didn't sound in the least bit sorry. "I'm not going to make a big deal out of this now, Olivia. Maybe you really are ill. I'll give you the benefit of the doubt. But I'd really like your support in this. Mum told me you've had a tough time lately, and I'm sorry for that. But for once, I'd like you to try and be happy for me."

I slumped down against the bathroom door and tried to keep breathing.

He covered it so quickly, his own reaction. When he walked in through Mum's door, that first time we "met," there was maybe a split second of shock. One that maybe only I would have noticed. The flicker of an eyelid, a slight tightening of the jaw. Nothing more than that. He covered it up so well, he was so smooth.

So you see, I can't think of him as Will. To me he'll always be Steven. I hadn't thought of that, when I renamed myself for the dating app. I hadn't thought that he might have lied too.

At their engagement drinks, I decided I wouldn't run away and hide like before. I'd spent the couple of months in between thinking of all the ways I could have reacted that would have been so much better, so much less pathetic, than scarpering and throwing up. I hadn't done anything wrong, after all. This time I'd confront him. He was the one that had all the explaining to do, to me, to Jules. He was the one who should be feeling pretty fucking sick. I had let him win that first one. This time, I was going to show him.

He threw me off at the beginning. When I arrived he gave me a big grin. "Olivia!" he said. "I hope you're feeling better. It was such a shame we didn't get to meet properly, last time."

I was so shocked I couldn't say anything. He was pretending we'd never met, right to my face. It made me even start to doubt myself. Was it really him? But I *knew* it was. There was no doubt about it. Closer up I could see how the skin around his eyes creased the same, how he had these two moles on his neck, below the jaw. And I remembered, so clearly, that split second's reaction, when he'd first seen me.

He knew exactly what he was doing: making it harder for me to get my own version of the truth out. And he'd also banked on me being too pathetic to say anything to Jules, too scared that she wouldn't believe anything I said.

He was right.

HANNAH

The Plus-One

There was something weird about Will's speech just now. Something that felt strangely familiar, a sense of déjà vu. I can't quite put my finger on it but while everyone around me cheered and clapped I was left with an uneasy feeling in the pit of my stomach.

"Here we go," I hear someone at the table whisper, "is everyone ready for the main event?"

Charlie's not on my table. He's on the top table, right there at Jules's left elbow. It makes sense, I suppose: I'm not one of the wedding party after all, while Charlie is. But everywhere else husbands and wives seem to be seated next to one another. It occurs to me that I have barely seen Charlie since this morning, and then only outside at the drinks—which somehow made me feel more disconnected from him than if we hadn't seen one another at all. In the space of a mere twenty-four hours, it feels as though a gulf has opened up between us.

The guests sitting near me have done a poll on how long the best man's speech is going to last. Fifty quid for a bet, so I declined. They've also designated our table "the naughty table." There's a manic, intense feeling around it. They're like children who have been cooped up for too long. Over the last hour or so they've knocked back at least a bottle and a half each. Peter Ramsay—who's sitting on the other side of me—has been speaking so quickly that it's starting to make me feel dizzy. This might have something to do with the crusting of white powder around one of his nostrils; it's everything I can do not to lean over and dash it off with the corner of my napkin.

Charlie rises to his feet, resuming his MC role, taking the mic from Will. I find myself watching him carefully for any sign that he might have had too much to drink. Is his face drooping slightly in that telltale way? Is he a little unsteady on his feet?

"And now," he says, but there's a scream of feedback as people—especially the ushers, I notice—groan and jeer and cover their ears. Charlie flushes. I cringe inwardly for him. He tries again: "And now . . . it's time for the best man. Everyone give a big hand for Jonathan Briggs."

"Be kind, Johnno!" Will shouts, hands cupped around his mouth. He gives a wry smile, a pantomime wince. Everyone laughs.

I always find the best man's speech hard to watch. There's so much expectation. There's that tiny, hair-thin line between being too vanilla and causing offense. Better, surely, to stay on the PC side of it than to try and nail it completely. I get the impression Johnno's not the sort to worry about offending anyone.

Maybe I'm imagining it, but he seems to be swaying slightly as he takes the mic from Charlie. Beside him, my husband looks sober as a judge. Then, as Johnno makes his way round to the front of the table, he trips and nearly falls. There's lots of heckling and catcalling from my table companions. Next to me Peter Ramsay puts his fingers in his mouth and lets out a whistle that leaves my eardrums ringing.

By the time Johnno gets out in front of us all it's pretty clear he's drunk. He stands there silently for several seconds before he seems to remember where he is and what he's meant to be doing. He taps the mic a few times and the sound booms around the tent.

"Come on, Johnners!" someone shouts. "We're growing old waiting here!" The guests around my table start drumming with their fists, stamping with their feet. "Speech, speech, speech! Speech, speech, speech!"

The hairs on my arms prickle. It's a reminder of last night: that tribal rhythm, that sense of menace.

Johnno does a "calm down, calm down" motion with his hand. He grins at us all. Then he turns and looks toward Will. He clears his throat, takes a deep breath.

"We go a long way back, this fella and I. Shout-out to all my Old Trevellyans!" A cheer goes up, particularly from the ushers.

"Anyway," Johnno says as the sound dies down, sweeping a hand to indicate Will. "Look at this guy. It would be easy to hate him, wouldn't it?" There's a pause, a beat too long, maybe, before he picks up again. "He's got everything: the looks, the charm, the career, the money"—was that pointed?—"and . . ."—He gestures to Jules—"The girl. So, actually, now I think about it . . . I suppose I *do* hate him. Anyone else with me?"

A ripple of laughter goes around the room; someone shouts: "Hear, hear!"

Johnno grins. There's this wild, dangerous glitter in his eyes. "For those of you who don't know, Will and I were at school together. But it wasn't any normal school. It was more like . . . oh, I don't know . . . a prison camp crossed with *Lord of the Flies*—thanks for giving us that one last night, Charlie boy! See, it wasn't about getting the best grades you could. It was all about survival."

I wonder if I imagined the emphasis on the last word, spoken as though it were a proper noun. I remember the game they told us about, at dinner last night. That was called Survival, wasn't it?

"And let me tell you," Johnno goes on. "We have got into our fair share of shit over the years. I'm talking about the Trevellyan's days in particular. There were some dark times. There were some mental times. Sometimes it felt like it was us versus the rest of the world." He looks over at Will. "Didn't it?"

Will nods, smiles.

There's something a bit strange about Johnno's tone. There's a dangerous edge, a sense that he could do or say anything and take it all completely off the rails. I look around the other tables, I wonder if the other guests are sensing it too. The room has certainly gone a little quiet, as though everyone is holding their breath.

"That's the thing about a best mate, isn't it?" Johnno says. "They've always got your back."

I feel like I'm watching a glass teeter on the edge of a table, unable to do anything about it, waiting for it to shatter. I glance over at Jules and wince. Her mouth is set in a grim line. She looks as though she's waiting for this to all be over.

"And look at this." Johnno gestures to himself. "I'm a fat fucking slob in a too-tight suit. Oh," he turns to Will, "you know how I said I'd *forgotten* my suit? Yeah, there's a little story behind that one." He swivels round to face us, the audience.

"So. Here's the truth—the honest truth. There was never any suit. Or . . . there was a suit, then there wasn't. See, at the beginning, I thought Will might get it for me. I don't know much about these things, but I'm pretty sure that happens with bridesmaids' dresses, doesn't it?"

He looks inquiringly at us all. No one answers. There's a hush in the marquee now—even Peter Ramsay next to me has stopped jiggling his leg up and down.

"Doesn't the bride buy them?" Johnno asks us. "It's the rule, isn't it? You're making someone wear the fucking thing. It's not like it's their choice. And old Will here especially wanted me to have a suit from Paul Smith, nothing less would do."

He's getting into the swing of things now. He's striding back and forth in front of us like a comedian at an open mic night.

"Anyway . . . so we're standing in the shop and I see the label and I think to myself—bloody hell, he's being generous. *Eight hundred quid.* It's the sort of suit that gets you laid, right? But for eight hundred quid? Better to pay to get laid. Like, what use do I have in my life for an eight hundred quid suit? It's not exactly like I've got some fancy do to attend every couple of weeks. Still, I thought. If that's what he wants me to wear, who am I to argue?"

I glance toward Will. He's smiling, but there's a strained look to it.

"But then," Johnno says, "there's this awkward moment by the till, when he sort of stands aside and lets me get on with it. I spend the whole time praying it goes through on my credit card. Total fucking miracle it did, to be perfectly honest. And he stands there, smiling the whole time. Like he'd really bought it for me. Like I should turn round and thank him."

"Shit's just got real," Peter Ramsay whispers.

"So, the next day, I returned the suit. Obviously I wasn't going to tell Will all this. So you see I concocted this whole plan, way before I got here, that I'd pretend I'd left it at home. They couldn't make me go all the way back to Blighty to get it, could they? And thank Christ I live in the middle of nowhere so that none of you lot could 'kindly offer' to go and get it for me—as that would have landed me in hot water, ha ha!"

"Is this meant to be funny?" a woman across from me asks.

"Eight hundred quid for a suit," Johnno says. "Eight hundred. Because it's got some random bloke's name stitched inside the jacket? I'd have had to sell a fucking *kidney.* I'd have had to sell this shit," he runs his hands down his body, lasciviously, to a few halfhearted catcalls, "on the street. And you know there's only limited interest in fat hairy slobs in their midthirties." He gives a big, wild roar of a laugh.

Following suit—like they've been given their cue—some of the audience laugh with him. They're laughs of relief, like the laughs of people who have been holding their breath.

"I mean," Johnno says, not done. "He *could* have bought me the suit, couldn't he? It's not like he's not *loaded*, is it? Mainly thanks to you, Jules love. But he's a stingy bastard. I say that, of course, with *all my love.*" He pretends to flutter his eyelashes at Will in a weird, camp parody.

Will's not smiling anymore. I can't even bring myself to look at Jules's expression. I feel like I shouldn't watch; this is not all that different to that horrible, dark compulsion you have to look at the scene of a car crash.

"Anyway," Johnno says. "Whatever. He lent me his spare, no questions asked. That's stand-up-bloke behavior, isn't it? Though I have to warn you, mate"—he stretches, and the jacket strains against the button holding it closed—"it may never be the same again." He turns to face all of us again. "But that's the thing about a best mate, isn't it? They've always got your back. He might be a tightwad. But I know he's always been there for me."

He puts a big hand on Will's shoulder. Will looks as though he's slightly buckling under the weight, as though Johnno might be putting some downward pressure on it. "And I know, I truly know, that he would never screw me over." He turns to Will, dips in close, as though he's searching Will's face. "*Would you, mate*?"

Will puts up a hand and wipes his face where it seems Johnno's saliva has landed.

There's a pause—an awkward, lengthening pause, during which it becomes clear that Johnno's actually waiting for an answer. Finally, Will says: "No. I wouldn't. Of course I wouldn't."

"Well that's good," Johnno says. "That's great! Because ha ha . . . the *things* we've been through together. The things I know about you, man. It wouldn't be wise, would it? All that history we share together? You remember it, don't you? All those years ago."

He turns back to Will again. Will's face has gone white.

"What the *fuck*," someone on the table whispers, "is Johnno going on about? Is he *on* something?"

"I know," I hear in reply. "This is *mental*."

"And you know what?" Johnno says. "I had a little chat with the ushers, earlier. We thought it might be nice to bring a bit of tradition to the proceedings. For old times' sake." He gestures to the room. "Chaps?"

As if on cue the ushers rise. They all move to surround Will, where he's sitting.

Will shrugs, good-humoredly: "What can you do?" Everyone laughs. But I see that Will's not smiling.

"Seems only fair," Johnno says. "Tradition, and all that. Come on, mate, it'll be fun!"

And between them they grab hold of Will. They're all laughing and cheering—if they weren't it would appear a whole lot more sinister. Johnno has taken his tie off and he wraps it around Will's eyes, tying it, like a blindfold. Then they hoist him up on their shoulders and march off with him. Out of the marquee, into the growing darkness.

JOHNNO

The Best Man

We drop Will on the floor of the Whispering Cave. I guess he won't be delighted about his precious suit touching the wet sand or the fact that the smell in here hits you like a punch in the face: rotting seaweed and sulfur. It's starting to get darker and you have to squint a bit to see properly. The sea's rougher than it was earlier, too: you can hear it crashing against the rocks on either side. The whole way here, as we carried him, Will was laughing and joking with us. "You boys better not be taking me anywhere messy. If I get anything on this suit Jules will kill me," and "Can't I bribe any of you with an extra crate of Bolly to take me back?"

The guys are all laughing. For them, this is all great fun, a bit of a blast from the past. They've been sitting in the marquee for a couple of hours getting drunker and more restless, especially those like Peter Ramsay who have powdered their noses. Before I did my speech I too had a bump in the toilets, with some of the blokes, which was maybe a bad idea. It's only made me more jittery. It's also made everything weirdly clear.

The others are all just excited to be outside. It's a bit like the stag. All the boys together, like it was back in the day. The wind, blowing a gale now, makes it all the more dramatic. We had to bend our heads low against it. It made carrying Will all that much harder.

It's a good spot, here, the Whispering Cave. Pretty out of the way. You can imagine, if there had been a cave like this at Trevellyan's, it would have been used in Survival.

Will is lying on the shingle: not *too* close to the water. Don't know what the tides are like around here. We've bound his wrists and ankles with our ties, as per old school tradition.

"All right, boys," I say. "Let's leave him here for a bit. See if he can make his own way back."

"We're not going to actually leave him there, are we?" Duncan whispers to me, as we climb out of the cave. "Until he works out how to untie himself?"

"Nah," I tell him. "Well, if he hasn't returned in half an hour we'll come get him."

"You better!" Will calls. He's still acting like this is all a big joke. "I've got a wedding to get to!"

I head toward the marquee with the rest of the ushers. "Know what," I say, as we pass the Folly. "I'm gonna peel off here. Gotta take a leak."

I watch them all return to the marquee, laughing and jostling each other. I wish I could be like one of them. I wish for me it was only harmless school memories, a bit of fun. That it could still be a game.

When they're all out of sight, I turn around and start walking back to the cave.

"Who's that?" Will calls, as I approach him. His words echo in the space, so it sounds as though there are five of him saying it.

"It's me," I say. "*Mate.*"

"Johnno?" Will hisses. He's managed to sit up, is leaning against the cave wall. Now the boys have gone he's dropped the act. Even with his eyes covered I can see he's fairly pissed off, his jaw tight. "Untie me, get this blindfold off! I should be at the wedding—Jules will be livid. You've had your joke now. But this isn't funny."

"No," I say. "No, I know it's not. See, I'm not laughing either. It's not that much fun when you're on the other end of it, is it? But you wouldn't know, not up until now. You never did a Survival, did you, at Trevs? Somehow got out of that one too."

I see him frown behind the blindfold. "You know, Johnno," he says, his tone light, friendly. "That speech . . . and now this—I think you might have had a bit too much of the good stuff. Seriously, mate—"

"I'm not your mate," I say. "I think you might be able to guess why."

I played drunker than I am, during the speech. I'm not actually all that drunk. Plus the coke has sharpened me. My mind feels very clear now, like someone's turned on a big bright spotlight in my brain. Lots of stuff is suddenly lit up, making sense.

This is the last time anyone plays me for the fool.

"Up until about two this afternoon I was your mate," I tell him. "But not now, not any longer."

"What are you talking about?" Will asks. He's starting to sound a bit unsure of himself. Yeah, I think. You're right to be scared.

I could see him looking at me the whole way through that speech, wondering what the fuck I was doing. Wondering what I was going to say next, tell all his guests about him. I hope he was shitting himself. I wish I'd gone the whole hog in my speech, told them everything. But I chickened out. Like I chickened out all those years ago—when *I* should have gone to the teachers, too, backed up whichever kid it was that snitched on us. Told them exactly what we had done. They wouldn't have been able to ignore two of us, would they?

But I couldn't do it then, and I couldn't do it in the speech. Because I'm a fucking coward.

This is the next best thing.

"I had an interesting chat with Piers earlier," I say. "Very *educational*."

I see Will swallow. "Look," he says, carefully, his tone very reasonable, man-to-man. It only makes me more angry. "I don't know what Piers said to you, but—"

"You fucked me over," I say. "Piers didn't actually need to say all that much. I worked it out for myself. Yeah, me. Stupid Johnno, must try harder. You couldn't have me there, could you? Too much of a liability. Reminding you of what you once were. What you did."

Will grimaces. "Johnno, mate, I—"

"You and me," I say. "See, it was meant to be you and me, sticking up for each other, always. Us against the world, that's what you said. Especially after what we'd done, what we knew about each other. I had your back, you had mine. That's how I thought it was."

"It is, Johnno. You're my best man—"

"Can I tell you something?" I say. "The whole whiskey business?"

"Oh yeah," Will says quickly, eagerly. "Hellraiser!"

He's remembered it this time. "See, there you go! You're doing so well for yourself. No need for all this bitterness—"

"Nah." I cut him off again. "See, it doesn't exist."

"What are you talking about? Those bottles you've given us . . ."

"Are fakes." I shrug, even though he can't see me. "It's some single malt from the supermarket, decanted into plain bottles. Got my mate Alan to make up labels for me."

"Johnno, what—"

"I mean, I did actually think I could do it at the beginning. That's what makes it so tragic. It's why I got Alan to mock the design up at first, to see how it might look. But do you know how hard it is to launch a whiskey brand these days? Unless you're David Beckham. Or you have rich parents to bankroll you, or connections with important people? I have none of that. I never did. All the other boys at Trevs knew it. I know some of them called me a pikey behind my back. But what *we* had, I thought that was solid."

Will's shifting on the ground, trying to sit up. I'm not going to help him. "Johnno, mate, Jesus—"

"Yeah, oh, and I didn't leave the wilderness retreat to set up the whiskey brand. How pathetic is this? Wait for it . . . I got fired for being stoned on the job. Like a teenager. This fat bloke on a team-bonding course—I let him go down too fast on the rope and he broke an ankle. And do you know why I was stoned?"

"Why?" he asks, wary.

"Because I have to smoke it, to get by. Because it's the only thing that helps me forget. See, it feels like my whole life stopped at that point, all those years ago. It's like—it's like . . . nothing good has happened since. The one good thing that's happened to me in the years after Trevs was that shot at the TV show—and you took it away from me." I pause, take a deep breath, prepare to say what I've finally come to realize, after nearly twenty years. "But it's not like that for you, is it? It's like the past doesn't affect you. It didn't matter to you at all. You carry on taking what you need. And you always get away with it."

HANNAH

The Plus-One

The four ushers explode back into the marquee. Peter Ramsay does a knee-slide across the laminate, nearly crashing into the table bearing the magnificent wedding cake. I see Duncan leap on to Angus's back, his arm making a tight headlock around his neck so his face begins to turn purple. Angus staggers, half-laughing, half-gasping for breath. Then Femi jumps on top of both of them and they collapse in a tangled heap of limbs. They're pumped up, excited by their stunt I suppose, carrying Will out of the marquee like that.

"To the bar, boys!" Duncan roars, leaping to his feet. "Time to raise hell!"

The rest of the guests follow them, taking this as their cue, laughing and chattering. I stay sitting in my seat. Most seem thrilled, titillated, by the speech and the spectacle that came after it. But I can't say I feel the same—though Will was smiling there was a disturbing undertone about it all: the blindfold, tying his hands and feet like that. I look across to the top table and see that it is almost completely deserted apart from Jules, who is sitting very still, apparently lost in thought.

Suddenly there's a commotion from the bar tent. Raised voices.

"Whoa—steady on!"

"What the fuck is your problem, mate?"

"Jesus, calm down—"

And then, unmistakably, my husband's voice. Oh God. I get to my feet and hurry toward the bar. There's a press of people, all avidly watching, like children on a playground. I shove my way through to the front as quickly as I can.

Charlie is crouched on the floor. Then I realize that his fist is raised and he's half-straddling another man: Duncan.

"Say that again," Charlie says.

For a moment I can only stare at him: my husband—geography teacher, father of two, usually such a mild man. I haven't seen this side of him for a very long time. Then I realize I have to act. "Charlie!" I say, rushing forward. He turns and for a moment he just blinks at me, like he hardly recognizes me. He's flushed, trembling with adrenaline. I can smell the booze on his breath. "Charlie—what the hell are you doing?"

He seems to come to his senses a little at this. And, thank God, he gets up without too much fuss. Duncan straightens his shirt, muttering under his breath. As Charlie follows me, the crowd parting to let us pass, I can feel all the guests watching silently. Now that my immediate horror has receded I simply feel mortified.

"What on earth was that?" I ask him as we return to the main tent, sit down at the nearest table. "Charlie—what's got into you?"

"I had enough," he says. There's definitely a slur to his speech and I can see how much he's drunk by the bitter set of his mouth. "He was mouthing off about the stag, and I've had enough."

"Charlie," I say. "What *happened* on the stag?"

He gives a long groan, covers his face with his hands.

"Tell me," I say. "How bad can it be? Really?"

Charlie's shoulders slump. He seems resigned to telling me, suddenly. He takes a deep breath. There's a long pause. And then, at last, he begins to talk.

"We got a ferry to this place a couple of hours' ride from Stockholm, made a camp there on an island in the archipelago. It was very . . . you know, boy's own, putting up tents, lighting a fire. Someone had bought some steaks and we cooked them over the embers. I didn't know any of the blokes other than Will, but they seemed all right, I suppose."

Suddenly it's all tumbling out of him, the booze he's drunk loosening his tongue. They'd all been to Trevellyan's together, he tells me, so there was a lot of boring reminiscing about that; Charlie just sat there and smiled and tried to look interested. He didn't want to drink much, obviously, and they mocked him about that. Then one of them—Pete, Charlie thinks—produced some mushrooms.

"You ate mushrooms, Charlie? *Magic* mushrooms?" I nearly laugh. This doesn't sound at all like my sensible, safety-conscious husband. I'm the one who's up for trying stuff out, who dipped her foot into it a couple of times in my teenage years on the Manchester club scene.

Charlie screws up his face. "Yeah, well, we were all doing it. When you're in a group of blokes like that . . . you don't say no, do you? And I didn't go to their posh school, so I was already the odd one out."

But you're thirty-four, I want to say to him. What would you say to Ben, if his friends were telling him to do something he didn't want to? Then I think of last night, as I downed that drink while they all chanted at me. Even though I didn't want to, knew I didn't actually have to. "So. You took magic mushrooms?" This is my husband, Deputy Head, who has a strict zero-tolerance policy of drugs at his school. "Oh my God," I say, and I do laugh now—I can't help it. "Imagine what the PTA would say about that!"

Next, Charlie tells me, they all got into the canoes and went to another island. They were jumping in the water, naked. They dared Charlie to swim out to a third tiny island—there were lots of dares like that—and then when he got back, they'd all gone. They had left him there, without his canoe.

"I had no clothes. It might have been spring, but it's the fucking Arctic Circle, Han. It's freezing at night. I was there for hours before they finally came for me. I was coming down from the mushrooms. I was so cold. I thought I was going to get hypothermia . . . I thought I was going to die. And when they found me I was—"

"What?"

"I was crying. I was lying on the ground, sobbing like a child."

He looks mortified enough to cry now and my heart goes out to him. I want to give him a hug, like I would Ben—but I'm not sure how it would go down. I know men do stupid stuff on stags, but this sounds targeted, like they were singling Charlie out. That's not right, is it?

"That's—horrible," I say. "That's like bullying, Charlie. I mean, it is bullying."

Charlie has a fixed, faraway expression. I can't read it. The arrogance of having always assumed I know my husband inside out. We've been together for years. But it has taken less than twenty-four hours in this strange place to show that assumption up for the illusion it is. I've felt it ever since we made that crossing over here. Charlie has seemed increasingly like a stranger to me. The stag do is one more confirmation of this: the discovery of a horrific experience that he has kept from me, that I now suspect might have changed him in some complex, invisible way. The truth is, I don't think Charlie is quite himself at the moment: or not the self I know. This place has done something to him—to us.

"It was all *his* idea," Charlie says. "I'm sure of it."

"Whose idea? Duncan's?"

"No. He's an idiot. A follower. Will. He was the ringleader. You could tell. And Johnno too. The others were all acting on instructions."

I can't quite imagine Will making the others do that. Anyway, the stags are normally the ones to call the shots, not the groom. Yeah, I can see *Johnno* being behind it, no problem, especially after that stunt just now. He has that slightly wild air about him. Not malicious, but like he might push things too far without really meaning to. Definitely Duncan. But not Will. I think Charlie prefers to hang the blame on Will simply because he doesn't like him.

"You don't believe me, do you?" Charlie says, his expression darkening. "You don't think it was Will."

"Well," I say. "If I'm honest, not really. Because—"

"Because you want to screw him?" he snarls. "Yeah, did you think I hadn't noticed? I saw the way you looked at him last night, Hannah. Even the way you say his name." He does a horrible little falsetto. "Oh Will, tell me about that time you got frostbite, oh, you're so masculine . . ."

The ferocity of his tone is so unexpected that I recoil from him. It's been so long since Charlie's been drunk that I'd forgotten the extent of the transformation. But I'm also reacting to the tiny element of truth in it. A flicker of guilt at the memory of how I found myself responding to Will. But it quickly transforms itself to anger.

"Charlie," I hiss, "how . . . how *dare* you speak to me like that? Do you realize how offensive you're being? All because he made some effort to make me feel welcome—which is a hell of a lot more than *you* did."

And then I remember last night, that flirting with Jules. That slinking into our bedroom in the small hours when he definitely hadn't been drinking with the men.

"Actually," I say, my voice rising, "you haven't got a leg to stand on. That whole horrible charade with you and Jules last night. She's always acting like she has you wrapped around her little finger—and you play along. Do you know how it makes me feel?" My voice cracks. "Do you?" I'm caught between anger and tears, the pressure and loneliness of the day catching up with me.

Charlie looks slightly chastened. He opens his mouth to speak but I shake my head.

"You've had sex with her, haven't you?" I've never wanted to know before. But now, I'm feeling brave enough to ask it.

There's a long pause. Charlie puts his head in his hands. "Once," he says, voice muffled through his fingers. "But . . . ages and ages ago, honestly . . ."

"When? When was it? When you were teenagers?"

He lifts his head. Opens his mouth, as though to speak, then closes it again. His expression. Oh my God. *Not* when they were teenagers. I feel as though I have been punched in the stomach. But I have to know now. "Later?" I ask.

He sighs, then nods.

My throat seems to close up so that it's a struggle

to get the words out. "Was it . . . was it when we were together?"

Charlie folds over into himself, puts his face in his hands again. He lets out a long, low groan. "Han . . . I'm so sorry. It didn't mean anything, honest. It was so stupid. You were . . . it was, well, it was when we hadn't had sex for ages. It was—"

"After I had Ben." I feel sick to my stomach. I'm suddenly certain. He doesn't say anything and that's all the confirmation I need.

Finally, he speaks. "You know . . . we were going through a rough patch. You were, well . . . you were so down all the time, and I didn't know what to do, how to help—"

"You mean, when I had borderline postnatal depression? When I was waiting for the stitches to heal? Jesus Christ, Charlie—"

"I'm so sorry." All the bluster has gone out of him now. I could almost believe he's completely sober. "I'm so sorry, Han. Jules had just broken up with that boyfriend she had at the time—we went out for drinks after work . . . I had too much. We both agreed it was a terrible idea, afterwards, that it would never happen again. *It didn't mean anything.* I mean, I barely remember it. Han—look at me."

I can't look at him. I won't look at him.

It's so horrible I can barely begin to think about it clearly. I feel like I'm in shock, like the full hurt of it hasn't sunk in yet. But it throws all that flirting, all that physical closeness, into a new, terrible light. I think of all the times I have felt Jules has purposefully excluded me—cordoning off Charlie for herself.

That bitch.

"So all this time," I say, "all this time that you've been telling me you've only ever been friends, that a bit of flirting means nothing, that she's like a sister to you . . . that's not fucking true, is it? I have no idea what the two of you were doing last night. I don't want to know. But how *dare* you?"

"Han—" He reaches out a hand, touches my wrist, tentatively.

"No—don't touch me." I snatch my arm away, stand up. "And you're a state," I say. "An embarrassment. Whatever they did to you on the stag, there's no excuse for your behavior just now. Yeah, maybe it was awful, what they did. But it didn't do you any lasting harm, did it? For Christ's sake, you're a grown man—a father . . ." I almost add "a husband" but can't bring myself to. "You've got responsibilities," I say. "And you know what? I'm sick of looking after you. I don't care. You can sort out your own bloody mess." I turn and stride away.

JOHNNO

The Best Man

"Johnno," Will says, with a little laugh. The cave walls echo the laugh back at us. "I really don't know what you're talking about. All this talk of the past. It isn't good for you. You have to move on."

Yeah, I think, but I can't. It's like some part of me got stuck there. As much as I've tried to forget it, it has been there at the center of me, this toxic thing. I feel like nothing has happened in my life since, nothing that matters anyway. And I wonder how Will has been able to carry on living his life, without even a backward glance.

"They said it was a tragic accident," I say. "But it wasn't. It was us, Will. It was all our fault."

"I've been tidying the dorm," Loner said, when we came in from rugby practice. I'd told him to do it, as

I'd run out of other stuff for him to do. "But I found these." He held them in his hand as though they might burn him: a stack of GCSE exam papers.

He looked at Will. You'd think from Loner's expression that someone had died. I suppose for him someone had died: his hero.

"Put them back," Will said, very quiet.

"You shouldn't have taken them," Loner said, which I thought showed courage, considering we were both about twice his height. He was a pretty brave kid, and decent, too, when I think about it. Which I try not to. He shook his head. "It's—it's cheating."

Will turned to me, after he'd left the room. "You're a fucking idiot," he said. "Why'd you get him to tidy it when you knew they were there?" He was the one that had stolen them, not me. Though I'm sure now that he'd have let me take the blame if it got out.

I remember how he gave a grin then that wasn't really a grin at all. "You know what?" he said. "I think tonight we'll play Survival."

"You couldn't bear it," I say to Will. "Because you knew you'd get expelled if it got out. And your fucking reputation has always been so important to you. It's always been like that. You take what you want. And fuck everyone else, if they might get in your way. Even me."

"Johnno," Will says, his tone calm, rational. "You've had too much to drink. You don't know what you're saying. If it had been our fault, we wouldn't have got away with it. Would we?"

It only took the two of us. There were four boys in Loner's dorm that night—a couple of them had got sick and were in the infirmary. That helped. I felt like maybe one of them stirred when we came in, but we were quick. I felt like an assassin—and it was fucking brilliant. It was fun. I wasn't really thinking. Just adrenaline, pumping through me. I shoved a rugby sock into his mouth while Will tied the blindfold, so that any noises he made were pretty muffled and quiet. It wasn't hard to carry him: he weighed nothing at all.

He struggled a bit. He didn't wet himself, though, like some of the boys did. As I say, he was a pretty brave kid.

I thought we'd go into the woods. But Will motioned to the cliffs. I looked at him, not understanding. For one horrible moment it felt like he might suggest we throw the kid off them. "The cliff path," he mouthed at me. "Yeah, OK." I was relieved. It took us ages, climbing down the cliff path, with the chalk disintegrating with every step, our feet skidding, and we couldn't even use the handrail, hammered into the rock, because our hands were full. The kid had stopped struggling. He'd gone very still. I remember I was worried he couldn't breathe, so I went to take the gag out, but Will shook his head. "He can breathe through his nose," he said. Maybe it was around then that I started feeling bad. I told myself that was stupid: We had all been through it, hadn't we? We kept on going.

Finally we were on the beach, down on the wet sand. I couldn't work out how we were going to make this hard. It would be obvious where he was, once he'd got the blindfold off, even without his glasses. It wasn't that far from the school and anyone could climb up that cliff path—a little kid, especially. Boys went down to the beach all the time. But I thought: maybe Will wanted to make it easy for him, after all, because of all the stuff he'd done for us—cleaning our boots and tidying our dorm and all of the rest. That seemed fair.

"You know it, Will," I say. A noise comes up from somewhere deep inside my chest, a sound of pain. I think I might be crying. "We *should* have paid for it, what we did."

I remember how Will pointed to the bottom of the cliff path. That was when he produced some laces. Nothing fancy, the laces from a pair of rugby boots.

"We're going to tie him up," he said.

It was easy in the end. Will got me to tie him to the handrail at the bottom of the cliff path—I was pretty good with knots, that sort of thing. *Now* I got it. That would make it a bit more difficult. He'd have to do a Houdini to get out of there, that was the part that would take the time.

Then we left him.

"For *God's* *sake,* Johnno," Will says. "You heard what they said, at the time. It was a terrible accident."

"You know that isn't true—"

"No. That is the truth. There isn't anything else."

I remember waking up the next day and looking out of the window in our dorm and seeing the sea. And that was when I realized. I couldn't believe how stupid we'd been. The tide had come in.

"Will," I said, "Will—I don't think he could have untied himself. The tide . . . I didn't think. Oh God, I think he might be—" I thought I might throw up.

"Shut up, Johnno," Will said. "Nothing happened, OK? First of all, we need to work that out between us, Johnno. Otherwise, we're in big trouble, you get that, right?"

I couldn't believe it was happening. I wanted to go to

sleep and wake up and none of it be real. It didn't seem real, something so fucking terrible. All for the sake of a few bits of stolen paper.

"OK," Will said. "Do you agree? We were in bed. We don't know anything."

He'd jumped so quickly ahead. I hadn't even thought about that stuff, telling someone. But I guess I would have assumed that was what we had to do. That was the right thing, wasn't it? You couldn't keep something like this secret.

But I wasn't going to disagree with him. His face kind of scared me. His eyes had changed—like there was no light behind them. I nodded, slowly. I guess I didn't think then about what it would mean, later, how it would destroy me.

"Say it out loud," Will told me.

"Yeah," I said, and my voice came out as a croak.

He was dead. He hadn't been able to get himself free. It was a Tragic Accident. That was what we all got told a week later in assembly after he had been found, washed up farther along the beach, by the school caretaker. I suppose the ties must have come undone after all, just not in time to save him. You'd have thought there would have been marks, anyway. The local police chief was a mate of Will's dad. The two of them would drink together in Will's dad's study. I guess that helped.

"I remember his parents," I say to Will now. "Coming to the school, after. His mum looked like she wanted to die, too." I saw her, from the dorm upstairs, getting out of her car. She looked up and I had to step out of sight, trembling.

I crouch down so I'm level with Will. I grip his shoulders, hard, make him look me in the eye. "We killed him, Will. We killed that boy."

He fights me off, throwing his arms out blindly. His fingernails catch my neck, scratching under my collar. It stings. I shove him against the rock with one hand.

"Johnno," Will says, breathing hard. "You need to get a grip of yourself. You need to shut the *fuck* up." And that's when I know I've gotten to him. He hardly ever swears. It doesn't fit with his golden boy image, I guess.

"Did you know?" I ask him. "You did know, didn't you?"

"Did I know what? I don't know what you're talking about. For Christ's sake, Johnno—untie me. This has gone on long enough."

"Did you know that the tide would come in?"

"I don't know what you're talking about. Johnno—

you're not making sense. I knew it last night, mate, and in the speech. You've been drinking too much. Do you have a problem? Look. I'm your friend. There are ways to get help. I can help you. But stop with this fantasizing."

I push my hair out of my eyes. Even though it's cold I feel the sweat come away on my fingers. "*I* was a fucking idiot. I've always been the slow one, I know that. I'm not saying it's an excuse. I was the one who tied him up, yeah, when you told me to. But I didn't think about the tide. I didn't think about it until the next morning, when it was too late."

"Johnno," Will hisses, like he's scared someone might come.

It only makes me want to be louder. "All this time," I say. "All this time, I've wondered that. And I gave you the benefit of the doubt. I thought: yeah, Will could be a dick at school at times, but we all were. You had to be, to survive in that place."

It made us into animals.

I think of the kid, how he was an example of what happened if you weren't—if you were too good, too honest, if you didn't understand the rules.

"But," I say, "I thought: 'Will's not *evil.* He wouldn't kill a kid. Not over some stolen exam papers. Even if it meant he might get expelled.'"

"I didn't kill him," Will says. "No one killed him. The water killed him. The game killed him, maybe. But not *us*. It's not our fault he didn't get away."

"Yeah," I say. "Yeah, that's what I've told myself, all these years. I've repeated the story you created. It was the game. But we *were* the game, Will. He thought we were his mates. He trusted us."

"Johnno." Now he's angry. He leans forward. "Get a *fucking* grip. I'm not going to let you ruin all of this for me. Because you've got some regrets about the past, because your life is a mess and you don't have anything to lose. A little kid like him—he wouldn't ever have survived in the real world. He was a runt. If it wasn't us, it would have been something else."

The term ended early, because of the death. Everyone turned their attention to the upcoming summer holidays and it seemed like the kid had never existed. I suppose he barely had for the rest of the school: he was a first year, a nonentity.

Except there was a snitch. One pupil who sneaked on us. I was always sure it was Loner's fat little friend. He said he'd seen us come into the dorm room, tie Loner up. It didn't get very far. Will's dad was headmaster, of course. He was a dick, most of the time—more to Will than anyone else. But for this, he had Will's back and mine too.

And we had each other's.

All these years we've stuck together—bound by memories, by the dark shit we went through together, the thing we did. I thought he felt the same way about it too, that we needed each other. But what the TV stuff shows is that all that time he wanted out of our friendship. I'm too much of a liability. He wanted to distance himself from me. No wonder he looked so fucking uncomfortable when I told him I would be his best man.

"Johnno," Will says. "Think about my dad. You know what he's like. That's why I was desperate to try and get those grades. I *had* to do it. And if he'd found out the truth, how I hid those papers—he would have killed me. So I wanted to scare the kid—"

"Don't you dare," I say. "Don't you start feeling sorry for yourself. Do you know how many free passes you've been given? Because of how you look, how you manage to convince people that you're this great bloke?" It's only made me angrier, his self-pity. "I'm going to tell them," I say. "I can't deal with it any longer. I'm going to tell them all—"

"You wouldn't dare," Will says, his voice changed

now—low and hard. "You'd ruin our lives. Your life too."

"Ha!" I say. "It already ruined my life. It's been destroying me ever since that morning, when you told me to keep my mouth shut. I never would have stayed silent in the first place if it weren't for you. Since that boy died there hasn't been a day when I haven't thought about it, felt like I should have told someone. But you? Oh, no, it hasn't affected you in any way, has it? You've just gone on, like you always have. No consequences. Well you know what? I think it's about time that there are some. It'd be a relief, as far as I'm concerned. I'd only be doing what we should have done years ago."

There's a sound in the cave then, a woman's voice: "Hello?"

Both of us freeze.

"Will?" It's the wedding planner. "Are you in here?" She appears around the bend of the rock wall. "Oh, hello, Johnno. Will, I've been sent to find you—the other ushers told me that they'd left you in here." She sounds totally calm and professional, even though we're all standing in a bloody great cave, and one of us is slumped on the ground tied up and blindfolded. "It's been nearly half an hour, so Julia wanted me to come and . . . well, rescue you. I should warn you that she's not—" She looks like she's trying to find a way to put it delicately. "She's not as delighted as she might be by this . . . and the band are about to start."

She waits, as I untie Will and help him up, watching over us like a schoolteacher. Then we follow her out of the cave. I can't help wondering if she heard or saw anything. Or what I would have done if she hadn't interrupted us.

AOIFE

The Wedding Planner

In the marquee the celebrations have moved into another gear. The guests have drunk the champagne dry. Now they are moving on to the stronger stuff: cocktails and shots at the temporary bar. They are high on the freedom of the night.

In the toilets in the Folly, refreshing the hand towels, I find telltale spills of fine white powder on the floor, scattered across the slate sink surround. I'm not surprised, I've seen guests wiping their noses furtively as they return to the marquee. They have behaved themselves for the rest of the day, this lot. They have traveled long distances to be here. They have come bearing gifts. They have dressed themselves appropriately and sat through a ceremony and listened to the speeches and worn the proper expressions and said the right things. But they're adults who have briefly left their responsibilities behind; they're like children without their parents present. Now this part of the day is theirs for the taking. Even as the bride and groom wait to begin their first dance they press forward, ready to make the dance floor their own.

An hour or so earlier, on a trip back to the Folly, I heard a strange noise, upstairs. The rest of the building was barricaded off, of course, but there are only so many measures you can take to stop drunk people going where they want. I went up to inspect, pushed open the door of the bride and groom's bedroom and found, not the happily married couple, but another man and woman, bent low over the bed. At my intrusion they scrambled to cover themselves, she yanking down her skirts red-faced, he covering his bobbing erection with his own top hat. Only a little while later, I saw them both returning innocently to different corners of the marquee. What particularly interested me about this was that they both appeared to be wearing wedding bands. And yet—and I've probably memorized the table plan as well as Julia herself now—I happen to know that all husbands and wives are seated opposite each other.

They weren't worried about me, though: not really. Their initial panic at my entrance gave way to a kind of giggly relief. They know I won't expose their secret. Besides, I wasn't particularly surprised. I've seen much of the same before. This extremity of behavior is very much par for the course. There are always secrets around the fringes of a wedding. I hear the things said in confidence, the bitchy remarks, the gossip. I heard some of the best man's words in the cave.

This is the thing about organizing a wedding. I can put together a perfect day, as long as the guests play along, remember to stay within certain bounds. But if they don't, the repercussions can last far longer than twenty-four hours. No one is capable of controlling that sort of fallout.

JULES

The Bride

The band have begun to play. Will—who returned to the marquee looking slightly unkempt—takes my hand as we step onto the laminate floor. I realize I'm holding his hand hard enough to hurt, probably—and I tell myself to loosen my grip. But I'm incensed by the interruption to the evening caused by the ushers and their stupid prank. The guests surround us, whooping, hollering. Their faces are flushed and sweaty, their teeth bared, their eyes wide. They're drunk—and more. They press forward, leaning in, and the space suddenly feels too small. They're so close that I can smell them: perfume and cologne, the sour, yeasty smell of Guinness and champagne, body odor, booze-soured breath. I smile at them all because that is what I am meant to do. I smile so much that there is a dull ache somewhere beneath my ears and my whole jaw feels like an overstretched piece of elastic.

I hope I'm giving an impression of having a good time. I've drunk a lot, but it hasn't had any discernible effect other than making me more wary, more jittery. Since that speech I've been feeling a mounting unease. I look around me. Everyone else is having a great time: their inhibitions truly thrown off now. To them the train wreck of a speech is probably a mere footnote to the day—an amusing anecdote.

Will and I turn one way, then the other. He spins me away from him and back again. The guests shout their appreciation of these modest moves. We didn't go to dance lessons, because that would be unspeakably naff, but Will is a naturally good dancer. Except that a couple of times he treads on the train of my dress; I have to yank it away from under his feet before I trip. It's unlike him, to be so graceless. He seems distracted.

"What on earth was all of that?" I ask, when I'm drawn to his chest. I whisper it as though I am whispering a sweet nothing into his ear.

"Oh, it was stupid," Will says. "Boys being boys. Messing around, you know. A little leftover from the stag, maybe." He smiles, but he doesn't look quite himself. He downed two large glasses of wine when he returned to the marquee: one after the other. He shrugs. "Johnno's idea of a joke."

"The seaweed was supposedly a little joke last night," I say. "And that wasn't very bloody funny. And now this? And that speech—what did he mean by all of that? What was all that about the past? About keeping secrets from each other . . . what secrets did he mean?"

"Oh," Will says, "I don't know, Jules. It's only Johnno messing around. It's nothing."

We turn a slow circle about the floor. I have an impression of beaming faces, hands clapping.

"But it didn't *sound* like nothing," I say. "It sounded very *much* like something. Will, what sort of hold does he have over you?"

"Oh for God's sake, Jules," he says sharply. "I said: it's nothing. *Drop* it. *Please.*"

I stare at him. It's not the words themselves so much as the way he said them—that and the way he has tightened his hold on my arm. It feels like as strong a corroboration as one could ask for that whatever it is, it's very much *not* nothing.

"You're hurting me," I say, pulling my arm out of his grip.

He is immediately contrite. "Jules—look, I'm sorry." His voice is totally different now—any hint of hostility immediately gone. "I didn't mean to snap at you. Look, it's been a long day. A wonderful day, of course, but a long one. Forgive me?" And he gives me a smile, the same smile I haven't been able to resist since I saw it that night at the V&A museum. And yet it doesn't have the same effect it normally does. If anything, it makes me feel more uneasy, because of the speed of the change. It's as though he's pulled on a mask.

"We're a married couple, now," I say. "We are meant to be able to share things with one another. To confide in each other."

Will spins me away under his arm, and toward him again. The crowd cheer this flourish.

Then, when we're facing one another once more, he takes a deep breath. "Look," he says. "Johnno has got this bee in his bonnet about this thing that he says happened in the past, when we were young. He's obsessed by it. But he's a fantasist. I've felt sorry for him, all these years. That's where I went wrong. Feeling I should pander to him, because my life has worked out, and his hasn't. Now he's envious: of everything I have, we have. He thinks that I owe him."

"Oh for God's sake," I say. "What could *you* possibly owe him? He's the one that's clearly been hanging on your coattails for too long."

He doesn't answer this. Instead he pulls me close,

as the song comes to its crescendo. A cheer goes up from the crowd. But they sound suddenly far away. "After tonight, that's it," Will says firmly, into my hair. "I'll cut him from my life—our life. I promise. I'm done with him. Trust me. I'll sort it out."

HANNAH

The Plus-One

I've wandered into the dance tent. The first dance is over, thank God, and all the guests who were watching have swarmed in to fill the space. I'm not sure what I want to find in here, exactly. Some distraction, I suppose, from the churn of thoughts in my head. Charlie and Jules. It's too painful to think about.

It feels as though every single guest is crammed in here, a hot press of bodies. The band's vocalist takes to the mic: "Are you ready to dance, girls and boys?"

They begin to play a frenzied rhythm—four fiddles, a wild, foot-tapping tune. Bodies are crashing around as everyone attempts, unsuccessfully, drunkenly, to do his or her version of an Irish jig. I see Will grab Olivia out of the crowd: "Time for the groom to claim his dance with the bridesmaid!" But they seem oddly out of step as they careen onto the dance floor, as though one of them is resisting the other. Olivia's expression gives me pause. She looks trapped. There was this bit in the speech. I thought that before. What was it? It had struck me as oddly familiar. I grope about in my memory for it, trying to focus.

The V&A museum, that was it. I remember her telling me last night about how she brought Steven there, to a party, held by Jules. And everything goes still as it occurs to me—

But that's completely crazy. It *can't* be. It wouldn't make any sense. It must be a weird coincidence.

"Hey," a guy says, as I push past him. "What's the hurry?"

"Oh," I say, glancing vaguely in his direction. "Sorry. I was . . . a bit distracted."

"Well, maybe a dance will help with that." He grins. I look at him more closely. He's pretty attractive—tall, black-haired, a dimple forming in one cheek when he smiles. And before I can say anything he takes hold of my hand and gives me a gentle tug toward him, onto the laminate of the dance floor. I don't resist.

"I saw you earlier," he shouts, over the music. "In the church, sitting on your own. And I thought: *She* looks worth getting to know." That grin again. Oh. He thinks I'm single, here by myself. He can't have caught that scene with Charlie in the bar.

"Luis!" he shouts now, pointing to his chest.

"Hannah."

Maybe I should explain that I'm here with my husband. But I don't want to think about Charlie right now. And holding this flattering new image of myself through his eyes—not the badly dressed imposter I thought I was, but someone attractive, mysterious—I decide not to say anything. I allow myself to begin to move in time with him, to the music. I allow him to move a little nearer, his eyes on mine. Perhaps I move closer, too. Close enough that I can smell his sweat—but clean sweat, a good smell. There's a stirring in the pit of my stomach. A little sting of want.

NOW
THE WEDDING NIGHT

Someone else out there. The thought has them spooking at shadows, cringing away from shapes in the blackness, which seem to loom up at them and then reveal themselves to be nothing more than tricks of the eye. They move in a tight, close pack, afraid of losing another of their number. Pete is still missing.

They seem to feel the prickle of unknown eyes upon them. They feel clumsier now, more exposed. They trip and stumble over the uneven ground, over hidden tussocks of heather. They try not to think about Pete. They can't afford to: they have to look out for themselves. Every so often they shout to one another for reassurance more than anything else, their voices like another light held against the night, uncharacteristically caring: "All right there, Angus?" "Yeah—you OK, Femi?" It helps them to keep going. It helps them forget about their mounting fear.

"Jesus—what's that?" Femi sweeps his flashlight in a wide arc. It illuminates an upright form, rising palely out of the shadows, nearly as tall as a man. And then several similar shapes, some smaller, too.

"It's the graveyard," Angus calls, softly. They gaze at the Celtic crosses, the crumbling stone forms: an eerie, silent army.

"Christ," Duncan shouts. "I thought it was a person." For a moment they all thought it: the round shape and thin upright base conspired briefly to seem human. Even now, as they retreat somewhat gingerly, it is hard to shake the feeling of being watched, reproachfully, by the many sentinel forms.

They continue for a time in a new direction.

"Do you hear that?" Angus shouts. "I think we've got too close to the sea now."

They stop. Somewhere near at hand they are vaguely aware of the crash of water against rock. They can feel the ground shuddering beneath their feet at the impact of it.

"OK. Right." Femi thinks. "The graveyard's behind us, the sea's here. So I think we need to go—that way."

They begin to creep away from the sound of the crashing surf.

"Hey—there's something there—"

Instantly, they all stop where they are.

"What did you say, Angus?"

"I said there's something there. Look."

They hold out their flashlights. The beams they cast tremble on the ground. They are bracing themselves to find a grisly sight. They are surprised, and rather relieved, when it reflects brightly off the hard gleam of metal.

"It's a—what is it?"

Femi, bravest among them, steps forward and picks it up. Turning to them, shielding his eyes from the glare, he lifts it so they can all see. They recognize the object immediately; although it is mangled out of shape, the metal twisted and broken. It is a gold crown.

EARLIER THAT DAY

OLIVIA

The Bridesmaid

I wander round the corners of the marquee. I move between the tables. I pick up half-full glasses, the remains of people's drinks, and down them. I want to get as drunk as possible.

I pulled away from Will as quickly as I could, after he grabbed me for that dance. It made me feel sick, being so close to him, feeling his body pressed up against me, thinking of the things I've done with him . . . the things he got me to do . . . the horrible secret between us. It was like he was getting off on it. Right at the end he whispered in my ear: "That crazy stunt you pulled earlier . . . that's the end of it, OK? No more. Do you hear me? No more."

No one seems to notice me as I go about minesweeping their discarded drinks. They're all pretty wasted by now and, besides, they've abandoned the tables for the dance floor. It's absolutely crammed in there. There are all these thirty-somethings slut-dropping and grinding on each other as though they're in some shit strip club dancing to 50 Cent, not a marquee on a deserted island with some guys playing fiddles.

The old me might have found it funny. I could imagine texting my mates, giving them a live running commentary on the absolute cringe fest going on in front of me.

A few of the waiters are watching everyone from the corners of the marquee, sort of hovering on the edges of things. Some of them are about my age, younger. They all hate us, it's so obvious. And I'm not surprised. I feel like I hate them too. Especially the men. I've been touched on the shoulder, on the hip and on the bum tonight by some of the blokes here, Will and Jules's so-called friends. Hands grabbing, stroking, squeezing, cupping—out of sight of wives and girlfriends, as though I'm a piece of meat. I'm sick of it.

The last time it happened, I turned around and gave the guy such a poisonous stare that he actually backed away from me, making a stupid wide-eyed face and holding his hands up in the air—all mock-innocent. If it happens again I feel like I might really lose it.

I drink some more. The taste in my mouth is foul: sour and stale. I need to drink until I don't care about that sort of thing. Until I can't taste or feel anymore.

And then I'm seized by my cousin Beth and dragged toward the dance tent. Other than earlier, outside the church, I haven't seen Beth since last year at my aunt's birthday. She's wearing a ton of makeup but underneath you can see she's still a child, her face round and soft, her eyes wide. I want to tell her to wipe off the lipstick and eyeliner, to stay in that safe childhood space for a while longer.

On the dance floor, surrounded by all these bodies, moving and shoving, the room begins to spin. It's like all the stuff I've drunk has caught up with me in one big rush. And then I trip—maybe over someone's foot or maybe it's my own stupid, too-high shoes. I go down, hard, with a crack that I hear a long time before I feel it. I think I've hit my head.

Through the fug, I hear Beth speaking to someone nearby. "She's really drunk, I think. Oh my God."

"Get Jules," someone says. "Or her mum."

"Can't see Jules anywhere."

"Oh, look, here's Will."

"Will, she's pretty drunk. Can you help? I don't know what to do—"

He comes toward me, smiling. "Oh Olivia. What

happened?" He reaches out a hand to me. "Come on, let's get you up."

"No," I say. I bat his hand away. "Fuck off."

"Come on," Will says, his voice so kind, so gentle. I feel him lifting me up, and it doesn't seem like there's much point in struggling. "Let's get you some air." He puts his hands on my shoulders.

"Get your hands off me!" I try to fight my way out of his grip.

I hear a murmur from the people watching us. I'm the difficult one, I bet that's what they're saying to each other. I'm the crazy one. An embarrassment.

Outside the marquee, the wind hits us full force, so hard it nearly knocks me over. "This way," Will says. "It's more sheltered round here." I feel too tired and drunk to resist, all of a sudden. I let him march me round the other side of the marquee, toward where the land gives way to the sea. I can see the lights of the mainland in the distance like a trail of spilled glitter in the blackness. They go in and out of focus: pin-sharp, then fuzzy, like I'm seeing them through water.

Now, for the first time in a long time, it's just the two of us.

Me and him.

JULES

The Bride

My new husband seems to have disappeared. "Has anyone seen Will?" I ask my guests. They shrug, shake their heads. I feel like I've lost any control I might have had over them. They've apparently forgotten that they're here for my big day. Earlier they were circling around me until it almost got unbearable, coming forward with their compliments and well-wishes, like courtiers before their queen. Now they seem indifferent to me. I suppose this is their opportunity for a little hedonism, a return to the freedom they enjoyed at university or in their early twenties, before they were weighed down with kids or demanding jobs. Tonight is about them—catching up with their mates, flirting with the ones who got away. I could get angry, but there's no point, I decide. I've got more important things to be concerning myself with: Will.

The longer I look for him the more my sense of unease grows.

"I saw him," someone pipes up. I see it's my little cousin Beth. "He was with Olivia—she was a bit drunk."

"Oh, yeah. Olivia!" another cousin chimes in. "They went toward the entrance. He thought she should get some air."

Olivia, making a spectacle of herself yet again. But when I go outside there's no sign of them. The only people hanging around in the entrance of the marquee are a group of smokers—friends from university. They turn toward me and say all the things you're meant to say about how wonderful I look, what a magical ceremony it was—I cut them off.

"Have you seen Olivia, or Will?"

They gesture vaguely around the side of the marquee, toward the sea. But why on earth would Will and Olivia go out there? The weather has started to turn now and it's dark, the moonlight too dim to see by.

The wind screams about the marquee and around me when I step into the brunt of it. Remembering the near-drowning scene earlier, I feel my stomach pitch with dread. Olivia couldn't have done something stupid, could she?

I finally catch sight of their faint outlines beyond the main spill of light from the marquee, toward the sea. But some intuition beyond naming stops me from calling out to them. I've realized that they're very close to one another. In the near-dark the two shapes seem to blur together. For a horrible moment I think . . . but no, they must be talking. And yet it doesn't make sense. I'm not sure I've ever seen my sister and Will speak to one another, beyond polite conversation at least. I mean, they barely *know* each other. They've met precisely once before. And yet they seem to have a great deal to say to one another. What on earth can they be talking about? Why come all the way round here, away from the sight of the other guests?

I begin to move, silent as a cat burglar, edging forward into the growing darkness.

OLIVIA

The Bridesmaid

"I'm going to tell her," I say. It's an effort to get the words out, but I'm determined to do it. "I'm going to . . . I'm going to tell her about us." I'm thinking of what Hannah said, earlier. *It's always better to get it out in the open—even if it seems shameful, even if you feel like people will judge you for it.*

He clamps a hand over my mouth. It's a shock—so sudden. I can smell his cologne. I remember smelling that cologne on my skin, afterward. Thinking how delicious it was, how grown-up. Now it makes me want to vomit.

"Oh no, Olivia," Will says. His voice is still *almost* kind, gentle, which only makes it worse. "I don't think you will, actually. And you know why? You won't do it because you would be destroying your sister's happiness. This is her wedding day, you silly little girl. Jules is too special to you for you to do that to her. And for what purpose? It's not like anything is going to happen between us now."

There's a burst of chatter from the other side of the marquee, and perhaps he's worried someone is going to see us like this because he takes his hand away from my mouth.

"I know that!" I say. "That's not what I mean . . . that's not what I want."

He raises his eyebrows, like he isn't sure whether he believes me. "Well, what do you want, Olivia?"

Not to feel so awful any longer, I think. To get rid of this horrible secret I've been carrying around. But I don't answer. So he goes on: "I get it. You want to lash out at me. I will be the first to admit, I haven't behaved impeccably in all of this. I should have broken it off with you properly. I should perhaps have been more transparent. I never meant to hurt anyone. And can I tell you what I honestly think, Olivia?"

He seems to be waiting for a reply so I nod my head.

"I think that if you were going to do it, you would have done it by now."

I shake my head. But he's right. I have had so much time to do it, really, to tell Jules the truth. So many times I have lain in bed in the early hours of the morning and thought about how I'd get Jules on her own—suggest lunch, or coffee. But I never did it. I was too chicken. I avoided her instead, like I avoided going to the shop to try on my bridesmaid dress. It was easier to hide, to pretend it wasn't happening.

I've thought about what I would do in this situation if I were Jules, or Mum. How I would have made a big display, probably the first time I saw him—embarrassed him in front of everyone at the engagement drinks. But I'm not strong like them, not confident.

So I tried with the note. I printed it out and dropped it through Jules's letterbox:

Will Slater is not the man you think he is. He's a cheat and a liar. Don't marry him.

I thought it might at least make her question him. Make her think. I wanted to sow a tiny bit of doubt in her mind. It was pathetic, I can see that now. Maybe Jules didn't even get it. Maybe Will saw it first, or it got swept up with a load of flyers and trashed. And even if she did see it, I should have realized Jules isn't the sort of person to be bothered about a note. Jules isn't a worrier.

"You don't want to destroy your sister's life, do you?" Will says, now. "You couldn't do it to her."

It's true. Even though at times I feel like I hate her, I love her more. She'll always be my big sister, and this would ruin things between us forever.

He has such confidence in his own story. My own version of it all is falling apart. And I suppose he's right in saying that he didn't lie, not really. He just didn't tell the truth. I don't seem to be able to hold on to my anger anymore, the bright burning energy of it. I can feel it slipping away from me, leaving in its place something worse. A kind of nothingness.

And then, suddenly, I think of Jules, the smile on her face as she stood next to him in the chapel, not having a clue about who he really is. Jules never lets anyone make a fool of her . . . but he has. I feel angry for her in a way I haven't been able to for myself.

"I've kept your texts," I tell him. "I can show them to her." It's the last thing I have over him, the last bit of power I hold. I hold my phone out in front of him, to emphasize it. I should see it coming. But he's been speaking so softly, so gently, that somehow I don't. His arm darts out. He grabs my wrist in midair. He grabs my other wrist, too. And in one quick motion he's got my phone off me. Before I can even work out what he's doing he's hurled it, far away from us, into the dark water. It makes a tiny *plop*! as it enters.

"There'll be backups—" I say, even though I'm not sure how I'd find them.

"Oh yes?" He sneers. "You want to mess people's lives up, Olivia? Because you should know that I have some photos on my phone—"

"Stop!" I say. The thought of Jules—of anyone—seeing me like that . . .

I felt so uncomfortable when he was taking them. But he was so good at asking for them, telling me how sexy I looked while I was performing for him, how much it would turn him on. And I was worried that not doing them would make me look like a prude, a child. And he wasn't in them at all—not his face, not his voice. He could claim I sent them to him, I realize, that I had shot them myself. He could deny it all.

His face is very near to mine, now. For a crazy moment I think he might be about to kiss me. And even though I hate myself for it, a tiny part of me wants him to. Part of me wants *him*. And that makes me sick.

He's still got ahold of my other wrist. It hurts. I make a sound and try to pull away but he only grips me harder, his fingers digging into my flesh. He's strong, so much stronger than me. I realized that earlier, when he carried me out of the water, looking like the big hero, playing to the crowd. I think of my little razor blade, but it's in my beaded bag, somewhere in the marquee.

Will gives me a yank forward and I trip over my feet. My shoe comes off. It is only now that I realize it's not all that far to the cliff edge. And he's pulling me toward it. I can see all the water out there, glossy black in the moonlight. But . . . he wouldn't, would he?

NOW

THE WEDDING NIGHT

The ushers stare at the mangled gold crown in Femi's hand. It seemed so out of place where they found it—sitting on the black earth, in the midst of the storm—that it takes all of them a few moments to work out where they have seen it before.

"It's Jules's crown," Angus says.

"Shit," Femi says. "Of course it is."

Each wonders silently what violence it might have taken to so brutally deform the metal.

"Did you see her face?" Angus asks. "Jules? Before she cut the cake? She looked really angry, I thought. Or . . . or maybe really frightened."

"Did anyone see her in the marquee?" Femi asks. "After the lights came on?"

Angus quails. "But surely you can't think . . . you

don't mean you think something really bad could have happened to her?"

"Fuck." Duncan lets out a hiss of breath.

"I'm not saying that exactly," Femi answers. "I'm only saying—does anyone remember seeing her?"

There's a long silence.

"I can't—"

"No, Dunc. Neither can I."

They look about them in the darkness, eyes straining for any movement, ears pricked for any sound, breath catching in their throats.

"Oh God. Look, there's something else over there." Angus bends to retrieve the object. They all see how his hand trembles as he lifts it to the light, but none of them mocks him for his fear this time. They are all afraid now.

It's a shoe. A single court pump in a pale gray silk, a jeweled buckle on the toe.

SEVERAL HOURS EARLIER

HANNAH

The Plus-One

This guy, Luis, is a great dancer. The band is whipping the guests into a frenzy, forcing us closer together as bodies careen around us. And I find myself thinking about how bloody stressful and lonely my whole day has been. Charlie's largely responsible for that. I don't want to think about him right now, though. I'm too angry with him, too sad. Besides, when was the last time I abandoned myself to some music . . . when was the last time I had a really good dance? When was the last time I felt this desired, this bloody sexy? It feels like I lost that part of myself somewhere along the way. For these few hours I'm going to enjoy having it back. I put my hands above my head. I swing my hair, feel it brush the bare skin of my shoulders. I feel Luis watching me. I find the rhythm of the music with my hips. I was always a good dancer—those years of practice in Manchester clubs in my teens, raving to all the latest anthems from Ibiza. I'd forgotten how much in tune it makes me feel with my own body, how much it turns me on. And I can see how good I look reflected in Luis's approving expression, his gaze only leaving mine to travel down the length of my body as I move.

The music slows. Luis pulls me closer. His hands are on my waist and I can feel his heartbeat through his shirt, the heat of his chest beneath the fabric. I can smell his skin. His lips are inches away from mine. And I'm becoming aware, now our bodies are touching, that he's hard, pressing against me.

I pull away a little, try to put a few centimeters of space between us. I need to clear my head. "You know what," I say. My voice has a tremor in it. "I think I'm going to go and get a drink."

"Sure," he says. "Great idea!"

I hadn't meant him to come with me. I feel all of a sudden as though I need a bit of space, but at the same time I don't have the energy to explain. So we head to the bar tent together.

"How do you know Will?" I shout, over the music.

"What?" He moves closer to hear, his ear brushing my lips.

I repeat the question. "Are you from Trevellyan's too?" I ask.

"Oh," he says. "You mean the school? Nah, we went to the same uni in Edinburgh. We were on the rugby team together."

"Hey, Luis." A guy standing at the bar raises a hand and envelops him in a hug as we draw near. "Come join a lonely bloke in a drink, won't you? I've lost Iona to the dance floor. Won't be seeing her till the bitter end now." He catches sight of me. "Oh, *hello.* Pleased to meet you. Been keeping my boy company, have you? He spotted you in the chapel, you know—"

"Shut up," Luis says, flushing. "But yeah, we've had a dance, haven't we?"

"I'm Hannah," I say. My voice comes out a little strangled. I'm wondering what I'm doing here.

"Jethro," Luis's friend says. "So, Hannah, what you fancy drinking?"

"Er—" I waver, thinking I should be sensible. I've already had so much to drink today. Then I think of Charlie, and what he told me about him and Jules. I want to regain that sense of freedom I felt, briefly, on the dance floor. I want to be a lot less sober. "A shot," I say, turning to the barman: it's Eoin, from earlier. "Of . . . er—tequila." I don't want to mess around.

Jethro raises his eyebrows. "Okaaay. I'm in. Luis?"

Eoin pours us three tequilas. We down our shots. "Christ," Luis says, slamming his down, his eyes tearing up. But I feel like mine hasn't done anything. It might as well have been water.

"Another," I say.

"I like her," Jethro says to Luis. "But I'm not sure my liver does."

"I think it's fucking sexy," Luis says, beaming at me.

We do another shot.

"You weren't at Edinburgh," Jethro says, squinting at me. "Were you? Know I'd remember you if you had been. Party girl like you."

"No," I say. That place again. The mere mention of it makes me feel a whole lot more sober. "I—"

"We were," Jethro says, slinging an arm around Luis's neck. "Time of our lives, right, Lu? Still miss it. Miss playing rugby too. Though it's probably good for my own safety that I don't." He points at the bridge of his nose, which is flattened, clearly an old break.

"I lost a tooth," Luis says.

"I remember!" Jethro laughs. He turns to me. " 'Course, Will never got a scratch on him. Played winger, the bastard. Pretty boy position. That's why he's so disgustingly handsome."

"He was the worst blocker," Luis says, "when we went out after a match. You'd be there trying to chat up some girl and then Will would trundle over to ask if you wanted a round and they'd only have eyes for him."

"His hit rate was insane," Jethro says, nodding. "Only reason he joined the Reeling Society, because of the totty. Let's not forget he wasn't always such a player, though. Remember the one who got away?"

"Oh, yeah," Luis says. "I'd forgotten about that. The Northern girl, you mean? The clever one?"

Oh God. It feels as though horrible is coming into focus. And I can only stand here and watch it.

"Yeah," Jethro says. "Like you." He winks at me. "He got his own back, though, when she dumped him. Remember, Luis?"

Luis squints. "Not really. I mean . . . I remember she left uni. Didn't she? I remember him being pretty cut up when she broke it off. Always thought she was a bit too smart for him."

The sick feeling in the pit of my stomach grows.

"That video that did the rounds, remember?" Jethro says.

"Shiiiiit," Luis says, eyes widening. "Yeah, of course. That was . . . savage."

"It's probably found its way onto PornHub now," Jethro says. "Vintage section, obviously. Wonder what she's doing now. Knowing it's out there somewhere."

"Hey," Luis says suddenly, looking at me. "You all

right? Jesus—" He puts a hand on my arm. "You've actually gone white." He grimaces, sympathetically. "That last shot go down the wrong way?"

I shove him away and stumble away from them. I need to get outside. I barely make it out in time before I fall onto my hands and knees and vomit onto the ground. My whole body is trembling as though I am running a fever. I'm dimly aware of a couple of guests, standing inside the entrance, murmuring their shock and disgust, the tinkle of a laugh. I vaguely register that the weather out here has become so much wilder, whipping my hair away from my head, stinging the tears from my eyes.

I vomit again. But unlike with my seasickness on the boat I don't feel any better. This sickness cannot be alleviated. It has gone down deep inside me, the poison of this new knowledge. It has found its way to my very core.

NOW

THE WEDDING NIGHT

"Who was wearing this?" Angus holds the shoe up. His hand shakes.

"I know I've seen it before," Femi replies. "But I can't think where—it all seems so long ago." It is the day that feels surreal now. This: the night, the storm, their fear, has become all that exists for them.

"Should we take it with us?" Angus asks. "It might—it might be some sort of clue as to what happened."

"No. We should leave it where it is," Femi says. "We shouldn't have even touched it. Or the crown, to be honest."

"Why?" Angus asks.

"Because, you idiot," Duncan snaps, "it could be evidence."

"Hey," Angus says, as they leave the shoe and carry on. "The wind—it's stopped."

He's right. Somehow, without their noticing it, the storm has worn itself out. In its wake it leaves an eerie stillness that makes them long for its return. This quiet feels like a held breath, a false calm. And they can hear their own frightened breathing now, hoarse and shallow.

It has been difficult to make much progress when they're checking in all directions—anxiously scanning the velvet darkness for any threat, any sign of movement. But now, finally, the Folly looms into view in the distance, its windows reflecting a black glitter.

"There." Femi stops short. The others behind him freeze.

"I think—" he says, "I think there's something there."

"Not another fucking shoe," Duncan shouts. "What is this? Cinderella? Hansel and bloody Gretel?" None of them is convinced by this attempt at a joke. All of them hear the rattle of fear in his voice.

"No," Femi says. "It's not a shoe."

All of them have heard the edge to his voice. It makes them want very much *not* to look, to cringe away from whatever it is. Instead they force themselves to stand

and watch as he moves his flashlight in a slow arc, the beam traveling weakly across the ground.

There is something there. Though it's not a something, this time. It's someone. They look on in growing horror as a long shape appears in the light upon the earth. Prone, terrible, definitely human. It lies fairly close to the Folly, on the edge of where the peat bog takes over from the more solid ground. In the wind the edges of the body's clothing fidget and snicker, and this, along with the wavering light from the phone's flashlight, gives an unnerving impression of movement. A macabre trick, a sleight of hand.

To the ushers it doesn't seem likely that there can really be a human being inside those clothes. A human who was, until recently, talking and laughing. Who was among them all, celebrating a wedding.

EARLIER
AOIFE

The Wedding Planner

With the help of several of the waiting staff, and infinite care, we have lifted the great cake into the center of the marquee. Shortly the guests will be called in here to gather around it, to witness the cutting of the first slice. It feels as much of a sacrament as the ceremony in the chapel earlier.

Freddy emerges from the catering area, carrying the knife. He frowns at me. "Are you all right?" he asks, looking closely at me.

"I'm fine," I tell him. I suppose I must be wearing the tension of the day on my face. "Just feeling a little overwhelmed, I suppose."

Freddy nods, he understands. "Well," he says. "It'll all be over soon." He passes me the knife, to place beside the cake. It's a beautiful thing, finely wrought:

a long blade and an elegant mother-of-pearl handle. "Tell them to be really careful with this. It could give you a nick from the slightest touch. The bride asked for it to be sharpened specially—madness really, as a knife like this is really meant for cutting through meat. It'll go through that sponge like it's butter."

JULES

The Bride

Olivia and Will, by the cliff edge: I heard it all. Or, at least, enough to understand. Some of it was snatched away by the wind and I had to move so close to them that I was certain that they would glance in my direction and see me. But apparently each was too intent on the other—their confrontation—to notice. I couldn't make sense of it at first.

"I'll tell her about us," Olivia shouted. At first I resisted understanding. It couldn't be, it was too horrific to contemplate—

I thought then about Olivia, when she came out of the water. How it seemed, for a moment, like there was something she was trying to tell me.

Then I heard the way his voice changed. How he put his hand over her mouth. How he grabbed her arm.

That shocked me even more than the actual substance of what he was saying. Here was my husband. Here was also a man I barely knew.

As I watched them from the shadows I noticed a kind of physical familiarity between them that spoke more eloquently than any words.

When I saw them by the cliff edge the whole hideous shape of it began to coalesce before me.

There wasn't time for anger at first. Only for the huge, existential shock of it: the bottom dropping out of everything. Now I am beginning to feel differently.

He has humiliated me. He has played me for a fool. I feel the rage, almost comforting in its familiarity, blossoming up inside of me and obliterating everything else in its wake.

I rip off my gold crown, cast it to the ground. I stamp down until it is reduced to a mangled piece of metal. It's not enough.

OLIVIA

The Bridesmaid

"Will!" It's Jules's voice. And then a bright bluish light—the flashlight on her phone. It feels like we've been caught in a spotlight. Both of us freeze. Will drops my arm, straightaway, like my skin has burned him, and steps quickly away from me.

I couldn't tell anything from the way she said his name. It was completely neutral—maybe a bit of impatience. I wonder how much she has seen, or, more important, how much she has heard. But she can't have heard all that much, can she? As otherwise—well, I know Jules. We'd probably both be lying at the bottom of that cliff by now.

"What on earth are you two doing out here?" Jules asks. "Will, everyone's wondering where you are. And Olivia—someone said you fell?" She comes closer.

Something's different about her, I think. She's missing her gold crown: that's it. But maybe there's another change, too, something that I can't quite put my finger on.

"Yes," Will says, all charm again. "I thought it best if I took her out for a bit of air."

"Well," Jules says. "That was kind of you. But you should come inside now. We're going to cut the cake."

NOW
THE WEDDING NIGHT

The ushers move toward the body carefully.

It lies a little off the tract of drier land, where the peat takes over. Already the bog has begun to gather itself around the edges of the corpse, hemming it in diligently, lovingly—so that even if the dead one were suddenly to miraculously come to life, to stir itself and try to stand, they might find it a little more difficult than expected. Might struggle to free a hand, a foot. Might find themselves held close and tight to the wet black breast of the earth.

The bog has swallowed other bodies before, swallowed them whole, yawned them deep down into itself. This was a long time ago, though. It has been hungry for some time.

As they creep closer, disparate parts are revealed in

the sweeps of light: the legs, splayed clumsily outward, the head thrown back against the ground. The vacant, sightless eyes, gleaming in the beam. They glimpse a half-open mouth, the tongue protruding slightly, somehow obscene. And at the sternum a stain of dark red blood.

"Oh fuck," Femi says. "Oh fuck . . . it's Will."

For the first time, the groom does not look beautiful. His features are contorted into a mask of agony: the staring clouded eyes, that lolling tongue.

"Oh Jesus," someone says. Angus retches. Duncan lets out a sob: Duncan, who none of them have seen moved by anything. Then he crouches and shakes the body—"Come on, mate. Get up! Get up!" The movement creates a horrible pantomime of animation as the head rolls from side to side. "Stop it!" Angus shouts, grabbing at Duncan. "Stop it!"

They stare and stare. Femi's right. It is. But it *can't* be. Not Will, the anchor of their group, the untouchable one, loved by all.

They are all so focused upon him—their fallen friend—so caught up in their shock and grief, that they have let their guard down. None of them notice the movement a few feet away: a second figure, very much alive, stepping toward them out of the darkness.

EARLIER

WILL

The Groom

Jules and I walk back to the marquee together. I leave Olivia to make her own way. For one crazy moment there, realizing how near we were to the cliff edge, I was tempted. It wouldn't have come as that much of a surprise. She tried to drown herself earlier, after all—or that's certainly how it looked, before I saved her. And with this wind—it's really blowing a gale now—there would have been so much confusion.

But that's not me. I'm not a killer. I'm a good guy.

It's all somewhat out of control, though, everything getting out of hand. I'll have to sort things out.

Obviously I could never have told Jules about Olivia. Not by the time I made the connection between them that day at her mum's house, not when it had gone so far. What would have been the point in hurting Jules unnecessarily? The thing with Olivia—that was never going to be real, was it? It was a temporary attraction. With her it was all based on lies, hers as much as mine. In fact it was the pretense that got me going when we met on that date, her trying to be someone she wasn't. Pretending to be older, pretending to be sophisticated. That insecurity. It made me want to corrupt her, rather like a girlfriend I had at uni once, who was one of the good girls—smart, a hard worker, who came from some crummy school and didn't think she was good enough to be there.

When I met Jules at that party, however, that was different. It was like Fate. I saw how good we would be together straightaway. How good we'd *look* together—physically, yes, but also in how well-matched we were. Me, on the brink of a promising new career, her, such a high flyer. I needed an equal, someone with self-confidence, ambition—someone like me. Together we'd be invincible. And we are.

Olivia will keep quiet, I think. I've known that since the beginning. Knew she wouldn't feel anyone would believe her. She doubts herself too much. Except—and perhaps I'm simply being paranoid—it does feel like she's changed since we've been here. Everything seems changed on this island. It's as though the place is doing it, that we've been brought here for a reason. I know that's ridiculous. It's the fact of having so many people in one spot at once: past and present. I'm usually so careful, but I admit I hadn't thought it all through, how it might play out having them all here together. The consequences of it.

So. Olivia: I think I'm fine there. But I'll have to do something about Johnno, soon as I get back to the marquee. I can't have him running his mouth off to anyone and everyone. I underestimated him, perhaps. I thought it was safer to have him here than not, to keep him close. But Jules invited Piers without my knowing. Yes, actually, *that's* where it all went wrong. If she hadn't, Johnno would never have known about the TV thing and we could have carried on as normal. It would never have worked, him on the show, he must know that. He does, in fact: he put it so well himself. He's an absolute liability. With his pot smoking and his drinking and his long fucking memory. He'd have had some sort of freak-out in front of a journalist and it would all have come out. If he can see that—what a disaster he would have been—then I don't really understand why is he so cut up about it. Anyway, he's dangerous. What he knows, what he could tell. I'm fairly sure no one would believe him—some absurd story from twenty years ago. But I won't run that risk. He's dangerous in other ways too. I have no idea what he was about to do in the cave, because I had the blindfold on, but I'm bloody glad Aoife found us when she did, otherwise who knows what might have happened.

Well. This time, he's not going to catch me unawares.

HANNAH

The Plus-One

I'm trying to look at it rationally, what I learned from Jethro and Luis. Is there the smallest chance it's a coincidence? I am trying to listen to my sensible voice. Imagining what I would tell Charlie in a similar situation: You're drunk. You're not thinking coherently. Sleep on it, think again in the morning.

But really—even without having to reflect properly—I know. I can feel it. It fits, too neatly to be any coincidence.

The video of Alice was posted anonymously, of course. And we were too lost in grief at the time to think about seeking out her friends, who might have been able to help us find the culprit. But later, I vowed that if I ever had a chance to get my revenge on the man who ruined my sister's life—who *ended* her life—I would make him suffer. Oh God . . . and to think I fancied him. I dreamt about him last night—the thought makes more bile rise into my mouth. It is yet another insult, that I fell for the same charm that destroyed Alice.

I think of Will at the rehearsal dinner. *Did we meet at the engagement drinks? You seem familiar. I must have seen you in one of Jules's photos.* When he said he recognized me, he didn't recognize *me.* He recognized Alice.

Beneath my calm exterior, as I step back into the marquee, is a rage so powerful it frightens me. The man responsible for my sister's death has flourished, has carved a career out of false charm, out of essentially being good-looking and privileged. While Alice, a million times brighter and better than him—my clever, brilliant sister—never got her chance.

I'm surrounded by a sea of people. They're drunk and stupid, bumbling about. I can't see through them, past them. I push my way through, at times so forcefully that I hear little exclamations, sense heads turning to look at me.

The lights seem to be failing again. It must be the wind. As I walk through the crowd they flicker and go out, then come on again. Then out. Earlier, when it was twilight, you could still see pretty well. But now without the electric lights it's nearly pitch-black. The little tea lights on the tables are no use. If anything it's more confusing, being able to see vague shapes of people, shadows moving this way and that. People shriek and giggle, bump into me. I feel like I'm in a haunted house. I want to scream.

I clench and unclench my fists so hard I feel my nails puncture the flesh of my palms.

This is not me. This is a feeling like being possessed.

The lights come on. Everyone cheers.

Charlie's voice, amplified by the mic, echoes from the corner of the room. "Everyone: it's time to cut the cake." Over the guests crowding in front of me I stare at my husband, holding his microphone. I have never felt so far away from him.

There is the cake, white and glistening and perfect with its sugar flowers and leaves. Jules and Will stand, poised, next to it. And in fact, they look like the perfect figurines atop a wedding cake: him lean and fair in his elegant suit, her dark and hourglass-shaped in her white dress. I would never say I have hated anyone before. Not properly. Not even when I heard about Alice's boyfriend, what he had done to her, because I didn't have a real figure to focus it on. Oh, but I *hate* him, now. Standing there, grinning into the flashes of a hundred mobiles. I move closer.

The wedding party is clustered around them. The four ushers, grinning away, patting Will on the back . . . and I wonder: Have any of them glimpsed his true nature? Do they not care? Then there's Charlie, doing a pretty good impression—and I'm certain it's just that—of looking sober and in control of his faculties. Nearby stand Jules's parents and Will's, smiling on proudly. Then Olivia, looking as miserable as she has all day.

I move a little closer. I don't know what to do with this feeling, this energy that is crackling through me, as though my veins have been fed with an electric current. When I put out a hand I see my fingers tremble with it. It frightens me and excites me at the same time. I feel that if I were to test it out, right now, I'd find that I have a new, unnatural strength.

Aoife steps forward. She passes a knife to Jules and Will. It's a big knife, with a long, sharp blade. There is a mother-of-pearl handle to it, as though to make the whole thing look softer, to conceal its sharpness, as though to say: this is a knife for cutting a wedding cake, nothing more sinister than that.

Will puts his hand over Jules's. Jules smiles at us all. Her teeth gleam.

I move closer still. I'm nearly at the front.

They cut down, together, her knuckles white around the handle, his hand resting upon hers. The cake cleaves away, exposing its dark red center. Jules and Will smile, smile, smile, into the phone cameras around them. The knife is placed back on the table. The blade gleams. It is right there. It is within reach.

And then Jules leans down and picks up a huge handful of cake. While smiling for the cameras, quick as a flash, she smashes it into Will's face. It looks as violent as a slap, a punch. Will staggers away from her, gaping through the mess at her as chunks of sponge and icing fall, landing on his immaculate suit. Jules's expression is unreadable.

There is a moment of appalled silence as everyone waits to see what will happen. Then Will puts a hand to his chest, does an "I've been hit" pantomime, and grins. "I better go and wash this off," he says.

Everyone whoops and cheers and shrieks and forgets the strangeness of what they just saw. It is all a part of the ceremony.

But Jules, I notice, is not smiling.

Will walks from the marquee, in the direction of the Folly. The guests have resumed their chatter, their laughter. Perhaps I am the only one who turns to watch him go.

The band begins to play again. Everyone spills toward the dance floor. I stand here rooted to the spot.

And then the lights go out.

OLIVIA

The Bridesmaid

He was right. I'm never going to tell Jules now.

I think about how he twisted it all around. How he made me feel it was my fault, somehow, everything that happened. He played on the shame he made me feel: the same shame I have felt ever since I saw him walk through the door with Jules. He has made me feel small, unloved, ugly, stupid, worthless. He has made me hate myself and he has driven a wedge between me and everyone else, even my own family—especially my own family—because of this horrible secret.

I think about how he grabbed my arm just now, by the cliff. I think of what might have happened if Jules hadn't come along. If she had seen, everything would be different. But she didn't and I've missed my moment. No one would believe me, if I told them now. Or they'd blame me. I can't do it. I'm not brave enough for that.

But I could do *something.*

And then the lights go out.

JULES

The Bride

The cake wasn't enough. It felt petty, pathetic. He has let me down, irrevocably. Like every other bloody person in my family. I overrode all of my carefully constructed security measures for him. I made myself vulnerable to him.

The thought of him smiling at me as we cut down, our hands joined on the cake. His hands that have been all over my own sister's body, that have—God, it's all too disgusting to contemplate. Did he think about her, when we slept together? Did he think I was too stupid to ever guess? He must have done, I suppose. And he was right. That's one more small part of what makes it so insulting.

Well. He has underestimated me.

The rage is growing inside me, overtaking the shock

and grief. I can feel it blossoming up behind my ribs. It's almost a relief, how it obliterates every other feeling in its path.

And then the lights go out.

JOHNNO

The Best Man

I'm outside in the darkness. It's blowing a bloody gale out here. It feels like things keep appearing out of the night. I put up my hands to fight them off. Most of all I'm seeing that face again, the same one I saw last night in my room. The big glasses, that look he wore in the dorm that last time, a few hours before we took him. The boy we killed. We *both* killed him. But only one of our lives has been destroyed by it.

I'm feeling pretty out of it. Peter Ramsay was passing stuff out like after-dinner mints—the effects are finally taking hold of me.

Will, that fucker. Going into the marquee like nothing had happened, like none of it had touched him: big fat grin on his face. I should have finished him off in that cave, I think, while I still had the chance.

I'm trying to get back to the marquee. I can see the light of it, but it's like it keeps appearing in different places . . . nearer then farther away. I can hear the noise of it, the canvas in the wind, the music—

And then the lights go out.

AOIFE

The Wedding Planner

The lights go out. The guests shriek.

"Don't worry, everyone," I shout. "It's the generator, failing again, because of the wind. The lights should come on again in a few minutes, if you all stay here."

WILL

The Groom

I'm washing the cake off my face in the bathroom at the Folly. Getting here was no picnic, even having the lights of the building to follow, because the wind kept trying to blow me off course. But perhaps it's good to have some space, to clear my thoughts. Jesus, there's icing in my hair, even up my nose. Jules really went for it. It was humiliating. I looked up afterward and saw my father, watching me. Same expression he's always worn—like when the first team was announced for the big match and I wasn't on it. Or when I didn't get into Oxbridge, or when I got those GCSE results and they were a whisker too perfect. More like a sort of grim satisfaction, like he'd been proven right about me all along. I have never *once* seen him look proud of me. That in spite of the fact that I've only ever tried to better myself, to achieve, as he always told me to. In spite of everything I *have* achieved.

Jules's expression when she picked up that slice of cake. *Fuck.* Has she worked something out? But what? Perhaps she was still just annoyed about the ushers carrying me off like that: the interruption to our evening. I'm sure it was that and nothing more. Or, if needs be, I'm sure I can convince her otherwise.

It wasn't meant to be like this. It all suddenly feels so fragile. Like the whole thing could come crashing down at any moment. I need to go back there and get a handle on everything. But what to sort out first?

I look up, catch sight of my reflection in the mirror. Thank God for this face. It doesn't show one bit of any of it, the stress of the last couple of hours. It's my passport. It earns me trust, love. And this is why I know I'll always win, in the end, over a bloke like Johnno. I wipe one last tiny crumb from the corner of my mouth, smooth my hair. I smile.

And then the lights go out.

NOW

THE WEDDING NIGHT

They crouch over the body. Femi—a surgeon in ordinary life, which feels very far away right now—bends down over the prone form, puts his face close to the mouth and listens for any sounds of breathing. It's futile, really. Even if it were possible to hear anything over the sound of the wind, it is quite clear from the open, cloudy eyes, the gaping mouth, the dark stain of crimson at the chest, that he is very dead.

They are all so focused on the motionless form in front of them that none of them has noticed that they are not alone, none of them glimpsing the figure that has remained shrouded in darkness on the edge of their circle. Now he steps into the light of their torches, looming out of the blackness like some terrible, ancient figure—Old Testament, the personification of vengeance. They don't even recognize him at first. The first thing they see is all the blood.

He appears to have bathed in it. It covers his shirt front: the garment now more crimson than white. His hands are steeped to the wrists in it. There is blood up his neck, blood crusted along his jaw, as though he has been drinking it.

They stare at him in silent horror.

He is sobbing quietly. He raises his hands toward them and now they catch the glint of metal. So the second thing they see is the knife. If they had time to think about it they might recognize it, the blade. It's a long, elegant blade with a mother-of-pearl handle, most recently seen slicing through a wedding cake.

Femi is the first to find his voice. "Johnno," he says, very slowly and carefully. "Johnno—it's all over, mate. Put the knife down."

EARLIER

WILL

The Victim

Fuck. Another power cut. I fumble in my top pocket for my phone, flick on the torch as I step out into the night. It's really blowing a gale out here. I have to put my head down and lean into it to make any headway. Christ, I hate it when my hair gets messed up by the wind. Not the sort of thing I'd ever admit out loud—it wouldn't be very on-brand for *Survive the Night.*

When I look up to check the direction I am walking in, I realize that there's someone coming toward me, visible only by the light of their phone. I must be lit up to them while they remain invisible to me.

"Who's there?" I ask. And then, finally, I can make the shape of them out.

Make her out.

"Oh," I say, in some relief. "It's you."

"Hello, Will," Aoife says. "Got all that cake off?"

"Yes, just about. What's going on?"

"Another power cut," she says. "Sorry about this. It's this weather. The forecast didn't say it would be nearly as bad as this. Our generator can't keep up with it. It should really have kicked in by now . . . I was going to see what had happened. Actually—you wouldn't be able to help me, would you?"

I'd really rather not. I need to get back, there are things to sort out—a wife to placate, a bridesmaid and a best man to . . . deal with. But I suppose I can't do any of those things in the dark. So I might as well be of help. "Of course," I say gallantly. "As I said this morning, I'm only too eager to be of assistance."

"Thank you. That's very kind."

"It's a wee way over here." She leads me off the path, round toward the back of the Folly. We're sheltered from the wind here. And then—odd—she turns to face me, even though we haven't reached anything that looks like a generator. She's shining the light in my eyes. I put up a hand. "That's a bit bright," I say. I laugh. "It feels like I'm at an interrogation."

"Oh," she says. "Does it?"

But she doesn't lower the light.

"Please," I say, getting annoyed now but trying to remain civil. "Aoife—the light is in my eyes. I can't see anything, you know."

"We don't have very much time," she says. "So this will have to be quick."

"What?" For a very strange moment I feel as though I am being propositioned. She is certainly attractive. I noticed that this morning, in the marquee. All the more so for trying to cover it up—I've always liked that, as I've said, that unawareness in a woman, that insecurity. What she's doing with a fat fuck of a husband like Freddy is anyone's guess. Even so, my hands are rather full right now.

"I suppose I just wanted to tell you something," she says. "Perhaps I should have told you when you mentioned it this morning. I didn't think it would be prudent, then. The seaweed in the bed last night. That was me."

"The seaweed?" I stare into the light, trying to work out what on earth she's talking about. "No, no," I say. "It must have been one of the ushers, because that was—"

"What you used to do at Trevellyan's—to the younger boys. Yes. I know. I know all about Trevellyan's. Quite a bit more than I would like to, really."

"About . . . but I don't understand—" My heart is beginning to beat a little faster in my chest, though I'm not quite sure why.

"I looked for you for so long online," she says. "But William Slater—it's a pretty common name. And then *Survive the Night* came out. And there you were. Freddy recognized you instantly. And you hadn't even changed the format, had you? We've watched every episode."

"What—?"

"So. It's why I tried so very hard to get you here," she says. "Why I offered that ridiculous discount to be featured in your wife's magazine. I *would* have expected her to question it a little more than she did. But I suppose that's why she's so well suited to you. Entitled enough to believe that the world simply owes her something. She must have realized that there would be no way we could make a profit from it. But I am getting something out of it, so it happens."

"And what's that?" I am beginning to back away from her. This is suddenly feeling a little fishy. But my right foot lands upon a piece of ground that gives way beneath it. It begins to sink. We're right on the edge of the bog. It's almost like she's planned it that way.

"I wanted to talk to you," she says. "That's all. And I couldn't think of a better way to do it."

"What—than like this, in the middle of a gale, in the pitch-black?"

"Actually I think it's the perfect way to do it. Do you remember a little boy called Darcey, Will? At Trevellyan's?"

"Darcey?" The light in my face is so bright I can't fucking think straight. "No," I say. "I can't say I do. *Darcey.* Is that even a boy's name?"

"Surname Malone? I believe you used surnames only there."

Actually, come to think of it, it does ring a bell. But it can't be. Surely not—

"But of course you'll remember him as Loner," she says. "Malone . . . Loner. That was the name you called him by, wasn't it? I still have all the letters from him, you see. I have them here with me on this island. I looked at them only this morning. He wrote to me about you, you know. You and Jonathan Briggs. His 'friends.' I knew something wasn't right about the friendship—and I didn't do anything. That is my cross to bear.

"His grave's right here. Where we were all happiest. There's nothing in it, of course. My parents didn't have anything to put in there, but you'll know why."

"I—I don't understand."

And then I remember a photo, of a teenage girl on a white sand beach. The one Johnno and I used to tease him about. The hot sister. But it *can't* be—

"I don't have time to explain everything," she says. "I wish I did. I wish we had time to talk. All I *wanted* was to talk, really, to find out why you did what you did. That's why I was so keen for you to come here, to hold your wedding on the island. There were so many things I wanted to ask you. Was he frightened, at the end? Did you try to save him? Freddy says when you came into the dorm you seemed excited, the two of you. Like it was all some big lark."

"Freddy?"

"Yes, Freddy. Or, as I think you used to call him: Fatfuck. He was the only boy awake in the dorm that night. He thought you might be coming for him, to take him for his Survival. So he hid, and pretended to be asleep, and didn't say a word when you carried off Darcey. He's never forgiven himself. I've tried to explain to him that he carries no guilt for it. It was the two of you who took him. But you most of all. At least your friend Johnno feels sorry for what he's done."

"Aoife," I say, careful as I can, "I don't understand. I don't know . . . what are you talking about?"

"Only—maybe I don't need to ask all those questions now. I know the answer. When I came to find you earlier, in the cave, I got all my answers then. Of course, now I have other questions. Why you did it, for example. Stolen exam papers? Does that really seem like enough of a motive to take a boy's life? Just because you'd been found out?"

"I'm sorry, Aoife, but I really must be getting back to the marquee now."

"No," she says.

I laugh. "What do you mean, no?" I use my most winning voice. "Look. You don't have any proof of what you're saying. Because there isn't any. I'm terribly sorry for your loss. I don't know what you're thinking about doing. But whatever it is it wouldn't do any good. It would be simply your word against mine. I think we know who would be believed. According to all records it was just a tragic accident."

"I thought you'd say that," she says. "I know you won't admit it. I know that you don't regret it. I overheard you in the cave, after all. You took everything from me that night. My mother as good as died that night too. We lost my father to a heart attack a few years later, certainly due to the stress of his grief."

I'm not afraid of her, I remind myself. She has no hold over me. I have *slightly* bigger fish to fry here, things with real consequences. She's just a bitter, confused woman—

And then I catch a glimpse of something. A gleam of metal, that is. In her other hand, the one not holding the light.

NOW

JOHNNO

The Best Man

I couldn't save him.

I shouldn't have pulled the knife out, I know that now. It would only have increased the bleeding, probably.

I wanted to make them understand, when they found me out in the dark. Femi, Angus, Duncan. But they wouldn't listen. They had these burning torches that they held out like weapons, like I was a wild animal. They were shouting at me, screaming at me, to drop the knife, to just PUT IT DOWN and there was so much noise in my head. I couldn't get the words out. So I couldn't make them see that it wasn't me. I couldn't explain.

How I'd been coming down off whatever Peter Ramsay had given me, out there in the storm.

How the lights went out.

How I found Will, out there in the dark. How I bent over him and saw the knife, sticking from his chest like something growing out of him, buried so deep you couldn't see any of the blade. How I realized, then, that in spite of all of it, I still loved him. How I hugged him to me and cried.

They surrounded me, the other ushers. They held me like an animal until the Gardaí arrived on their boat. I could see it in their eyes, how they feared me. How they knew I had never really been one of them.

The Gardaí are here now. They've put me in cuffs. They've arrested me. They'll take me back to the mainland. I'll be tried back home, for the murder of my best friend.

Yeah, I did think about it, in the cave. Killing Will, I mean. Picking up a rock close to hand. And there was definitely a moment when I *really* thought about it. When it felt like it would have been the easiest thing. The best thing.

But I didn't kill him. I know that—even though things did go a bit hazy after I'd had that pill from Pete Ramsay, a couple of slightly blank spots. I mean, I wasn't even in the tent. How could I have grabbed the knife? But the police don't seem to think that's a problem.

I don't *think* of myself as a killer, anyway.

Except I am, aren't I? That kid, all those years ago. I was the one who tied him up, in the end. Will made sure of that, but I still did it. And it's not really an excuse that will stand up to anything, is it, saying that you were too thick to properly think out the consequences?

Sometimes I think of what I saw the night before the wedding. That thing, that figure, crouched in my room. Obviously there's no point in telling anyone about that. Imagine it: "Oh, it wasn't me, I think Will might actually have been stabbed with a great fucking cake knife by the ghost of a boy we killed—yeah, I think I saw him in my bedroom the night before the wedding." Doesn't sound all that convincing, does it? Anyway, it's more than likely that it came from inside my head, what I saw. That would make a kind of sense, because in a way the boy's been living there for years.

I consider that jail cell waiting for me. But when I think about it, I've been in a prison since that morning when the tide came in. And maybe it's like justice catching up with me, for that terrible thing we did. But I didn't kill my best friend. Which means someone else did.

AOIFE

The Wedding Planner

I lift up the knife. I told Freddy I only wanted to get Will here to speak to him. Which was true, at least in the beginning. Perhaps it was what I overheard in the cave that changed my mind: the lack of remorse.

Four lives destroyed by that one night. One guilty life in recompense for an innocent: it seems a more than fair trade.

I hope he sees the blade, catching in the flashlight beam. For a moment I want him—so golden, so untouchable—to feel a tiny fragment of what my little brother might have experienced that night as he lay on the beach, waiting for the sea to come in. The terror of it. I want this man to be more terrified than he has ever been in his life. I keep the light trained on him, on his widening eyes.

And then, for my little brother, I stab him. In his heart.

I have raised hell.

SEVERAL HOURS LATER
EPILOGUE

OLIVIA
The Bridesmaid

The wind has stopped, finally. The Irish police have arrived. We're all gathered in the marquee, because they want us in one place. They've explained to us what has happened, what they found. Who they found. We know that someone's been arrested, but not who, yet.

It's amazing how little noise a hundred and fifty people can make. People sit around at the tables, talking in whispers. Some of them are wearing foil blankets, for the cold and shock, and these are louder than the sound of voices, rustling as people move.

I haven't said anything at all, not to anyone, not since he and I stood by the clifftop. I feel like all the words have been stolen from me.

All I've thought about for months is him. And now he's dead, they say. I'm not pleased. At least, I don't think I am. Mainly I'm still just shocked.

It wasn't me. But it *could* have been. I remember how I felt the last time I saw him, cutting the cake with Jules. Seeing that knife . . . The thought was in my head. It was only for a couple of seconds. But I did think it, feel it, strong enough that a part of me wonders whether maybe I *did* do it, and somehow blanked it out. I can't catch anyone's eye, in case they see it in my face.

I jump in shock as I feel someone's hand on my bare shoulder. I look up. It's Jules, a foil blanket over her wedding dress. On her it looks like it's a part of the outfit, like a warrior queen's cape. Her mouth is set in such a thin line that her lips have disappeared and her eyes glitter. Her hand is on my shoulder, her fingers are gripping tight.

"I know," she whispers. "About him—you."

Oh God. So after all that soul-searching about whether to tell her, she somehow worked it out on her own, anyway. And she hates me. She must do. I can see it. I know there's nothing I can do to change Jules's mind once she's made it up, nothing I can say.

Then there's a shift and I think I glimpse something new in her expression.

"If I'd known . . ." I see her mouth the words more than hear them. "If I'd—" She stops, swallows. She closes her eyes for a long moment and when she opens them again I see that they have filled with tears. And then she's reaching for me and I'm standing up and she's hugging me. And then I tense as I feel her body begin to shake. She's crying, I realize, great loud, angry sobs. I can't remember the last time Jules cried. I can't remember the last time we hugged like this. Maybe never. There's always been that distance between us. But for a moment it's gone. And in the middle of everything else, all the shock and trauma of this whole night, it's just the two of us. My sister and me.

THE NEXT DAY

HANNAH

The Plus-One

Charlie and I are on the boat back to the mainland. Most of the guests left earlier than us, the family are staying behind. I look back toward the island. The weather has cleared now and there's sunlight on the water but the island is cast in the shadow of an overhanging cloud. It seems to crouch there like a great black beast, awaiting its next meal. I turn away from it.

I've barely been bothered by the movement of the boat this time. A little nausea is nothing compared to the deep sickness of the soul I felt when I made my discovery last night, that it was Will who as good as killed my sister.

I think of how I clung to Charlie on the ferry crossing to the island less than forty-eight hours ago, how we laughed together, despite my feeling so awful. The memory of it stings.

Charlie and I have hardly talked to one another. We have barely glanced at one another. Both of us, I think, have been lost in our own thoughts, remembering the last time we spoke before everything happened. And I don't think I'd have the energy to speak right now, even if I wanted to. I feel physically and emotionally shattered . . . too weary to even begin to organize my thoughts, to work out how I feel. No one slept at all last night, obviously, but it's more than that.

We'll have to face everything once we're home, of course. We'll have to see, when we return to reality, whether we can mend what has been ruptured by this weekend. So much has been broken.

And yet one thing has emerged, complete, from that wreckage. A missing part of the puzzle has been found. I wouldn't call it closure, because that wound will never fully heal. I am angry that I never got my chance to confront him. But I got my answer to the question I have been asking ever since Alice died. And in killing him, you could say that Will's murderer avenged my sister too. I am only rather sorry I didn't get the chance to plunge the knife in myself.

Acknowledgments

To my editors, Kate Nintzel, Kim Young and Charlotte Brabbin: This book has been such a collaborative effort that I definitely feel your names should be on the front of it too. Kate, thank you for your brilliant editorial eye and for being such a fantastic cheerleader for my writing from the outset.

To my U.S. publishing team—Liate Stehlik, Jennifer Hart, Kate Nintzel, Brittani Hilles, Kaitlin Harri, Imani Gary, Stephanie Vallejo, Elina Cohen, Jeanne Reina, Owen Corrigan and Molly Gendell—thank you for bringing my books to the U.S. audience!

To my agents, Alexandra Machinist and Cath Summerhayes: Thank you for championing me and my books at every opportunity. Thank you, too, for being such fun to work with!

To Luke Speed: Fantastic film agent and the loveliest man. Thank you for your vision and wisdom.

To all the booksellers who have hand-sold my book and who have such love of the written word and who create such exciting, welcoming spaces in which to discover it.

To all the readers who have read the book and told me they've enjoyed it: I love hearing from you—I can't tell you how much joy your messages bring.

To my parents, for your pride and love. For always encouraging me to do what I love best, right from the beginning.

To Kate and Max, Robbie and Charlotte: Thank you for making life such fun and for all your encouragement.

Last, but definitely not least . . . to Al: Always my first reader. Thank you for everything you do—your constant support and encouragement, your willingness to spend an entire six-hour car journey thrashing out a new book idea, for rescuing me from the despairing depths of a plot hole, for spending your whole weekend reading through my first draft. This book would not have been finished without you.